Dedication

I dedicate this series to all the readers of the Ruthless Storm Trilogy. It was their inquiry of the girls that made this series possible.

Books in the Evan's Girls series

Scarlett

Emily

Debbie

Chelsea

Felicia

Chrissy

Eden

Erica

The Evan's Girls Series is based on the children left behind after serial killer Evan O'Conner murdered their families. Each story is about one of his living victims – too young to identify him as a murderer. Too young to even remember their families. They are catapulted into lives that aren't forgiving. Some find along the way that they have supernatural gifts.

Chelsea is the story of her life. Her amazing foster family became the nuclear family she needed until dark secrets about her real family surface sending her on a wild, frightening chase.

Elle Klass

Chelsea Evan's Girls Volume 4

Copyright © 2021 by Elle Klass
Published by Books By Elle, Inc.
ISBN: 978-1-951017-26-2
All rights reserved
Cover art created by TL Katt
Editor Dawn Lewis

Author's Disclaimer

This book is entirely fictional. Any characters or events are purely figments of the author's imagination. Many city and business names are fictional as well. No part of this publication may be reproduced, transmitted or redistributed either in its entirety or in part without the author's express written consent.

Chelsea

I remembered nothing of my childhood. It was a void. The place all my bad and sad memories existed, separate from my conscious mind. My parents died when I was a child and I became a ward of the state while they searched for a living relative. When none were found, they sent me to live with the first family. I was completely mute and so they gave me back to the state. I guess it scared them. Charice – my social worker – says my loss of speech was trauma induced.

She placed me in a different home. One that had more experience with traumatized children. This family had an older child who was very good to me – Phoebe. One day, while building a block village, I spoke. That day marks the start of my memories. I was six years old. It's like as long as I didn't talk, I wouldn't remember. I suppose there was nothing good to remember until Phoebe gave me something good to hold onto.

I stayed with the family who took great care of me. They loved me like their own child and my bond with Phoebe was sisterly. It was my eighteenth birthday that marks the day everything started, throwing me into a mystery and a past my mind refused to remember.

Part 1

Unheard and Unseen

Adulting

"**B**reakfast is the most important meal of the day," Judy called as I tossed my backpack over my shoulder. Her tone of voice reflected a mother hen watching over her chick.

"No time. I'm already late. I'm meeting Charice, turning eighteen stuff," I called as I pulled the front door open. A pitter patter of steps moved swiftly towards the front door and a hand touched my shoulder, halting my rush.

Friendly brown eyes, thin wrinkles webbing from the corners, set inside her round face stared at me. "You're never too busy for breakfast." A small brown paper bag hung between her fingers. She wasn't about to let me go without making sure she did her maternal duty, even though it was my eighteenth birthday.

I grabbed it. "Thanks, Judy."

"You'll be home for dinner tonight?" she called after me as I opened the door on the white Kia and threw my backpack onto the passenger side, sliding myself into the driver's seat.

I unrolled the window. "Yes," I called and backed out of the driveway. Taking one last glance, Judy's full figure filling the doorway. I waved at her and sped off. She always made a big deal about birthdays and holidays and probably had a big dinner planned.

The strip of offices were a welcome sight to me as I whipped my Kia into a parking space beside the handicap since it was early enough no one was there to grab it. The door opened with ease. I rushed past the familiar doctors' offices, dentist office, and CPA to the back of the building where Charice's office was located.

It was a comfortable setting as I dropped into the red fabric chair I'd been sitting in for years now. My eyes, as always, went to the snowy painted mountain scene behind her desk. She'd been with me since my parents' death, took care of me, made sure I was in the right home. Today marked the end of that journey.

Gold-rimmed glasses framed her blue eyes, her hair pulled into a messy bun, and cheeks as rosy and bright as they'd been every time I visited her for the past twelve years that I remembered. A short sleeved blue blouse hung over her shoulders and she smelled heavily of Entice – her favorite perfume. "Happy Birthday," she crooned, wrapping her arms around me in a hug.

This was it. The moment my life became mine. I was graduating high school in two days and next year onto college. She quickly went through the paperwork and asked me how I was doing, was I ready for graduation, college. She was like a second mom in many ways.

"You've come a long ways. You were one of my first cases. We've been together since the beginning. I'm not at liberty to say…" she started, rifling through my file. "Where is… oh my," she mumbled. She licked her finger, flipping pages, then glanced up at me. "It seems I've misplaced it. I'll get another one." She stood and exited the room, mumbling to herself.

I couldn't remember a time she was organized, she was always forgetting something. My file was left open on her desk. It was the size of a Stephen King novel. My eyes immediately went to the picture of a forlorn little girl. Her eyes hollow, no smile, wisps of dull hair framed her face. She looked like a ghost. It took a moment for me to realize I was looking at me.

Beneath the picture was a police report. My eyes drawn to the word *fire*. Charice wasn't in the room so I could glance through and read the contents of the folder: beneath the police report, a psychologist's analysis. I'd never been interested in my past but seeing myself triggered a curiosity I was suddenly keen on understanding. Considering my options, I could read through everything, but I'd never get through all the information before she got back. I could take it, but that might get her into trouble, and I'd feel as if I was betraying her trust.

I pulled out my phone and took pictures of the police report, the psychologist's report, and myself.

"I got another one," she said loudly.

I stuffed the phone into my pocket in time for the door to open. Her blue blouse fell over jeans and green painted toenails peeked out from her tan sandals. I avoided her face, riddled with guilt over taking pictures.

She dropped the paper in front of me. "This one is important. It ensures you get a check every month to help with living expenses."

I signed the paper, still not looking her in the eye.

"I have one more thing." From the corner of my eye she leaned to her left. Using both hands, she pulled something wrapped in yellow paper with a white bow. "This is for you."

A present. Guilt ate me up, tied my stomach in knots, but I didn't say a word about what I'd done. "Thank you." I took the present and stood.

She leaned her head down, meeting my eyes. "Is something wrong? You know you can talk to me about anything." Concern filling every syllable.

I could but I couldn't. She was bound by some type of confidentiality. I adored and trusted her, but I couldn't tell her everything. She was a social worker and her job came first. I met her gaze. "I… uh… I'm going to miss you. That's all."

She brought a hand to her chin. "Why don't you open that?"

I met her gaze and pulled the gift closer, unwrapping the pretty yellow paper. Inside was a thirteen inch, two-in-one computer. My mouth dropped open. These weren't cheap. I couldn't believe she'd spent that kind of money on me. Yes, she'd known me longer than I remembered knowing her. She made many home visits over the years, even staying for dinner. There wasn't a time in my life I didn't remember her not being part of it. "I can't take this."

A smile wrinkled the thin skin on her face. "Yes, you can." She came around the desk and folded her hands over mine.

One Toke, Two Tokes

I completed both my finals and escaped outside. Above my head, leaves rustled in the spring breeze as I stared at the picture of the hollow girl. No wonder the first six years of my life were a void. My mind was consumed as I'd worked through my exams. It didn't matter if I passed or failed them because my grades in the classes were both good.

"Got some chronic," James said as he dropped onto the bench beside me, lacing an arm around the wooden back of the bench. Dishwater unkempt blond hair fell over his eyes. He lived behind me. For years we'd pushed up the loose board in the fence between our houses and hid in his father's shed, getting high.

His mother disappeared when he was a baby; he lived alone with his disabled father. An accident at work injured his back. He was barely able to walk and was on a combination of medications that included narcotics. Physically he never harmed James, but mentally he belittled him. 'You'll never amount to anything. You're worthless.' I'd heard plenty.

I stood. "Not today."

He grabbed my hand. "What fun is turning eighteen if you don't get high?" he urged, always the huge pothead.

I blew the air out of my mouth slowly in contemplation. "What's the first memory you have of me?"

"That's a strange question. Come on." He jumped off the bench and walked towards the student parking lot.

The gravel crunched under his tires as he pulled the three-toned, rust-bottomed Gremlin off the road.

We ran to the lake. I picked up a stone and bounced it across the water's surface.

"Nice one," he said, pulling a pipe from his pants. He laid it on a log and dug into his pocket again. Finding a bag of pot, he drew it out. He smoked morning, noon, and night; always high. I couldn't remember a time when he wasn't. It defined our relationship.

He handed the full pipe to me. "Six years ago. I heard you crying through the fence."

Phoebe had left for college. I was lost, couldn't imagine how I'd carry on without her. She promised she'd be back for summers and holidays and I could call her anytime. James. That's how I carried on without her. We became fence friends – best friends.

That day, he pushed the loose slice of fence and slipped through. My face stained in tears, he found a way to cheer me up, make me laugh. I think he needed it as an escape from his father more than I needed him. His father unable to chase him, James'd slip out the back door and hide in the shed. That's how he'd heard me crying. I was on the opposite side of the fence to the shed.

I inhaled deeply, drawing the pot into my lungs. After passing the pipe back and forth, I lay back on the grass. A couple white cotton clouds drifted across the blue sky.

He lay on his back, his head touching mine. "I'm getting out of here too. Got a job. Construction."

"That's good." I meant that. He needed to get away from his father. There was potential in him, but if he stayed here, he was bound to land in jail. "I guess everybody moves on."

We lay for several minutes, silence between us. "James."

"Yeah."

"Do you ever think of trying to find out what happened to your mom?" I asked. His mom was a sore subject. Her case cold after all these years. No answers for him and no leads. She vanished, that was it. Really, I think it was the trauma that brought us together. The pictures on my phone could lead me to answers but did I want to know? *Would they give me peace or nightmares?*

"No, she left us. I hate her."

The pain in his voice tiptoed over my soul. If I chose to read through the reports I was on my own. I couldn't ask him for help.

Echoes of the Past

Like every other sleepy southern town, it appeared the perfect place to raise a family. A quaint, quiet place where bad things didn't happen… until a triple homicide erased that vision. Opening people's eyes to the fact crime happened everywhere. It had no preference.

A tall, thin man with a tight brown mustache stood behind a glass window. His uniform fit loose and his nametag read Deputy Greene. What a boring name. I sighed and counted my steps as I approached the glass window. I pressed the red buzzer on the wall.

"How can I help you?" Deputy Greene asked.

Anxiety bubbled in my guts. "I'd like… to speak with… Officer Sugda." The words caught in my throat. His was the name on the police report. My instincts fighting my efforts to relive the memories stuck in the void.

He ran his tongue over his bottom lip. "What's the name?"

"Chelsea Mora," I said as if my name was a bad word. In this town I imagined it was.

His eyes narrowed as he picked up a phone. "A Chelsea Mora here to see you, Chief." He pointed towards the plastic chairs with metal legs along the wall.

Misgivings crossed my path as I considered running. The door wasn't far. It wasn't too late. I could get in my car and drive home to safety. I didn't need to do this. *No. I did.* My heart raced as a door opened along the wall with the glass window.

A dark-skinned man with a thick chest stood in the doorway. "Come with me."

The plain white walls and weak odor of pine cleaner did little to ease my tensions. I followed him around a corner then another. I wasn't sure I'd find my way out. After four or five turns he came to a stop, guiding me into an office.

It was far more inviting, with creamy walls and pictures of children, some young, others older. I imagined they were his children. A picture of a young couple on his desk. The man resembled him but was much younger, and the woman must be his wife. I sat in a cloth chair, more comfortable and encouraging than the plastic ones in the lobby.

He took a seat in a plush ergonomic computer chair. "I haven't heard your name in a few years. I s'pose you're here searching for answers." His voice deep with an edge, a warning.

I shook my head, my words caught in my throat. Nervous, I clutched my car keys so hard the tip dug into my palm.

"It was a house fire. Took your entire family. I'm sorry." His voice didn't sound remorseful, more as if he'd rehearsed it, expecting one day I'd return.

"Do you remember them?" I asked meekly.

He raked a hand over his balding head. "I don't. They were private people. Never heard their names until that day." He leaned forward with a stern face, his arms resting on top of the desk between us. "It took people around here a long time to forget what happened. I suggest you go home and forget it too Miss Mora."

Forget, yes, I'd forgotten it all right. I shouldn't dig it back up but, driven by curiosity, I couldn't stop. If I left and dropped it, my mind would nag at me. "I can't, sir."

He nodded then stood. "I guess you should come with me then."

I thought he'd show me a police report or evidence, something at the station. Instead I followed him through the maze of the police station, through a door exiting the back of the building. He walked towards a cruiser and opened the passenger door. "Get in."

Streetlights on thick wires hung in the still, summer air. We swept past small houses with porches giving way to mailboxes and gravel driveways, houses so far from the road they could barely be seen. He finally slowed, pulling onto a dirt road, rutted and grown over with grass.

The car stopped and he cut off the engine. "This is it. Where it happened."

He pushed the car door open. I followed suit and toddled nervously around the car. The grass crunched beneath our feet as he led me towards a weed covered patch. Twelve years later, there wasn't much to see. The frame existed around the weeds and a sprinkling of wildflowers.

He stopped short of the home's moss covered frame. "You were right here. It still haunts my dreams. A tiny thing you were."

My voice caught in my throat, the words came out breathy, "What happened?"

"The fire was intentional, but you wouldn't be here I s'pect if you didn't already know that. Gasoline was used as an accelerant. This was the case that made the Hurricane Killer famous, Miss Mora." He folded his arms across his chest.

I knew about the accelerant, but not the Hurricane Killer. "Was he ever caught?"

"He was caught alright, murdered, couple years ago." Satisfaction lingered in his voice.

I shifted on my feet. "What else can you tell me?"

"You weren't the only child made it out of that house alive. Now, I'm taking you back to your car and you're going to leave town without talking to other folks. You hear me?" He demanded in a strong, stern voice.

Nuclear

hief Sugda's words echoed in my head. I couldn't help but think about them on the long drive home. They were a warning not to pursue what he knew I was determined to. He didn't want the sleepy little town turned upside down, but what could he do if I started poking around? Was there anyone in the town that knew anything? Was it futile?

No, the fact that he warned me told me it wasn't futile, someone knew something and he didn't want it, whatever black cloud it was hanging over his town. That made me more determined, at the same time there were other avenues I could pursue first; the internet, the files, newspapers, and old news broadcasts.

By the time I pulled the Kia into the driveway it was dark. A cheek to cheek smile crossed my face as I parked behind the blue colored Honda taking up my normal spot. Phoebe! Thrusting the backpack over my shoulder I rushed towards the door. She'd made no promise to be here; currently working on her dissertation she rarely had free time.

I flung the door open. My ears welcoming Judy and Phoebe's cheerful voices racing through the halls from the kitchen. Phoebe stopped cold when she saw me, placed the dishes and silverware in her hands on the yellow doily tablecloth.

Her arms swallowed me in a generous hug, and she said, "You didn't think I'd miss this, did you?" She must have read the shocked and elated expression on my face.

I squeezed her tightly before letting go and taking in her messy appearance. Her shoulder-length dishwater blonde hair tied back in a messy half bun, loose T-shirt and sweats hanging over her large-boned, curvy frame. She was dressed for comfort not fashion.

The house was permeated with a lemon-herb blend. As we set the table together, we talked. She caught me up on the details of her work in environmental protections for endangered animals. It was her passion in life.

Roy, my foster father, cleared his throat as he entered the kitchen, still in his scrubs. He was a radiologist. Judy had been a therapist. After Phoebe was born she returned to work part time and, after they took in me, she stopped working altogether, claiming it was more important to spend time raising her daughters. I didn't think that was entirely true. I think she quit because I was high maintenance, and I would always be eternally grateful for what the family gave up for me.

After a quick hug and kiss to Phoebe, Roy flipped through the mail in his hand. Pulling one letter from the group he handed it to me. "Looks like you have something from the university."

Three sets of eyes stared at me expectantly as I opened the letter. I couldn't imagine what it was. I'd already received the acceptance letter and packet. I scanned it, returning to the sets of eyes burning a hole in my head in anticipation. "They're inviting me to summer school. I would be able to bring my car and keep it in the fall and even keep my dorm room." That was a perk, since the rule for incoming freshman in the fall was to be carless for a year.

"That's great!" Judy said, with a painted smile on her round face. There was a hint of something else, a pervading agony in the soft edges of her words. A sorrow that resounded inside me. As ready as I was for the next step in my life, I also hoped for one last summer with the beautiful family that took in the poor distraught girl in the photo. Seeing myself and the ashes of my babyhood home had awoken a deep loss and a resounding gratitude to the family that surrounded me.

Phoebe painted on a smile. "You don't have to decide tonight." Her words always comforting, as if she had a direct line to my thoughts.

I nodded.

It was Judy who changed the subject as she placed the lemon butter tilapia on the table, "You're late tonight. Did your meeting with Charice go well?"

I shrugged. "I guess." I didn't think bringing up visiting my childhood home would help the somber mood hanging over the room. "She gave me a laptop."

"Nice!" Phoebe piped in, her sentiments echoed by Judy and Roy.

Dinner was filled with laughter, creating a layer of ease over the tension. It was as if Judy knew why I was late, as if they all did. Possibly it was the guilt I was feeling, as if keeping a huge secret that would destroy this nuclear family from the inside out.

A leg under my rear, the other hanging over the side of the padded window bench in my bedroom, I unpacked the laptop and pressed the power button. Charice had thought of everything, as it was already fully charged. I'd been pretty lucky to get stuck with a rookie social worker who put the effort into my case. Plugging my phone in, I downloaded the photos I'd taken in her office.

I lifted my head as the door creaked open – Phoebe. She strolled towards my bed, her wet hair soaking into the extra-large T-shirt that hung from her shoulders. "Nice computer."

I lowered the screen so she wouldn't catch a glimpse of my downloads and gave her my full attention.

"I'm heading to Huntington Park tomorrow – Edisto Beach. It's part of my research, keeping up with the loggerhead population. You want to ride with me?"

"Sure." Like any little sister I admired my big sister, even if we weren't blood related.

She wrinkled her nose. "Be ready by eight. We'll stop for breakfast on the way."

Once she departed I checked the progress and, as I assumed, the pictures were downloaded. I packed them all into a file, then separated them into more files. I was by all means anal when it came to certain things and organizing was one of them. I'd meticulously catalogued the DVDs in the living room by genre, sub-genre, title, and even year. I even went so far as to use the label maker and ID them all so everyone knew what order to return a movie after watching.

Once organized, I closed that window and opened an internet browser. Sugda's words resonated in me; another child made it out alive. It was the only tangible thing he gave me. It didn't take long to find the headline articles. Tyrus Reed, an eight-year-old boy, went missing only to be returned to his family home. The child's story was that someone had kidnapped him as he walked home from school. They put a bag over his head and shot a needle into his arm. He woke up in a dark room. It was an elderly man that returned him. The elderly man was never found.

I wasn't an investigator but that sounded fishy to me. Why would someone find a child and not call the police, instead return him and leave? It didn't make sense but, as I perused the articles by date, the story unfolded and connections were made to the Mora family.

I read with bated breath. The Moras were tied to child abduction and the black-market sale of young children. There were several people arrested. I bookmarked the page on the internet browser. I wanted to follow-up and see if they were prosecuted, maybe put to death. Death seemed more appropriate for anyone involved with ripping young children from their families and subjecting them to a life of slavery or... I pushed the thoughts from my head, not wanting to imagine the horror.

It was the next paragraph that really turned my world upside down; *including the*

Mora children… DNA evidence… not related. Tremors shook my body and I swallowed hard, trying to wet my drying throat. My hands shook profusely, and I felt sick to my stomach.

I leaned forward and dragged myself onto my bed, unable to process or even think. I squeezed my eyes shut, but the words crawled across the backs of my eyelids like scrolling text on a billboard.

Seaweed Floats and Marshes

The annoying, familiar squawk of my alarm woke me. I didn't remember falling asleep, nor had I dreamt, but the feeling inside me was empty. I hadn't dwelled on my parents over the years because I didn't remember anything about them. I didn't miss them, but in light of the information the Moras weren't my parents... *Who were my parents?*

Why hadn't I been returned, like Tyrus, to my family? It wasn't fair! I was a toddler left outside a burning home during a hurricane and he was returned. I was sent to foster care! Anger blazed over me like the fire that burnt the Moras home. I hated them and him. I knew deep down my feelings were inappropriate, but that didn't stop the anger from boiling to the surface. I felt hate like I never had before.

I took several deep breaths to try and reach my sensible side. The little part of me that understood it wasn't Tyrus's fault or my foster family's or even Charice's. It was the fault of the people I thought were my parents. The fault of the *Hurricane Killer,* as Sugda called him. Sugda. Without warning I'd taken the title off his name. He should have done something. It was his town and he swept it under the rug, dismissed me.

After several minutes, I was able to gain control. I needed to find Tyrus Reed. He lied, and had continued his lie, but maybe I could appeal to him as a victim. It was that hope that got me out of bed and through the motions of getting dressed as I refocused my energy.

Phoebe was the ray of light that kept the darkness at bay. She helped me squelch the anger in me and focus on the good in my life. There had to be a logical reason I wasn't placed with my biological family, like they were dead, or I was given up at birth by young parents who couldn't care for me.

The car ride was filled with the birds I might find on the trails and the increase in the loggerhead population. How their efforts to save the population were working.

The breeze from the ocean and ample shade from the trees took away most of the smoldering South Carolina heat as I walked one of the trails, leaving Phoebe momentarily as she spoke the language of turtles, eggs, and nests with the scientists.

I don't remember it, but years ago we went on vacation to Edisto Beach on

Huntington Island and saw the sea turtles. My cheesecloth memory, I relied on the stories they told of how I was at first scared of them then wanted to bring them home.

Birds, heard but unseen, thrived in the marshes and trees. I had my eye on finding a painted bunting with their bright blue heads and red chests but so far hadn't seen one. I wasn't versed enough in birding to know one bird call from another.

The fresh air and hiking trails hadn't taken my mind off things but had centered my thoughts. Finding Tyrus Reed was my first step. I wouldn't pay Sugda another visit because I was too angry at him and that anger would only get me in trouble.

I thought about the letter from the university. I'd have access to my car, a large library, and no interference and needed explanation to my foster family. They wouldn't inquire why I was late or what I was doing with my time. I convinced myself summer classes and pursuing the memories that slipped through the cheesecloth in my brain was the answer. In retrospect, it probably wasn't, but one can't see the future.

I stopped at a bench and dropped my backpack, pulling out a Phoebe-made bottled water. She was serious about the environment and only used refillable metal bottles. She stuck a few in the freezer last night. I watched as she pulled them out this morning as we filled our backpacks.

Taking a seat on the wooden bench next to my pack, I stared through the full trees, their leaves packed together leaving little room, it appeared, for anything else, but through them I spotted a flash of gray-blue. I craned my neck as if it would help me see better. Of course, it didn't, and I finally found a spot of gray-blue then my eyes made out the rest of the little bird. Its head gray-blue and breast white, with yellow wings.

I watched the bird, in silence so as not to scare it, for several minutes, seeing more and more in the trees. My mind boggled at how nature was happening all around me, I just had to stop and enjoy it for five seconds to see it.

I pulled my phone out and snapped a couple pictures. They weren't the best, but I was able to enlarge, upload, and add them to the image identifying app on my phone. A Blue-headed Vireo. In seconds I was able to identify a bird yet, at eighteen, how was it I didn't know who I was? How come I couldn't simply upload a picture of myself and *bam* identity.

I packed up the water bottle and kept my phone out, snapping pictures to take my mind off everything else. I continued on the trail and veered off on a smaller trail. Human voices grew quieter as I followed the trail deeper, until silence surrounded me.

It was the snap of a branch that brought the silence to my attention, like standing inside a void. I stopped there, noting I was no longer on a trail but deep in the trees. The snap rattled my ears again, followed by crunching. I hadn't given an ounce of thought to what animals might live in the woods.

Turning quick on my heel, I came face to face with a tall, sturdy-built man in a green tank top, denim shorts, and camouflage ball cap. At first I felt relief that I wasn't alone but, taking in the set of his pointed jaw, sternness in his eyes, and ominous stance, fear raced up my spine.

"You shouldn't wander off the trails," he stated. His voice demanding and coarse.

I stepped to the side to walk around but was blocked by his large frame. I stepped to the other side but was again blocked. *What did he want?* My heart pounded so hard in my chest I heard it in my ears. I considered my next move. He wasn't letting me by and wasn't here for chit chat. There was nothing friendly about him and he was far larger than me.

I stepped backwards and, without giving it another thought, I did the only thing I could. I ran. Holding the straps of my backpack tight around my shoulders I dodged tree branches, birds fluttering from the trees as I disturbed their space.

I didn't look back or even forward as my legs carried me further and further away, hoping I was quicker. I had small size and agility on my side. I couldn't hear anything but my heart thumping wildly in my ears until the familiar sound of voices moved through the trees. I followed them until I came to a campground. I slowed my pace as I emerged from the woods.

A group of four adults took no notice of me as I swiftly walked past their campground situated right off a trail. Seeing more people ahead, I took that path, putting more distance between me and the man with the camouflage ball cap.

My heart leaped from my chest when my phone rang. Digging it out of my pocket, Phoebe's face lit up the screen. "Hey."

"Where you at?" she asked, her cheerful voice sending a wave of calm over me.

Checking the GPS, I wasn't far from her. "Not far."

"OK."

Her bright smile calmed my still electrified nerves as I reached her. "You look a little winded and why do you have twigs and leaves in your hair?" she asked as she pulled one out and dropped it to the ground.

I laughed nervously. "I got a little off the trail. I was taking pictures of birds and didn't pay attention to where I was going."

She chuckled. "If I didn't know better, I'd think you were a city girl."

It wasn't like the small town we lived in was anything more than a small town where everyone knew everyone, but we had a few subdivisions, a few schools, several gas stations, and numerous churches. It wasn't much, but I didn't venture into the woods alone but with James.

I didn't see the man again nor did I tell Phoebe about him. There wasn't much to say. We stayed close to the crowds and others and that evening we went for a sea turtle walk that she'd booked. The whole time I'd thought she happened to be free and our trip to Edisto Beach was spur of the moment for her thesis. I was wrong. She spent the time thinking about spending this weekend with me and booked the turtle walk. My foster family was my family, but I couldn't drop the search for more or finding the memories that eluded the cheesecloth in my mind.

Everyone equipped with red lights so as not to disturb or disorient the turtles, we watched the loggerheads nest under the cover of darkness to avoid predators.

Each nest holding approximately 150 eggs, I didn't think the turtles would wonder in the future who their siblings were, or even their parents, when they hatched and made their way offshore, spending their early years in seaweed floats and marshes. Those that weren't eaten by predators, anyways. They had numbers on their side as sea birds, raccoons, and crabs ate them for a late-night snack.

The similarity between my life and the turtles' wasn't so astonishing. I survived the predators, found a safe home in a salt marsh, and was now ready to head into the ocean.

Sleep Baby

The quiet hum of the Honda was drowned by pop music on the radio. I plugged my phone into the car charger and used the time to search for Tyrus Reed. I found a few and narrowed them down using social media. There was only one located on the East Coast. He was a defense attorney in Atlanta who was also a black belt in Karate. It was cliché and maybe too cliché. A kidnapped child who grows up to defend those who commit hideous crimes such as the one perpetrated against him. The black belt was icing on the cake. No one would take him again.

On a deep, systemic level, I understood his choices. I was just as bad. A foster child seeking financial independence and a career in a field that gave me a false sense of control. It was robotics club that had driven home the idea of being a computer software designer. I joined because I was head over heels for Zayden. His hazel green eyes melted me every time he looked my way. There was never any sign the feeling was mutual and we ended up as friends and I fell in love with designing apps and coding.

I opened the picture album on my cell to glance through the ones I'd taken at Edisto Beach. The photos of my psych report glared at me. I hadn't yet peaked at them. My finger hovered over the words written on the page, unsure whether it wanted to push on it.

Phoebe's phone rang before I made a choice. A picture of a young man, no more than thirty, his smile friendly, with a dimple on the left side of his cheek and deep brown eyes, stared from her screen. The name Doug displayed on the dashboard of the Honda. "Hey, babe," she answered, glancing my way with a quick smile.

"How are the loggerheads?" Doug's deep voice answered.

"Good. I'm here with Chelsea."

"Hi, Chelsea, Phoebe talks about you constantly."

I could see the silly look on her face as if she'd been caught doing something she shouldn't. "Hi…uh… Doug."

His friendly voice continued, "I hear you code?"

Phoebe glimpsed at me, her cheeks flush but not as flush as mine. I felt the heat rising, not with anger but in disbelief that Phoebe talked about me enough to tell him my career goal. "Yeah."

Phoebe interjected then and took the conversation in another direction. I clicked the first picture of the psychologist's report to occupy my mind. My eyes scanning the information as the two carried on their conversation. I think her flush cheeks were more her slight embarrassment, or even guilt, at not mentioning him to me. We'd spent the entire day together and not once had she brought him up.

Their voices drowned as a word on the report caught my eye – fentanyl. It was found in my system, along with various minute amounts of other drugs such as melatonin. A quick internet search showed fentanyl was used to ease children to sleep. Melatonin was also used to help people sleep. *Did the Moras drug me or the Hurricane Killer? Was it both?*

I made a mental note to find as much as I could about the Hurricane Killer because it might help me understand what happened to me. Was he a type of vigilante Dexter psychopath or was his agenda more self-serving?

I took a deep breath and attempted to take the "me" out of what I was reading and think about it in terms of someone else. Fentanyl has shown with continued use that it can cause memory problems. It was almost a relief to think I'd found the missing link to my cheesecloth brain, and truly disturbing to think anyone would drug a small child.

"Chelsea." A hand waved between my face and the phone screen.

I glanced up, first noting through the windshield we were surrounded by non-moving, non-occupied cars then the blinking neon light *Buzzee's* and *open* on the outside of a large farmhouse-shaped building caught my eye before I glanced Phoebe's way.

Her and Doug's conversation had been drowned by my own thoughts, I didn't even notice when it ended.

"I'd thought we'd stop for coffee and a small snack."

I nodded and followed her lead, exiting the car. I supposed it was about explaining Doug as much as it was grabbing coffee. She'd think she owed me an explanation but, really, she didn't. It was her life.

Several big rigs were parked alongside the truckstop. My eyes went to their trailers and I thought of the children the Moras kidnapped and smuggled. There was no mention in the articles of how they moved the children around. *Was it by truck? Boat?* My mind envisioned the pictures often displayed in the movies of children crowded into a trailer or container. I shuddered visibly at the thought and was glad Phoebe wasn't looking at me.

Inside, the establishment appeared more as a mom-and-pop country restaurant with red checkered curtains and table coverings. An old-fashioned jukebox player that dropped 45s stood in the corner, lit up with blue and red tube lights. You're So Vain by Carly Simon could be heard in every corner.

I followed Phoebe to a small table where she ordered coffee from a waitress in a uniform that matched the coziness of the truck stop. I expected jeans and a T-shirt, not a button up dress, white collar, and a white apron over the front. The black loafers on her feet seemed far more practical.

It all added to the ambience and I figured maybe the push back in time somehow gave the place a feel that truckers on the road for long hours might be more comfortable with. I wasn't much of a coffee drinker, so ordered a strawberry milkshake. After a long day in the sun, it was appetizing.

"So, hey." Here came her apology that she didn't owe me. I shut my mouth and let her talk. "I'm sorry I hadn't told you about Doug. We've been dating about six months. He designed the software we use to track endangered species. I really wanted to bring him but it's your day."

I read between the lines. She thought bringing him would overpower my moment. I didn't think she knew her parents as well as I did. They'd always had room for me and had made me feel like part of the family. "He seems nice. You could have brought him, maybe he could teach me a thing or two."

A wide smile stretched across her round face. "He works for Indigo and they did the entire project for free! I didn't think big corporations even did that, especially when they can pick up government funding to pay for development. We worked closely together, and he designed it to our specifications." The light in her eyes brighter than the jukebox.

The server placed our drinks on the table with a smile and small talk with her very southern drawl. I shoved the straw into my shake and stirred the whipped cream into the icy mixture below. "That's great."

"Are you and James planning on the annual rite of passage grad party..." she paused as she glanced at her phone, "tonight? It's after midnight!"

"We should probably be going or I won't be awake to go," I joked.

Our drinks in to-go cups, we headed out the door. I glanced again at the trailers. I couldn't get the picture of children packed together, no food, no water, no comfortable place to rest their head, and fear gripped me. *How many children?*

Fleeing the Scene

Sometimes there are things best left unknown, unseen and unheard. All of that pertained to my life before Charice and my foster family. The fentanyl may be partially responsible for my memory loss but, after what I learned about the Moras, I figured the lack of memories shielded me from everything a person shouldn't remember about a horrifying experience in their life. It was a brick wall safety net that kept me sane.

After graduation practice, we had about an hour of down time before the ceremony. James grabbed my hand and leaned down to my ear whispering, "Let's get out of here."

I couldn't stop the devious smile that crossed my face as we slowly backed away from the other graduates busy conversing about the grad party, presents they expected, and the valedictorian rehearsing her speech. When we reached the cafeteria doors and no one was watching, we slipped through and ran once the door closed like two small children sneaking extra cookies before dinner.

We stopped in the business hallway. It was located in the back of the school, several hallways from the crowded cafeteria. In the quiet hallway we settled against the wall, our tushes on the floor. I'd worn shorts and hiked my gown up so it wouldn't collect the dirt.

It was my moment to tell James everything from the last couple days. I wasn't sure how he'd take it but I needed someone to confide in because I felt like I was about to burst like a balloon. He didn't interrupt as I spoke, but didn't hide his emotions either. They were painted all over his face as he narrowed his eyes in skepticism then widened them in concern with an upper lip quiver.

"Have you talked with your foster parents?"

Now that was a silly question coming from him. A guy who never spoke to his dad or had any confidence in adults.

"No, you know how I am. I'd feel guilty. They've taken care of me. Do you know any other foster children that have it as good as me? They're all packed into houses." I thought of the trucks again and took a deep breath to force the image away.

"But not you. You ever wonder why?" he asked.

No, I never had. Not really. It was just a thing that I got lucky. "I was high maintenance." It was an easy answer that was my way of diverting the focus.

"All kids are high maintenance and don't give me the martyr bit. Look, they got paid for having you there." He rubbed his hands along his jeaned legs, turning away from me.

"I guess so." Silence persisted between us for a few moments before I spoke again. "The other child who got out – Tyrus – I want to meet him."

He sighed and spoke low, "Why? What is he going to tell you?"

Pushing a curl behind my ear I said, "I don't know, but we're both victims. Maybe he remembers something."

"He was rescued by a killer and you were left outside a burning home. He went back to his family and you to a life of foster care." His words hit the nail on the head. That was exactly it.

I leaned forward and drew circles on the tile. "Yeah. Why him and not me? It makes me angry. I was three years old, drugged and left to die!"

"I get it, Chelsea." He brought a hand to my chin and lifted my head as my eyes focused on the invisible circles my fingers drew on the tile. I glanced away and into his eyes. "You're not doing this alone. OK, I'm coming with you."

I gave him a quick hug. It wasn't the response I expected but it was me and him against the world for a few years now so it shouldn't have surprised me. If he wanted to find his mom, I'd be right there with him.

He stood, dusting his robe off and offered me a hand. "Come on, we better get back before they notice we're gone."

A welcome breeze swept over the stadium during the ceremony, keeping me comfortable in my cap and gown, otherwise we would have melted in the heat. Even at seven pm the sun was still bright in the early summer evening. Scanning the crowd, I found my family. The smiles on their faces proud. They were my family. I was one of the lucky ones.

After the ceremony, Roy gave me a bouquet of flowers that I guessed was customary, but I was greeted with a second bouquet when Charice found us.

"Congratulations," she said as she handed me the mixed flower arrangement. I gave her a hug and a thank you. Her blue eyes sparkled under the stadium lighting. I hadn't expected her to be at the ceremony but was glad she made it. That's the kind of person she was.

After graduation and dinner with my family, James included, we headed to the graduation party.

Like any small southern town, everyone knew about the party. Every year the graduates met in the woods by the river. It was a rite of passage and this year was our year. James grabbed a tree and whirled around, confronting me.

I stopped abruptly. His face a twist of sorrow and tension. He opened his mouth to speak and froze as if the words missed the exit.

"What's going on?" I asked, searching his eyes.

Raking a hand through his hair he shifted on his feet and licked his lips as if forcing the words out. "This is our last night together…"

His words hung in the air and I understood their meaning. I was really his only friend and now he'd be alone. Music and voices carried on a light breeze through the night air as I contemplated what that meant for him. He had no one to come back to and I'd be starting classes soon. I'd told him earlier I was planning on beginning my college career this summer. We still had whatever our adventure finding Tyrus would entail, but this was our last real hoorah. After tonight our lives would be changed forever. If I only knew then how true that statement was the entire evening might have turned out different.

We'd never return to the lake and get high, he wouldn't be waiting for a ride before and after school because my car had air conditioning and heat that worked, we wouldn't be meeting at the fence anymore. The childhood chapter of our lives was closing. It wasn't a loss of innocence for either of us and I'd faced a horrible life my mind locked away in a shady, cobwebbed corner but that was no different than the pain of losing his mother and an abusive father.

I took his hand. "We make a pact tonight, right now," I said. "Every last weekend in May for the rest of our lives we meet at the log by the river."

He dug a hand into the pocket of his loose-fitting jeans, drew out a Swiss army knife, flipped it open and pricked his finger. He then handed the small blade to me. "A blood pact."

James had a flare for the overdramatic, his melancholy words seeping through my pores. I pricked my finger. "A blood pact."

We pressed our fingers together and repeated, "Every last weekend in May."

By surprise, tears exploded from my eyes. James grasped my wrist, pulled my body to his and wrapped his arms around me with ferocity. The scent of soap on his skin was drowned when my nose stuffed up. I couldn't stop the water pouring from my eyes. I didn't understand yet why the tears flowed hard and heavy like a wild river.

I wrapped my arms tight around him, my head pressed beneath his chin. I swore in that moment I heard him whisper, "I love you–"

The words and moment were interrupted by a male voice, "Party is at the river!"

The stolen moment gone, we pulled apart as the long, lanky teen approached us. Dillon was a guy that was everyone's friend, star long distance runner, and all-around nice person. "James, my man." He held up his fist for a bump. "Chelsea," he acknowledged me. "Gotta take a piss. Meet you at the river," he stated then jogged off.

We followed the music and voices. Teens littered the waterfront and dock. A couple trucks were pulled up, tailgates open as makeshift bars.

"James, brah, we got a bong like you've never seen," Franco said. His large chest pushing at the fabric around his torso as if his shirt would burst wide open. He was a naturally big guy, north of six feet tall.

James guffawed. "What are we waiting for?" He turned towards me. "Coming?"

"Nah, you go ahead," I said, giving him my blessing, but they were gone before I finished my sentence as Franco hooked an arm around James's neck and pulled him backwards.

I searched one of the tailgate bars, stocked with some type of red punch, a keg, and plenty of red plastic cups, undecided between the mystery spiked punch or beer.

"You look like a punch kind of girl," a young man said as he leaned against the tail gate. Dark hair covered his head in unruly waves and his green eyes sparkled under the moonlight.

"I was thinking beer, no mystery ingredients."

He chuckled. "Your friend is popular tonight."

Who was this guy? Not only had I never seen him, I'd certainly remember if I had since he was mouthwatering gorgeous, but everyone knew James even if James wasn't their friend. He was the school pothead, and it was a small town. "He's the guy you want at a party," I said, streaming beer from the keg into a plastic cup. "You want one?"

His lips curled into a smile, revealing straight white teeth like you'd see on a magazine model. "Sure, thanks."

I handed him the beer then took a sip of my own. Curiosity eating at me. He wasn't a town cop. They condoned the party. The whole town rolled up after graduation every year. By nine everyone was home but the grads. I guessed they figured it was safer we have this night and never once had there been an accidental death or incident. "How come I've never seen you?"

He shrugged as we stepped away from the makeshift bar to give the next customers room. "I transferred in spring semester."

I stopped short. "Of your senior year?"

"Yeah, Mom wanted out of the city and accepted an offer here. It was my choice, I could have stayed with Dad in the city but wanted a fresh start."

"Oh, what kind of trouble were you in?"

He chuckled. "I have to be in trouble to get a fresh start?"

I tilted my head back and met his green eyes. "Yup." I was a sucker for green eyes.

"No trouble."

I didn't completely buy it even though I read sincerity in his face and eyes. Something drove him here the last semester of his senior year. Maybe it was divorce. He did say his mom moved here but his dad was in the city. "Not much here."

"College in the fall. I'll be gone again and Dad's working on getting me an internship this summer."

We strolled onto the dock stretching over the slow-moving water. Trees reflecting on its glassy surface. I paused and leaned my arms against the wooden railing. "An internship, what's your interest?"

He leaned against the railing beside me. The warm flesh of his arm touching mine. A mixture of aftershave and the flowery scent of the gentle summer breeze tingled my nose. Tremors of desire flooded through me as I tried to play it cool. "I don't know yet, but an internship of any kind will look good on a resume."

I expected at any time he'd leave but instead donated the night to me as we talked under the stars. James busy doing what James does, I didn't fret. He'd catch up to me when he was ready to hang out. Our shoes off and feet dangled in the water at the edge of the dock, the night could not have been more perfect.

The slight breeze off the water carried a chunk of hair over my face. He brushed it away and pushed it behind my ear, the feel of his hand against my cheek crippled my senses into jelly. His face moved closer to mine; his lips close enough to almost taste him.

"Time to go," James's voice interrupted. The moment dissipated and vanished as I craned my neck upwards at James. Gathering my feet from the water, I pushed off the weathered wooden deck, glanced down at the hot guy who'd entertained me all evening then turned and followed James.

Footfalls behind us and a hand on my shoulder made me stop in my tracks and whirl around.

"Your shoes," he said, the guy from nowhere who made my night something unforgettable. His expression expectant and stance confident as if expecting I'd stay with him instead of letting James determine my evening.

I smiled sheepishly. "Thanks." It wasn't that I didn't want to spend more time with him but James was the guy that was always there for me and we'd taken my car.

James grabbed my hand, "We gotta go," and pulled me with him as I couldn't take my eyes off the amazing stranger. His frame growing smaller the further from him I got.

"What's your hurry?" I asked, clearly annoyed as I pulled my hand from his and stopped.

He continued walking. "I'm ready to go. We have a long drive to Atlanta."

This wasn't James. He was never in a hurry, never worried about school or studying or even pot. He was laid back and carefree, but that was mostly in appearance. Underneath he was a troubled guy. "I'm not moving until you tell me what's going on." I folded my arms around my chest.

He swung around. "Nothing. I told you, I have to get home."

It was graduation night. He wasn't worried about driving to Atlanta or even meeting Tyrus. I was nervous about it, but not him. It wasn't his problem. He was support. The biggest party in this small one-horse town every year and we were finally seniors and he wanted to choose tonight to be responsible. I narrowed my eyes and searched his face and stance. His shoulders back, hands at his sides, straight lips, hair falling over his eyes; he was unreadable. It was something I'd never seen in him.

I jogged towards him and, noting my movements, he continued his fast pace towards my car as if fleeing a crime.

Green-Eyed Flare Up

I put the keys in the ignition but didn't turn the car over. "Are you jealous?" It was the only thing that made any amount of sense. He didn't like another guy paying me attention.

He flung the hair back out of his eyes. "No." From his pocket he pulled out a blunt. "We can talk about it over this."

We went to our usual spot at the log by the river. The party far enough away we couldn't hear the music or voices.

He lit the blunt, took a long drag, and handed it to me. I sucked in as much as my lungs would hold. I might as well make the most of the moment since there wouldn't be many left. One day we'd be married with kids and we wouldn't hold true to our pact.

I blew out. "Are you sure nothing is bothering you?"

He took the blunt and twisted it in his fingers. "It didn't feel right, ya know?"

I watched him blow the smoke in rings. He had a knack for that. I'd never figured it out. I blew out something that looked more like half-moons. "Was it that guy I was with?"

He appeared to stare at the reflection of the moon over the water. "I don't know." He shrugged and inhaled again, holding in for a few seconds before releasing. "Have you ever met him?"

"No." Really, that was maybe what attracted me the most. He hadn't been born and raised in this one-horse town.

"Exactly, no one at the party recognized him. If he was a student, someone would have known him, had a class with him."

"Wait." I turned towards him. "You asked around?"

He met my gaze. "Hell yeah. Chelsea, you're like this beautiful innocent girl. The freckles on your nose that move across your face. It's like they dance when you talk and are a perfect match to your strawberry blonde curls and you have no idea that you're a bombshell. If this guy is hitting on my best friend than I'm going to find out about him."

He was right. I was insecure about my looks and didn't have the best taste in guys. I dated a guy my sophomore year, really nice guy but he turned out gay. That did a number on my self-esteem. I didn't care that he was gay. I cared that he led me on and that I was so easily led on. Every guy I ever dated, there was always something wrong with him or me.

"He just moved here this semester. I'm sure that's why no one knew him."

James let out a deep drag. "The woods, back there, something felt off. It wasn't just him. It was like something's in the woods." He let out an aggravated breath. "I'm sure it was nothing."

I chuckled. "Kids in the woods partying. It's the perfect set up for a horror flick."

He put the blunt out and stuffed it in his pocket. "And if we don't get out of here, we'll be first to go. It's always the ones that wander from the pack."

We laughed together as we ran back to my car, sufficiently freaked out.

I didn't have to knock on his door the next morning. He was sitting at the kitchen table with Judy eating scrambled eggs and drinking coffee. He glanced at me when I entered the room.

"Make yourself at home," I joked, taking the seat next to him and across from Judy.

She lifted her coffee mug. "He says you two are going on an adventure today."

I flashed him a faux smile as I kicked his shin. "It may be one of our last opportunities to spend time together."

She reached a hand across the table and I met it with my own. She squeezed. "Honey, life passes too fast. Enjoy being young." Her smile filled the room and her words hung in the air. If only she knew. "Oh, and I packed you sandwiches."

It was surprising to me that I was so skinny. She always made sure I had more than enough food and the house always smelled of the herbs she cooked with.

The drive to Atlanta, we listened to music, singing, and hardly spoke until I finally turned down the radio, craving conversation. I wanted something to take my mind off what I would say or do when I met Tyrus. "Tell me about your job."

"It's a job, construction," he said then turned the radio back up.

I lowered the volume again. "Look, I'm nervous. I don't know if I can do this. It seemed like a better idea yesterday."

"I don't think it's a good idea at all but I think it's brave and I think it should be done. If anything, it will ease your mind."

"You think? What am I going to say? Do I just walk into his office and say 'hey, we were kidnapped by the same assholes. Tell me what was your experience like?'"

"Not everything in life fits into little boxes. You can't organize and control everything. You just have to do this. We can catch him outside of the office. We'll figure it out."

Yeah. We needed a plan. I handed James my phone. "Find him on social media. Does he have a routine?"

For the rest of the drive, we worked out a plan. James knew I couldn't fly by the seat of my pants like he does. My life has to have structure and order. Tyrus, twice a week and on Saturdays, volunteered at a dojo after work. He didn't appear to be married, have children, or even a girlfriend. We figured finding him at work was the worst idea. Confronting him when leaving the dojo was the best idea that we could come up with.

By the time I pulled the car into the parking lot, my nerves were all over the place and felt like needles pricking every centimeter of my skin. Through the glass, I saw Tyrus's thick frame. Not weightlifter bulky but thick with definition and the children were lined up practicing kicks and punches. Watching him, seeing how he interacted with the children eased my mind until the parking lot started to fill up and I knew class was ending.

We waited until the building was empty except for Tyrus and headed in. Nerves wracked my body and I stopped a few feet from the door.

James grabbed my sweaty hand. "I'm right here."

I nodded and clutched his hand tight as we walked into the dojo. Tyrus leaned over a duffle bag, glanced up as we entered. "We're closed."

I let go of James's hand and twisted mine together. "A… are you Tyrus Reed?"

He lowered his eyebrows in curiosity. "Can I help you?"

I took in a deep breath and searched my mind for words, but none came.

James started, "The same Tyrus Reed that was kidnapped as a child?" That was direct enough. I felt the heat in my cheeks.

He folded his arms across his chest as if sizing us up.

"I'm Chelsea Mora," I spluttered.

That caught his attention, his gaze softened and he dropped his arms. "The Chelsea Mora."

I nodded.

"What can I help you with?" His words didn't show fear or anger and my tensions started to ease.

"I know the Moras weren't my parents and I want to know what happened that night," I spit out, waiting on pins and needles for his response.

"That's all in the papers." The edges of his words laced in lies.

I stepped closer to him, my gaze searching his. "We're both victims of the same crime, only you went home to your family and I went into foster care. I know an old man didn't find you and take you home. It was the killer, right?"

He glanced from me to James, who stood a couple steps behind me. "They kept me drugged and I don't remember much, but you're right, he brought me home. I'll never know why he didn't kill me. You were different."

"How?" I demanded, finding control in my words, courage rising in me.

"You can find this in the papers. His MO was killing the parents and older brothers while always leaving the youngest, a daughter, behind. He was a sick man. I'm not defending him, but I think he assumed, at least at first, that you and that boy were the Moras children. It would have ruined his night to accept something else, moreover, he probably didn't know who your parents were." His words cut sharp and deep and I barely noted the empathy in them.

It was as if he was defending the Hurricane Killer. He was a defense attorney… Everything he said was probably true, but he hadn't answered my question. "What happened?"

"There's a coffee shop two doors down. Why don't you meet me there in ten minutes and I'll tell you what I remember?"

"No, you can tell us now," James demanded in a powerful voice. "She deserves to know." It was a side of James I hadn't seen and it took me off guard.

Tyrus scooted his bag and sat on the bench. "This conversation doesn't leave this room," he stated before telling his story which wasn't much different than what I read in the papers. They'd drugged him twice and locked him in a room. It was the killer who took him from the room. He was scared and did what he was asked without asking any questions.

An eight-year-old boy, he was frightened. Most children would have done the same thing. He'd seen me once when he was taken to the restroom, but he never saw the boy. He was locked in the room again and wasn't let out until the killer opened the door and led him out of the house and he followed the dirt road and waited by the car exactly as he asked him.

My mind carried me back to the day Chief Sugda took me there. Nothing about it was familiar, but I imagined a small, scared young boy who wanted to get home to his family, who wanted to feel safe again in his parents' arms. I took his hand. "Thank you."

He smiled and wrapped a hand on top of mine. "You're welcome. There's one more thing. It might not mean anything, but I remember the word talbot. My mind was cloudy but I'm sure I heard one of them say it. I don't know what it means. It could be a road, a restaurant, a boat, or someone's name. I just don't know."

Talbot – the word didn't mean anything to me either. Thinking back to the article with the arrests, I didn't remember anyone having the first or last name of Talbot. I gave his hand one more squeeze and we left. After opening the car door I gave the dojo one last glance. Tyrus stood by the door and flipped the light switch as he stepped outside into the moist warm air.

James closed the door as I started the engine. "Social Services would have looked for your parents, for a living relative. They place children with their families first right."

"I guess unless they can't be found or are dead." The parking lot was empty except for us and the black Mercedes Tyrus climbed into so I pulled forward.

His next words were filled with mischievousness: "We need to get your file."

Serving Leftovers

We discussed it over burgers. The sandwiches Judy made us devoured hours ago. It wasn't really a discussion, but me defending Charice and whatever was left of the life my foster family had built. His argument was how come she'd never shown me the file even at my last visit. I was eighteen, why didn't she come forward. The logical answer was that the investigation never turned up a relative, or at least a relative suitable to raise a child. I couldn't help but remember Charice's behavior during our last visit.

She'd been different, left my file wide open. I took it for her normal harebrained behavior. She was an organized, disorganized mess. She'd gone in the back because she forgot something, leaving me alone with my file where I'd taken pictures. She'd even announced her return, giving me time to put the file back together. James's argument made more sense than mine. Four hours later I parked behind her office and we were walking towards the back door.

He pulled out his Swiss army knife. Somehow I didn't doubt he'd picked a lock before, but what shocked us both is when the door opened as soon as he pushed one of the gadgets into the lock. I gasped and he stared at me wide eyed.

"We should go," I mouthed, instantly following the lead of the shackled hair on my arms.

He rested his ear against the door and after several seconds opened the door the rest of the way. If my nerves hadn't been edgy enough earlier, they certainly were now. He slid along the door and into the dark building. I followed right behind him, more scared to be outside alone than inside next to him. I handed him the flashlight I always kept in my car and motioned him to Charice's office.

The building was eerily quiet. It was a place that always gave a sense of comfort because I associated it with Charice and her always welcoming smile and demeanor. He went to the file cabinet and I to her desk. Both of us coming up empty handed. "Maybe she took it home," I whispered.

"Why? Her job with you is mostly done. Wouldn't she have another child to take your place?"

Why was he thinking so logical? "Maybe she sent it somewhere else, since I'm eighteen?" I knew that wasn't the answer. I was in college and, even though an adult, I was still under the state's thumb as they were paying me a monthly check and for my college. Perhaps she had taken it home.

He pointed at her computer. I was good at coding, not hacking. I blew out a breath, the warm air filling my hands over my mouth and thought about what her password might be. She had children but I didn't know their birthdays. Finally, I shrugged. "I don't know what her password could be, and I don't think it would be wise for me to touch the computer. Think about it, the back door was open."

That's the first time I said what I was trying to avoid thinking. Someone had already been there before us.

He nodded, conceding that I was right and there was something more wrong with this situation than a young woman attempting to read her social services file. He wiped the file cabinet where he'd opened the drawers and we left. He wiped the doorknob with his T-shirt as well. Once inside my car, the chills running over my spine subsided and the shackled hairs on my arms relaxed. I wasted no time in starting the engine.

The drive was quiet until I turned the corner into our subdivision. "I think you need to be careful," James stated.

I didn't respond, unsure even what to say.

"I mean it. If someone was there before us, why would they take *your* file?" His voice lacking its usual jovialness and fringing on concern.

"It's probably like you said, she took it home and we don't know anyone else had been there. Maybe she just forgot to lock the door."

That should have been the ah-ha moment when the moving pieces started coming together but I was so desperate to put everything in my life back into neat little boxes. What happened next took both of us, and the entire town, by surprise.

Peach Cobbler

The TV was on I noted by the bouncing light against the blinds in the living room. I parked in my usual spot. Phoebe had gone home this morning before I woke up. When I entered, Judy and Roy nearly jumped out of their seats, ebbing wrinkles of apprehension sewn into their faces.

I dropped my keys on the small round glass top table by the door and entered the living room. "What's going on?"

It was Roy who spoke. "A senior was attacked in the woods last night."

His statement so profound and alarming the pesky arm hairs shot back up. I heard James's words of warning and blame in my head.

Judy stood and wrapped her arms around me and Roy joined in a large foster family hug.

When we pulled out of the large foster family hug Judy spoke, wiping the tears leaking from her eyes. "Leandra Wittings. Physically, she's fine, but I can't imagine the emotional pain that girl will go through." I imagined Judy overstated that comment.

She'd been a child therapist before she became my foster mom and probably had a good idea of the trauma it induced.

Roy took my hand and led me to the couch. Both he and Judy sat beside me. "The police were here earlier. They wanted to know if you remembered anything strange, maybe a person that didn't belong." He reached over to the coffee table and picked up a card that he flipped in his fingers. "We told them you and James returned before midnight. The attack was after one a.m."

He handed me the card. "That's the officer. He asked you to call or come by the station if you saw anything out of place." His tone one of questioning, as if he knew I spent the evening talking to someone who *didn't* belong.

Like a stab to my heart. A pointed finger at the young man I'd spent the evening talking with. I didn't know Leandra well. We'd had a couple classes together over the years and she joined the robotics club her sophomore year but left after a few weeks. We had a running inside joke as *school twins* because everyone mistook us for sisters, even occasionally mistaking one of us for the other. She had darker hair and neither of us saw the resemblance.

So much for never an incidence at the grad party. I'd spoken too soon. James's words of warning grew louder in my head. I left early, but what did the dangerously too hot guy I was talking with do? *Did he stay? Had he lied to me? Who was he?* James was in my head. He'd said something seemed off, like something was in the woods...

Nonsense. The guy was easy to talk with and I felt good in his presence. Was he the kind of person that would attack someone, and why? *What would he have to gain?* There was no answer to that question or even a great excuse like those I made for my file not being where it should be. I knew absolutely nothing about him, not even his name, so I had nothing to offer the police.

"We're glad you're OK," Judy said, her voice sincere and filled with unease.

I cradled the card in my hand. "If I think of anything, I'll call, but there's nothing I can think of. It was as normal as an alcohol party with a bunch of graduates could be; loud music, makeshift bars, and dancing."

When I got to my room I took several deep breaths. All the little organized boxes in my brain were opening, their contents spilling out in a disjointed fashion. My breathing sped up as I collapsed against the closed door. The bed in front of me, moving closer, the walls closing in. I was having a panic attack.

I used to get these when I was younger and Judy's voice spoke in my head, *deep breaths, control your breathing, close your eyes, focus on something that makes you happy.* I focused on deep breathing and my childhood happy spot. Sitting with Phoebe on the couch as she read me a story and we ate Rice Krispy treats.

After several moments, I felt better and opened my eyes. The room was no longer threatening to squeeze me in and my bed welcomed my presence. I crawled across the floor, my hand brushing against something that triggered me to pull my hand away quickly and my eyes to search for the culprit – my shoes from last night.

Their soft light brown leather brought me back to last night when *he* chased me down and handed them to me as I'd left them on the dock. His fingerprints would be on them. My instinct was to wipe them down but what if he was guilty and I wiped away evidence. Instead, I grabbed a book from under my bed and pushed them towards the closet.

Rising onto my knees, I pulled the door open and forced them in then covered them with a hoodie so I wouldn't see them. Then I slammed the door and crawled into bed.

My dreams were filled with the monster in the closet that escaped and chased Leandra through the woods, only she turned into me. My eyes popped wide open as I was trying to scream but no noise left my mouth. Tears rolling down my cheeks.

It took a few moments for my mind to completely leave dream world and enter reality. Dark surrounded me, swathing me in a cold exterior that chilled me to the bone. I pulled the covers over my head and my knees into my chest.

My guts filled with unease and tension, I went to the fence after breakfast, sending James a text to meet me there. *Did he know?* I wondered as I waited.

The familiar sound of the screen door closing and the crunch of his steps across the grass told me he was on the way. I lifted the fence and he crawled through. Hair falling forward over his face, he flipped it back, revealing his eyes. Slowly, it fell back into place.

His dad hadn't told him anything. He claimed his dad was passed out snoring on the couch by the time he got home so he snuck into bed. Same thing the night of graduation. I assured him that Roy and Judy vouched for both of us. It wasn't like we were suspects anyways.

I twisted the blades of grass in my fingers. "I think I should go to the police."

"Why would you do that?"

"I thought about what you said about that guy. I don't know him. You said nobody knew him. Maybe it was him."

He folded his legs to his chest. "You know his name?"

"No."

"Then what are you going to tell them?"

I shrugged. "I guess, nothing."

I knew it was my guilt eating at me, telling me I should go to the police, but truly I didn't know anything, not even about the attack. All I knew is I was talking with a guy who wasn't a familiar face and whose name I didn't know. I was seeking confirmation that silence was the best answer.

I had other problems and spent the afternoon refocusing my energy on me. I watched movies in my bed to take my mind off the last week but that didn't work. The lies and secrets unfolding about my past were like watching part one of a movie that ended in a cliffhanger and having to wait another year to see part two. I opened my laptop, placing it on my lap, and searched for the *Hurricane Killer*.

Tyrus was right: I was part of his MO. During East Coast hurricanes, he stalked and killed families of at least four or even five; killing both parents and the oldest children, always boys, leaving the youngest, a daughter, alive.

The first family noted to die, only circumstantial evidence to say he did it, was his own family. He killed his mother, stepfather, and younger brother but his younger sister had crawled under her crib. The police had shown up and carted him off to psych care. His final victims were his sister Emily and her family. He left their daughter, his niece, Erika, alive.

A healthy swell of chills reached up my spine. He came back for her. Did that mean he planned on coming back for all the girls, including… me?

It was the same night he killed his sister that he met his fate. Someone killed him in the same fashion, by slashing his neck and letting him bleed out. His murderer was never found.

So he wasn't a Dexter type but a really twisted soul. Further reading revealed he'd been abused by his mother. The more I learned, the more I sided with Tyrus. Evan O'Conner, AKA the Hurricane Killer, despite how depraved his actions, saved my life and from something much worse than growing up in foster care. He saved me from further abuse from the Moras even though that was far from his motive.

The psych report supported I'd been abused, or at the very least neglected. My mind rationalized that the Hurricane Killer was the lesser of two evils. His victims died a quick death, unlike the Moras who stole children and sold them into awful fates. My own life would have turned out completely different if he hadn't killed the Moras that night.

The only pain I felt was for the boy who was my *pretend* brother. He not only never saw his family again but lost his life. DNA evidence eventually discovered his family and his remains were returned to them for a proper burial. The article didn't release his name.

The aromatic melody of beef stew and peach cobbler brought me out of my room and into the kitchen where Judy pulled the delicious dessert out of the oven. She placed it on the granite counter and slipped the thick green potholders off her hands.

I took a seat at the table and pulled a pie puffy out of the basket. Judy's happy place was making food and she always made extra pie crust, filled it with butter, sugar, and cinnamon, rolled it, pinched the ends and baked them.

"Hey, stranger," she said, taking note of my presence.

"Hey," I said between bites as the cinnamon butter melted onto my tongue. "Is Roy working tonight?"

"The hospital called him in but he should be home about nine."

I took another bite, watching her stir the stew. "You wanna grab a couple bowls?" she asked. "The stew is ready."

I set the silverware on the table as she leaned against the counter and took a break. "What have you been up to today?"

"Nothing. I watched a movie and... I filled out the form for summer classes," I said hesitantly.

"Oh." She didn't hide the sting in her voice.

I handed her a bowl which she set on the counter and taking mine first filled it with stew then ladled a few spoons into hers.

I didn't wait to sit before taking the first steaming bite of a carrot. After my tongue stopped burning I felt I needed to explain. It was important for them to understand and for me to have their blessing to push the guilt away. "It's a good opportunity. I can bring the Kia and won't have to change dorm rooms in the fall. I can also take the boring, repeat of high school classes now. I have to take two classes so I thought I would take US history and humanities." I was the high school student who had already earned almost two years of credits with CLEP exams. They were a simpler alternative to AP or dual enrollment and weren't overly costly.

"You've always had a logical head on your shoulders. When do classes start?" she asked between blows on her stew.

"The week after next. They have a summer orientation that Wednesday and classes start Thursday."

She gave a sorrowful, thoughtful smile. "Oh."

"Can I ask you something?"

"Of course."

"Why didn't you ever take other foster children?"

That question seemed to take her by surprise but she answered, "You were an easy sell," she jested. "Phoebe always wanted a sister and Roy loves children."

She paused for a moment. "By the time your case crossed my desk you were in your fourth home in less than a year. When they wanted to move you again, I put my foot down. You needed stability and a nuclear family. I knew we could provide that so I volunteered. Roy and Phoebe were as excited as me."

They did create the nuclear family. Judy, Roy, and Phoebe, along with James, were my center.

After a couple bites she continued, "You had such an obsession with Rice Krispy treats. I made a pan daily and when Phoebe came home from school, the two of you would squeeze into the big recliner with a plate and she'd read you stories." Her voice reminiscent.

I smiled. "I remember." It was the only possible memory I had before six but since that tradition continued when I was in grade school I figured the memories melted together.

"Can we do a movie night tonight?" I asked, feeling the pain of missing them already.

"I'd love that and we have a cobbler that needs our attention."

Big bowls of peach cobbler and ice cream, we curled up on the couch and watched Ted 2. As the movie was coming to an end, the front door opened and Roy stood in the entryway to the living room. Pain and sorrow filling his eyes.

Walking Away

I caught the concern on Roy's face and my first thoughts went to Phoebe, but that didn't make sense. If something happened to her why would they call her father at work and not try the home phone first? My mind then focused on Leandra. Did the person who attacked her come back to finish the job? That wasn't unheard of, at least not in police procedural TV.

Roy sat in the recliner, leaned forward, and folded his hands together. "There's no easy way to say this. Chelsea, your um. Charice." He cleared his throat, his eyes glassy with water. "She passed, sometime late last night. Her husband found her today."

I couldn't process the words or make any sense of them.

The couch bounced lightly as Judy moved closer to me and I felt her arm around my shoulder. As my head sorted through Roy's words, I felt my heart tighten in anguish.

"They think it was a heart attack," Roy said. His words far off and distorted.

"Chelsea?" I heard Judy but couldn't find my voice.

I remember getting up but don't remember going to bed.

When the light from the break in the curtain streamed over my eyes it woke me. A sense of numb crept over my body. I couldn't feel or move the parts for quite some time.

Slowly the feeling came back and so did Roy's words. My skin felt like fiery needles were poking every nerve ending.

I didn't move, not even when Judy entered. She scooted onto the edge of my bed and smoothed my hair back.

I finally sat up and wrapped my arms around her middle and cried into her shoulder.

I'm not sure at that moment if I actually understood Charice was gone or if it was the moment I began to put the pieces together.

She pulled her feet up and held me for a long time.

It was later in the day when I finally left my room, knowing I looked rough but didn't care. "What happened to her?" I asked Roy who was leaned back in the recliner watching a movie.

He stopped the movie and pushed the footrest down. "They think a heart attack."

"What else?"

"Her husband found her."

"Why wasn't he there and what about their kids?" I grilled him. It wasn't his fault but I wanted to know everything.

He didn't get angry for the questions or even flinch. "He took the kids camping overnight Saturday. They came home yesterday and she was..." He didn't say the words but he didn't need to.

"When?"

"Around 11 pm."

I stood and wandered into the kitchen then slumped in a chair.

Roy's footfalls followed me. He opened the refrigerator and pulled out the peach cobbler and two bowls from the cabinet. After microwaving them he set one in front of me with a fork. "You should eat."

I didn't resist and we ate our cobbler in silence.

When I returned to my room I checked my phone. It was dead so I plugged it in and curled into bed under my covers until a tapping sound alerted me. It took my mind a minute to register what the sound was. Someone was tapping on my window. Apprehensively, I went to the window and pulled the curtain from the corner.

Peace melted over me when I saw James.

I opened the window and he crawled inside. I scooted over and gave him room on the bench.

"I hadn't heard from you," he said as if he had to explain himself. It was a small town, and everybody knew everything, especially something like this. Of course, he and everyone else knew.

I leaned back against the wall. "It's been a rough day."

He nodded in agreement. "I've been thinking about it and you all day and um... I uh..." He struggled to find the words. I didn't have the mental energy to figure it out.

"I was worried, that's all."

"I'll be OK, I think. I keep thinking about her and her family."

That seemed to be the window of opportunity he was looking for. "It happened Saturday night. I don't think it's a coincidence."

I thought back to Saturday night. We went to her office to break in, but the door was already open. Guilt, a huge gob of guilt, chomped away at me. I wasn't ready to put both those things into the same thought so I changed the subject. "I think we should go see Leandra tomorrow. She probably could use a friend right now, or friends."

I couldn't help Charice but I could help Leandra feel better anyways. I imagined she felt kind of like me, numb, confused, angry, and sad all at once.

He nodded again then flipped his hair out of his eyes. "You'll be going alone. I'm leaving in the morning."

With everything that happened fighting for space in my weary mind I'd forgotten tomorrow was Monday but it seemed I remembered him saying he was leaving Sunday night. "You're still here."

He shrugged. "Call Leandra. I'll text you in a couple days," he said then crawled back out the window.

"James."

After planting his feet on the ground, he turned towards me. I held out my arms and wrapped him in them tightly. The next week without him was going to be tough. I sat on the bench and watched him walk across the yard and flip the fence up. In the moment it seemed normal, like I'd see him again the next day. Later I'd realize how it was anything but normal.

White Roses

I told myself to keep moving and everything would be OK: just don't stop. After a quick shower I slipped into a pair of shorts and a tank. Then I threw the tank off. It made me look as rough as I felt, and that wasn't the impression I wanted to give someone I was trying to console.

Finding a cute blouse, I slipped it on and took my phone off the charger. Two years ago in robotics club we all exchanged phone numbers. I crossed my fingers it was still her number as I sent her a text then brushed my hair. The curls sprung through the wires in the brush and not wanting to mess with it today I tied them back in a ponytail.

My phone pinged a few minutes later with a message from Leandra. After a couple more texts back and forth I headed to her house.

It was a large, brick, two-story home with double front doors and a porch held up by green pillars that matched the shutters on every window. A couple large shade trees in the front yard, one on each side of the driveway, and a neatly manicured and honeysuckle fragrant walkway.

I rang the doorbell. Immediately I heard a dog and a few minutes later a tall middle-aged man I assumed was her father answered the door. Leandra quickly joined him.

After a quick introduction, we left. I volunteered to drive since it was my invite. We spent that day thrift shopping and putting together various retro 80s and 90s outfits that we purchased for fun and ended the day with fast food and milkshakes that we ate in my car.

I learned that she would be attending the same university as me. Not a big surprise since it was close, about a two-hour drive, and would be convenient for coming home for long weekends and holidays.

"Thank you, you know, for today. I really needed this. After Friday, my parents have been watching my every move," she said, her brown eyes reflecting sincerity.

I shrugged. "It was nothing. I figured you could use a friend."

"You know, the worst thing was he saw me pee. That's why I left the group and as soon as I stood and zipped my pants I felt his arms around me. I'm sure it was a guy. He pulled me against him and his arms were hairy and strong. I kicked his shin hard and that gave me enough time to get away but I never saw his face." It wasn't fear in her voice but violation of her privacy.

It reminded me of the incident at Edisto Beach with the guy in the camo hat, but of course the events weren't related and I wasn't attacked, but the guy was big. "It's a good thing you have a hell of a shin kick."

She smiled and raised her eyebrows. "I wish we could get together again but I'm leaving for Australia with my mom tomorrow evening for two weeks."

I was a bit jealous. I'd always been curious to travel to foreign lands. For me, it would have to wait until after college. Cementing my financial independence was my goal now. "We have the fall."

We followed each other on social media where she'd be posting pictures, and then I took her home.

Judy accompanied me to Charice's funeral which was a far larger event than I expected. There were so many people it was like the whole town came to say goodbye to her. Young children stood side by side with their foster parents like I did with Judy. The enormity of the good she brought to the world was broadcast through the small town that day.

Her husband and family spoke, tears leaked from my eyes. I'd never again sit in her office or hear her voice or see her joyful smile. She'd been a staple in my life. A white casket that held her lifeless body was lowered into the ground. A display of white roses lay on the top, signifying to me the hope she'd given so many.

Judy squeezed my hand as tears also streamed her cheeks. I glanced at Charice's family, her two boys and husband. I'd grown up looking at them grow up through pictures on her desk, little league, boy scouts, elementary and junior high graduations, and family vacations.

After the funeral was a reception. I attended alone as I'd asked Judy to sit it out. It was something I felt I had to do alone to pay my respects to her family. To tell them how much she meant to me. It was held at their home; a modest, newer home with wood instead of brick construction and a back yard that stretched to the woods.

Inside was cozy with warm, bright colors that reminded me of her personality. The expansive kitchen and living room held the large number of people who attended. I wandered around, a little small talk here and there, and eventually went out the open French doors onto the covered wooden deck, overlooking the field and trees. I rested my arms on the railing.

"Beautiful day, isn't it?" asked a male voice.

I turned to see her husband resting his arms on the railing beside me. "It is. It's the kind of day she loved."

"You're Chelsea?" he asked. The gentle breeze catching wisps of his thinning brown hair. He wasn't an overly handsome man but had something about him that was attractive.

I was a bit taken aback that he knew who I was but I guessed after being one of her cases for fifteen years it made sense that she talked about me, at least on occasion. "And you're Mr. Adams."

He turned towards me. "She always talked about you. You were the one. She cared about all these children here, every one of them, but you were something special."

"She was something special."

"That she was." There was a moment of silence between us before he spoke again. "What do you think of the computer?"

I smiled. "I love it! But she didn't have to do that."

That brought a smile to his face and I realized that was what made him attractive. It was a smile like hers. "But that's what made her *her*. I should be getting back to the other guests," he said, reaching a hand on my shoulder before he departed.

On my way to the restroom, I noted the door across from it was wide open. There were two desks, each with a laptop and one cluttered in files. I guessed the cluttered desk was hers. I thought of how my file was missing from her office the other night and wondered if it was one of those on her desk. No one was around so I debated on taking a glance. What could it hurt? It might put my mind at ease if I looked and it was there.

I pushed my guilt aside and decided to take a quick peek, that would be it. There was a gorgeous view out the window and if anybody saw me, that's the excuse I'd use. Taking a deep breath, I scanned the names on the folders, not wanting to touch or disturb anything. My name wasn't one of them. Not willing to go all out and search the room, I scurried away from her desk and composed myself as I entered the hallway.

I hadn't confirmed or denied whether my folder was there or not. It didn't matter, I decided, and was done looking into a past I didn't remember. If my mind wanted me to know it wouldn't be made of cheesecloth. Next week would start a new chapter in my life, a fresh beginning. Forgotten things were best unseen and unheard.

Part 2

Seen and Heard

Blindfolds and Earplugs

My suitcase bounced against each step as I pulled it up the tiled stairs. The noise bouncing off the walls of the dorm building. Each room was furnished with two beds, a mini fridge, two built-in desks, and access to a shared Jack and Jill bathroom with the room next door.

Sweat beaded on my brow by the time I reached the final step and rested a moment, glad the building only had three floors. The emptiness of the halls reminded me the summer semester was beginning in two days.

I stopped when I found the room and slid the key into the lock, met with a kaleidoscope of colors when I opened the door. Obviously, my roommate liked color. The tie-died motif of her unmade bed matched the swirling culprit of the rainbow of colors spread over the room – a sun catcher. It was pretty, but I figured it would be disruptive when studying.

The wild color scheme, I assumed my roommate was an extroverted partier. Unlike me, as I contrasted my baby blue and tan bed motif. I was more conservative, levelheaded, and an introvert, who came to school to learn.

By the time I finished unpacking and making up my bed she still wasn't home. I figured I'd take a tour of the college on my own before summer school orientation tomorrow. I stuffed the map the college gave me in the back pocket of my jean shorts and my cell phone in the other pocket. I didn't plan on using the map unless I needed help getting back. This evening was an adventure to explore my new surroundings, my home for the next four years.

I passed a few students who stepped off at the second floor on the way down the three flights of stairs which were easier coming down without the large, hefty suitcase that I perched empty on the shelf in my small closet. It hadn't been easy, since the width of it nearly matched the door frame.

A sidewalk twisted from the dorms which I followed in curiosity. It led to the river and continued its path along it with benches sprinkled on the river's edge. Small groups and pairs of students hung out here and there. An older man sat on a bench eating a sandwich. I imagined he was one of the professors. It was a beautiful evening, even the air was agreeable and not steamy. A breeze came off the river, blowing chunks and curls of hair over my head.

I categorized the place as a good place to hang out or even catch some alone time but a bad place to study as the breeze would push any pages in a book. The Riverwalk led to a large, covered arena for all the indoor sporting events and, occasionally, bands.

A path led from the arena towards the center of campus and branched off in various directions to the admissions office and financial aid, to each building that housed each college and its classrooms. I stayed straight on the path that circled back to the food court. A trail connected it to the dorms.

The food court still open, I grabbed an iced coffee since there were no milkshakes. I settled on a seat beneath one of the umbrella tables and wondered if my roommate was back yet as I sipped my coffee. I choked down the first swallow as it had to be the worst iced coffee ever.

"I would have warned you if you'd asked," said a young woman who took the seat across from me. Her blonde hair pulled behind her head except for a pink chunk that rested against her cheek. "I don't know though, it is funny to watch everyone's first sip." She guffawed. "Don't worry. There's a better coffee shop in town and Ryde is in and out of the campus all day." She paused, "Anora," she introduced herself.

"Chelsea."

She continued, "The food here is OK. I hope you bought a food pass though, as the prices are high without one. They give you a discount if you pay for the semester. It's less for summer semester."

"Thanks," I responded, not sure what else to say.

"Leave that on the table, I'll buy you a real coffee."

I wasn't sure what to say but didn't want to pass up the opportunity to meet someone and learn more about the campus and area which she seemed to know something about. On the Ryde she filled me in on where to get anything I wanted in town from the best pizza, Chinese, best toilet paper prices, and even the local thrift shop, as well as the avoids.

The college was in the city but sat on so much land it was easy to forget how close it was to everything. The Coffee Bean, from appearance, was like any coffee shop. Inside was cozy; decorated in warm colors with large windows allowing the sun to fill the place during the day. The blinds drawn, I barely made out the street and passing cars from inside.

We sat at a seat in the middle, college students filled the crevices. She placed a tray with two coffees on it and a bag on the table then pushed one of the coffees my way. "Try that." From the bag she pulled out two boxes.

"They also have the best pie and cobblers. Their special today is peach cobbler. Their cheesecake is delish too and everything is eco-friendly and recyclable."

My first thought was how Phoebe would approve of this place. "Thank you," I said, my stomach grumbling as I eyed the cobbler, wondering if it was as mouthwatering as Judy's. It looked delish with a flaky topping and large peaches.

"They have a deal with a local fruit stand and buy only fresh and make fresh each day. I love this place and wish there was one back home." Anora wasn't shy and did most of the talking as we ate our cobbler and drank our iced coffee, which wasn't bad. I wasn't a coffee fan but had been won over. She was right: every town needed a place like this.

It turns out she graduated a few weeks ago with her bachelor's degree and is a bioengineering major. She wants to help make sustainable food as the population continues to grow. In the fall she's starting her master's work. For the summer, she's assisting in a research project, something about mtDNA, mutations, and genetic diseases. Most of what she said was over my head.

"You should join the study. There's a small grant for students. It's not much, but could pay for your fall books or food pass," she said, her eyes large and round.

Her words caught me off-guard. Was she asking me to donate DNA? "Maybe. I'll think about it." I really wasn't up for volunteering, but the extra money could come in handy.

In His Absence

Ihadn't heard from James since that last night at my window. He hadn't responded to my texts, so when my back pocket vibrated, my heart pumped rapidly and I grabbed it, hoping it was him. When I saw Phoebe's name pop up, my heart dropped. She'd sent a gif of a student rushing to class with a boatload of books.

I chuckled and, not watching where I was going, Anora talking my ear off, brushed past someone. The cologne laced summer scent was familiar. "Excuse me."

I glanced behind, recognizing the dark curls and vibrant green eyes as he turned his head. A cocky, open-mouthed smile stretched across his face.

"If it isn't Cinderella. I thought I was going to have to match your shoes to every girl in the kingdom to find you and all I had to do was get coffee."

I bit my lip. I couldn't help but remember what James said: that nobody at the party knew him. He was right, someone should have recognized him. New eye candy got noticed quickly in a small-town high school. "In the flesh."

"Can I buy you a coffee?"

"I just had one but um… maybe tomorrow?" I said, hoping he had plans already or work or anything else but to spend time with me. He was hot and I was flattered, but with James's words of warning, Leandra's attack, and an overall sense of unease, I wasn't sure I should trust him or even attempt to be his friend.

Anora's voice interrupted the conversation, "Hey, I'll catch you back at school."

I turned my attention to her. "No, no, it's late and I'm tired." I had to go. He could be Leandra's attacker. My eyes dropped to his arms. They weren't super hairy but that didn't mean anything, I reminded myself. Her idea of hairy and my idea might be two different things. And he was still at the party when James and I left. Worse: nobody knew him.

Anora put a hand behind her ear and shifted her eyes from me to him as if to say 'It's OK, spend time with the hot guy'.

"Ealon," he said, holding out a hand to Anora.

She shook his hand. "Anora. I gotta run. See ya girl."

I gave him a cheesy smile. "I gotta go." The words dropped from my mouth as I was taking steps away from him.

"Tomorrow, same time," he called after me.

I didn't respond as I turned and didn't look back. *What if he was the guy? What if he wasn't?* I didn't need to lead him on. Tomorrow was a busy day, orientation and buying books. I wouldn't have time to meet him for coffee, I told myself.

She looped an arm through mine and leaned into me. "You're in college, no need to rush home to mom and dad, not when someone who looks like *that* notices you."

I didn't completely understand yet what she meant, but my mind was focused on the *danger* of spending time with Ealon. "We've met before," I said, hesitantly.

Her eyes widened. "What? Spill!" she said, opening the car door of the Ryde and sliding across the bench seat.

I slid in next to her and gave her a quick version of the night we met. Not that there was much to say.

The driver stopped in the outermost parking lot; without a pass he wouldn't be able to take us directly to the dorms. We stepped out and strolled toward the dorms.

"Statistically you have a 1/328,000,000 chance of meeting the same person twice in this country. The odds become less when you figure in geographic location, age group, possible hangouts and interests, so I figure there is something like a 1/528,000 chance the two of you would meet again. You can't let opportunities like that slip away, yet here you are, going back to the campus with me instead of spending the night with a hottie like him."

Anora and her incessant talk, statistics, and science was growing on me quickly. Luck or not, statistically, what was the chance we'd meet? "I don't know. I don't really have time to date right now." Excuses, excuses. I didn't know her well enough not to lie about the situation. She didn't need to know more.

"I'm 22 and haven't dated in 2 years. It was a blind date as a favor for a friend and went horribly wrong. I have this uncanny ability to turn people away with nerd talk. Dates can't keep up so either they give me the deer in the headlight look and I know the inside of their head is hollow and I'm bored, or they run away. I'm a bio nerd and have more intelligent conversations with my computer. I thought I'd meet a higher intellectual group at college so I'm pretty disappointed." She paused and took a breath. "I know, I talk too much."

It wasn't hard to imagine Anora having a difficult time dating. In the past couple hours there were two things I learned about her; first, she talked incessantly, and second she saw science and numbers in everything. My mind was blown, but I liked her. She'd grown on me in a noticeably short time. I didn't understand half of what she said but wasn't bothered by it. She was interesting and like no one I'd ever met.

She was also pretty, and it was natural beauty as she wore no makeup. Her face was tear drop-shaped like mine, with elegant lines accentuating her cheek bones and a perfect sized nose that carried small freckles. I was confident men and women, found her attractive. It was also easy to believe people were intellectually intimidated by her. She wasn't one of those people who wanted you to think they were smart throwing out trivia mumbo jumbo. She was the real deal and had no dial to tone it down. "You do talk a lot," I giggled.

As we approached the backside of the dorms, I spotted what appeared to be, from my estimation, my dorm room illuminated, which meant my roommate was home. "Thanks for the coffee."

"You're welcome. What's your number so I can call you?"

She was forward too, but I'd enjoy hanging out with her again, so I gave her my number and she sent me a text: *Think about the study.*

I will. Night! I responded.

Don't pass up the hottie, she texted back, reminding me I should go for it. I thought about it as I jaunted up the steps to my room. Maybe I'd ask her to come with me. Tell her I like using the buddy system or something. Rapes weren't uncommon on college campuses, statistically she would know that. But was I scared of him as a perceived threat or scared of forming a relationship?

As far as the study, I didn't think I was really interested. The money could be helpful, but the idea of being a guinea pig for science wasn't appealing.

What would studying my mtDNA prove? The thoughts swirled in my head, mingling with the anticipation of meeting my roommate.

When I opened the door and spotted the small girl with board-straight black hair at a desk with a book opened, my anticipation vanished. She glanced away from her book and at me, her almond eyes meeting mine and a slight smile on her face.

She glimpsed away from me and I realized she had the same anticipation about meeting me. "I'm Chelsea."

Her eyes met mine again. "Hi. Kit."

I moved into the room and closed the door, as if that would make the awkward moment go away. "I like your rainbow sun-catcher." It was about the stupidest thing to say, but it was the only thing I could think of.

She shrugged. "If it bothers you, I can take it down."

"No, it's pretty. The colors surprised me, but I like it." A lie, OK, so maybe it would grow on me. I could tell from her eye glances and slumped posture she was an introvert like me, not the party girl I'd assumed. I didn't want our relationship to start out on the wrong foot.

She tugged at a chunk of hair and twisted it. "I saved you some room in the fridge and they are bringing us a new microwave. The other one didn't work."

A microwave too, how lucky was that? The fridge was small but large enough to have a freezer shelf. I hadn't looked inside it yet. "Great! So, how long have you been here?"

"Since yesterday. I came early. I think most of the new summer students will be here tomorrow."

"Yeah, the building was pretty empty today," I said, thinking back to the spooky quiet and echo of my steps in the stairwell when I made the first trip to the dorm room.

"I'm sorry I wasn't here. I went to the library. It's quiet and has plenty of study nooks. I started on a novel and lost track of time," she said as if she had to explain herself. That told me she wasn't only an introvert like me but also suffered from a guilty complex like me.

"Maybe you can show me tomorrow. I walked around the campus but didn't go in the library."

She nodded.

I concluded she was up waiting for me as she turned the light off and crawled into her bed soon after our conversation stopped. It had been a busy day and the events circulated in my head as I fell into a deep sleep. The last thought I remembered was seeing Ealon's face when we bumped into each other. Even his name was hot!

Buddy System

The next day proved to be busy. It started with Kit and me grabbing breakfast in the food court. I stayed away from the coffee and ordered a bagel and milk. Kit, on the other hand, went with a muffin and bowl of fruit. She didn't order coffee either, but orange juice. When I asked, she confirmed she'd tried the coffee too and wasn't impressed. We both giggled and I took that moment to invite her to the Coffee Bean with me that evening. When she agreed, relief poured over me. I didn't want to meet him alone, but thought maybe Anora was right and I should at least give it a shot.

Orientation was uneventful. After, they took us on a tour of the school. Kit and I detoured to the library. She was a bookworm extreme. I guessed that was how she dealt with anxiety. Her face lit up and almond-shaped eyes became large circles when she opened the door to the library. She transformed from shy girl to a walking encyclopedia on literature from Shakespeare to Mary Shelley to E.E. Cummings.

I left her there to purchase my books, promising to meet her back at the dorm by 5:30 so we could make it to the Coffee Bean. The bookstore was crowded, and the line didn't go quick as there were only two cashiers working. I held the books as I waited in line. A turtle moved faster than the line but, after an hour and a half, it was finally my turn. I laid the books on the counter and the cashier, a young woman, probably also a student with a short blonde bob and dark brown eyes, rang up the books.

"One sixty-eight and thirteen cents," she said with a smile.

That was the price on the used books. Since it was the summer session, they were using the same books as they had for fall and spring semester. "I have an account."

"What's your name?"

She typed it in and, after a couple clicks, her eyes darted back to me. "It shows the account but there's nothing in it yet. Sometimes financial aid can take a day or two to catch up."

My face dropped. I didn't have that amount of money in my checking account. I grabbed the books. She laid her hand on them before I could pick them up and spoke, "I'm not really supposed to do this but I work open to close the next two days. How about I hold these in your name for forty-eight hours?"

She must have read the expression on my face. "Thank you."

"No problem." She never lost her smile.

I ran to the financial aid office in hopes I could get the situation straightened out right away. Luckily, there wasn't a huge line, and the wait didn't take longer than a few minutes. At a quarter past four, I figured maybe I could even run back to the bookstore. The line was thinning when I left.

An older African American woman, her short hair styled neatly, asked my problem and my name. Her fingers, with long acrylics or maybe they were gel nails, flew across the keyboard before she informed me that the money was pending and should be in my account in no less than three business days. She gave me a card with information on how to check for myself.

That meant I should have it by Monday and classes started tomorrow. I tried not to look defeated. It wasn't her fault. If I got lucky it would be in the account by Friday and I could go back to the bookstore and get the books.

By the time I reached the dorm it was nearly five. Kit was in the room, her face buried in a book. She dropped it, looked at my hands, and asked, "Where're your books?"

I sighed as I dropped onto the edge of my bed. "My financial aid money isn't in the account yet. The worst thing is I dread waiting in that line again."

She agreed with her eyes before they shifted back to the book she was reading. I got on my computer and set up my account. I'd have to check it daily.

We took my car to the Coffee Bean. I didn't tell her about Ealon, mostly because of my guilty conscience. I didn't want her to think I was hanging out with her to use her, even though that's essentially what I was doing. After spending the day with her, other than being introverts we didn't have much else in common and shared several uncomfortable silent moments between us.

Anora had been so easy because she was outgoing and spoke constantly. There wasn't such a thing as a silent moment when she was around. I did want to know my roommate better, after all, we were living together.

We entered the Coffee Bean, apprehension filled me. As much as I wanted to see him, I didn't want to. My brain was twisted like a pretzel. Immediately, I scanned the establishment searching for him. Students sat in groups, talking over steamy and chilled coffee in their hands and on the tables. Empty plates and ones filled with pie and other high carb delicacies in front of them, but nowhere did I see him. My tension eased a little as I thought maybe he wouldn't show.

From across the room, I spotted Anora, the pink streak in her hair stood out more than her waving me over. I was comforted because she would fill the dead air that would inevitably exist between Kit and myself and on another level I was glad she decided to take me up on the invite. If I'd have known I wouldn't have invited Kit but I didn't lead on.

After grabbing our coffee, we joined her and, after introductions, she led the conversation. Kit, working towards a degree in psychology, was far more interested in the science than I was. I wouldn't say they hit it off but the conversation didn't dry up. She asked if we were ready for classes. If we got our books. Kit had purchased hers the day she arrived on campus, which was smart. No lines, no fuss. I told them my story, which included the long line in the bookstore only to find out my financial aid wasn't available yet.

"I can front you the money. I'm an only child and my dad adds more money into my account than I spend. You can pay me back by meeting me at the lab Saturday for a spit sample. Just pay me back when the stipend comes in," Anora offered, settling back into the cushy high-back chair.

The offer was generous. I mean, what if I chose not to pay her back? "I can't. I don't know, maybe. Financial aid said I should have it in three business days so I'd like to wait it out."

"Spit sample? Lab?" Kit questioned, her brows forming a V.

Raising a hand and rolling her eyes, Anora said, "I can't believe I haven't brought it up until now. I'm working on this study…" Her eyes drifted towards the door and she switched her train of thought mid-sentence. "I could use another coffee. It's going to be a late night. Come with me and I'll explain it."

They rose from their chairs, Anora's voice trailing as they walked away from me. Another voice filled the spot Anora's took.

"Hey," he said, taking a seat in the chair Kit just vacated. Ealon's green eyes melting me right away. "Sorry I'm late. My internship is more like errand duty." He rolled his eyes to show his disapproval.

That's why *Anora* needed another coffee. My back was to the door but she'd faced it, sitting across from me. "Hi," I said, noting the blue collared polo shirt and black slacks.

He set the coffee in his hands on the small table between us. "You never told me your real name, Cinderella."

"Chelsea." I glanced behind me and Anora was still talking to Kit by the counter, in front of the sugar and creamer station.

His smile was intoxicating. "Chelsea. It fits you."

"What does that mean?"

"The freckles, reddish-blonde curls, brown eyes. It's how I picture a Chelsea to look," he said with a cocky smile on his face.

I couldn't help but give him a quick grin in return as I studied him. "You don't exactly look like an Ealon."

Still cocky he asked, "What should an Ealon look like?"

"I don't know, redder hair, maybe not so wavy."

The ice broken, my tensions vaporized and I nearly forgot all about Anora and Kit until I felt a tap on the shoulder.

"My Ryde is here. Kit's coming back with me." Anora winked with a satisfied smile on her face as if to say 'I told you so'.

I gave her and Kit a thank you. I knew Anora figured out I brought Kit along so I wouldn't be alone, but she didn't mention anything to Kit and even took her off my hands so I could spend the evening with Ealon. I owed her big!

Talking with him was as easy now as it had been the night we met. He slyly invited me to join him for dinner and I didn't even catch it until we'd already walked the two blocks and were sitting in the restaurant. Over a basket of chicken fingers and coleslaw he joked about his job working for a bunch of uptight lawyers.

"So, what is it you'd rather do?"

"I mix music. You should come see me Saturday night at Flashers."

"Maybe. It depends on how much work I have." I glanced at my phone. "Oh shit! It's late and classes start tomorrow."

"I can give you a ride," he offered.

"I have my car."

"Let me at least walk you."

I gave him that. My car was parked in a well-lit parking lot and, really, any anxiety I had over him being Leandra's attacker had vanished. It couldn't be him, besides the non-hairy arms he was charming and jovial, not the kind of person who would attack someone in the woods or get off by resorting to peeping tom-ism. I cursed James in my head for putting the idea there.

The heat of the day was gone and even the humidity had decreased. When we reached my car he grabbed my hands. "Saturday," he said as he stepped closer, his face inching towards mine until our lips met. The kiss even better than I had imagined.

Ceramic Against a Wall

riday morning came, no money in the account. Friday afternoon came, no money in the account. I found the book PDFs online and was sure I had the technical finesse to pirate a copy each but I couldn't bring myself to do it. It would be stealing someone's intellectual property. "Stupid guilty conscience," I muttered under my breath as I closed my laptop.

I texted Anora. There was no other option. I could call my foster parents, but I wasn't their responsibility anymore. When Judy called yesterday to see how I was doing, I almost asked but couldn't bring myself to do it. The nuclear family still holding tight, I had to navigate my independent adult life. Find solutions to my own problems. *What would it harm to donate a little spit?* Anora met me at the bookstore an hour later and the friendly cashier with her always smile still had the books.

"Thanks. I really appreciate it," I said on our way out the door.

Anora turned toward me and stopped. "You don't have to be part of the study if you don't want to. I hope you don't feel like you have to."

I sighed. I did have to even if she wasn't pushing me. It really wasn't a big deal and I felt I owed her in some way. I couldn't pay her back directly from the school account once the money was there because it was only good at the food court and bookstore. "I'm helping further science."

Her face lit up. "I gotta run. You and Kit stop by the lab in building eighteen about ten tomorrow."

Kit? She hadn't mentioned Anora had talked her into it but, since Wednesday evening when we hung out at the coffee shop, I'd only briefly seen her, more in passing. Our schedules worked opposite it seemed and I was sure the rest of her time she spent in the library.

The light blue walls in the lab and fake marble-looking tile didn't make the place look entirely sterile, yet it didn't make it warm and inviting either. We wrote our names on stickers which Anora wrapped around the test tubes we spit in. I felt pretty silly, but it was harmless and didn't hurt. It wasn't like she needed blood.

I chuckled after and handed her the test tube.

"It feels ridiculous, right?"

Kit nodded. "It really does. Like the kids who picked their noses in class and everybody saw it and thought it was gross."

"Oh my gosh. That kid was in my class two years in a row and he sat next to me," Anora said with a laugh.

I thought about school, then James, followed by thoughts of Ealon. It was Saturday. Tonight was the night he did a show at Flashers. "What are you doing later, ladies?"

Kit chimed in right away, "My lit teacher is insane and by the end of the weekend my first book and paper are due."

Somehow, I figured that was right up her alley. I turned to Anora, ready to beg with my eyes but the look in hers showed me I didn't have to. "Whatever we're doing."

"Going to Flashers. Ealon invited me." When she lowered a brow in question I followed up with: "He's working. DJ-ing or something."

Kit groaned quietly as if she really wanted to come instead of study. I guessed she, like me, didn't have a multitude of friends. I turned to her. "We don't have to stay out long."

"I really can't. Maybe another weekend."

I had a lot of homework too and makeup reading, but it would wait until Sunday and Monday since I didn't have class again till Tuesday.

Flashers was in a typical brick building. A solid neon light announced the club's name. The bouncer at the entrance checked our IDs and gave me an orange wristband that revealed to everyone I was under 21. I wrapped my hand around it as we entered.

The music inside was too loud for real conversation. Sleek black tables and chairs spotted the floor except in front of the stage. College students and other adults our age danced. Colorful lights flashed overhead. I noticed plenty of others had orange wristbands too and I didn't feel so much like a brown rabbit in the snow.

We managed to find a couple chairs at the bar along the wall. I searched the crowd but didn't see Ealon. Anora had saved me from a fashion emergency when I realized I had nothing to wear. She'd set me up with a glittering black dress that found and hugged my small curves. We were roughly the same size – even her shoes fit me - and to top it off she let me borrow a small black bag that fit over my shoulder and around my torso.

Two hands on my shoulders grabbed my attention as I spun around in the stool to face Ealon. He was dressed more like the first night I met him. His hair freshly brushed, jeans and a T-shirt. He took my hand and led me to the dance floor.

The flashing colorful lights played across his chest as he moved with the music, accentuating the defined muscles beneath, matching the tone in his arms. I couldn't take my eyes off him, nor could I imagine what he saw in me; Chelsea – flat-chested and too skinny. I felt lucky our bodies moved together, hoping other women in the club were noticing the guy dancing with me.

The music vibrated between us as it slowed and he took my hands, lifting them high, his eyes focused on mine. The connection I felt with him was otherworldly. Like we'd known each other in the past. Maybe we were lovers before, reincarnating into our current bodies. I couldn't place it, but I knew him. My body felt it as it yearned for him.

He spun me and pulled me close, so close I felt his chest against my back as his hands trailed down my sides and for a moment the connection felt wrong, like we were doing something bad or immoral. As quickly as the feeling came it vanished.

After a few dances he walked me back to Anora.

"My turn," she said, or it looked like she did, as she dropped her small dress purse over my shoulder and rushed onto the dance floor.

I guessed that was my cue to babysit the bags, although both were small enough with long enough shoulder straps to hang sideways across our chests.

Ealon leaned close to my ear, his warm breath on my cheek as he said, "I'm up next but before I go I want something from you." He pulled away and placed a cold slim object in my hand.

I glanced down at a cell phone then back at him. His eyes urged me to input my number which I did without any more hesitation before handing him back his phone.

The left corner of his mouth turned up in a smile and he leaned in and placed a hand against the back of my neck. I tilted my head upwards, taking him in as his lips pressed against mine. My tongue quickly met his in a passionate kiss before he left.

I couldn't take my eyes off him as he made his way through the crowd and disappeared before reappearing in the DJ booth.

I slipped onto the stool and noted two drinks on the bar, one had Anora's pink lipstick on it. I grabbed the other and took a sip – water. It felt cool and refreshing as it drained down my throat.

Anora returned and grabbed the lipsticked drink. "What do you think?" she practically shouted.

I nodded my approval as Ealon introduced himself to the crowd. It was like a dream. Here I was with a damn hot guy who was also the DJ. I melted and particles rose to cloud nine.

Anora shouted at me again, "Let's dance!" With our drinks empty and our purses draped around our shoulders and chests, we made our way to the dance floor, dodging other college age students until we found an area. We let the music carry us away from our college woes, essays, and research to a place brimming with the freedom of youth.

After several songs, Anora made her way back to the bar and I to the restroom. The later it got, the fuller the place seemed to get, I noted as I weaved and dodged couples and small groups. There was a short line and plenty of young women stood in front of the sinks, glossing their lips and primping their hair in the mirror. The music quiet enough, I heard their conversations.

On my way out I caught a glimpse in my peripheral of a dish water blonde mop of hair I'd recognize anywhere, turning to make sure my eyes weren't playing tricks on me. A few feet away stood James. I gasped and my heart pounded as I walked towards him. He was buried in his phone. "James," I said, loud enough to be heard over the music.

His back against the wall. He lifted his head and met my eyes. Hair falling over his.

"Why haven't you returned my texts?" I asked, once close enough to talk instead of shout.

He shrugged. "Busy working," he said, as if I should know the answer. Those words made my heart drop. We leaned on each other for years. He was my sunshine and my moon. My thoughts poured over him daily. Something was out of place now.

I swallowed and dropped the subject. "How's your job?" He knew which university I was attending. I couldn't imagine why he wouldn't have told me he was going to be working in the same city, but I figured the club wasn't the place to give him the third degree. It burned deep down that he wouldn't say anything to me or even contact me. He couldn't work 24/7.

"It's work." He paused. "How's school?"

Who was this cold version of James? I swallowed my pain. "I don't know. Classes just started this week and I already have homework tomorrow." The words hung in the air and the moment was awkward, not something I'd ever felt in his presence. "I didn't know you'd be working here, maybe we can hang out sometimes."

"Looks like you got a guy to hang out with."

That comment took me aback. Was that it? Why he didn't mention he'd be in the city because of his thoughts about Ealon? Was it something more? It wasn't like I knew Ealon would be here. James saw me with Ealon, so he'd been here for a little while. "I'm not here with him but, yeah, we like each other," I said in defense. It was my own insecurity and the feeling of being dumped that overcame me, as James hadn't even told me he'd be in the city, much less asked to meet me anywhere. He hadn't even texted me since we parted the night before he left.

He pushed off the wall. "Did you find his name in the graduation program?" Beneath his shaggy hair I felt his eyes boring into mine.

He was still on Ealon being the attacker. I bolstered my position. "I hung out with Leandra after you left and she wasn't harmed and the guy had hairy arms. It's not him!"

James raked his hair back and walked away. He left me standing there. Twice now I'd watched him walk away. *What was happening between us?* I couldn't stop my eyes from glancing at the healed dot on my hand where I pricked it. So much for our blood pact!

My heart swam in sadness and I blinked away tears as I returned to Anora. I pulled the phone out of my purse and showed her the time. She nodded in agreement. It wasn't even that I really wanted to leave, more I wanted to bury my face under my pillow and cry.

I gave Ealon one last glance as we headed outside into the muggy summer heat. He winked at me as though he hadn't taken his eyes off me. *Did he see me talking with James?*

"Who's that guy you were talking with?" Anora asked, more than curiosity in each word.

"A guy from home. He's no one." What a lie. He was everything! I wanted to tell her how bad and betrayed I felt, but didn't know her well enough to dump my sadness on her shoulders.

"He's hot in a bad boy way. You sure he's no one?" I didn't get the gist of her message or prying. He smashed my heart like a ceramic vase against a brick wall. The pieces dropping to the floor.

I considered telling her more, but really didn't know where to even start. "He was my neighbor. We've known each other for years."

"So, it's not romantic?" she inquired.

"No," I assured her, my mind not even wondering where she was going with that.

"It seemed a little heated, but it's not my business," she said, then changed the conversation as we waited for our Ryde.

I pulled my phone out and sent Ealon a message: *Thanks for the invite.* My finger hovered over the send button. The message sounded stupid. I quickly went to erase it when a message from him came through. *I enjoyed seeing you tonight.* Warmth filled me up as I texted him back, barely paying any attention to Anora's words.

Summer Vacay

Kit was fast asleep when I returned to the dorm, so I tiptoed into the restroom, careful not to wake her, then buried myself under my blankets and let the tears flow. James wasn't like himself. He'd always been there and that was the realization I came to. He'd always been there/ but had I always been there for him? I'd thought so. I couldn't stop his father from being an ass, but my window and heart were always open for him.

I figured I'd give him time then I'd reach out again. Maybe before summer ended we could go back to the river, sit on our log and toke. Just us.

Kit was gone by the time I woke up. I pushed my hair back in a ponytail and pulled on a pair of cotton shorts and threw on a tank top. The sun was already bright, I noted as I fitted my sunglasses over my eyes and strolled to the food court. A bowl of fresh fruit and bran muffin in a bag, I took a seat at one of the benches along the river.

The breeze swept the heat and humidity away. Pulling the lid back, I stabbed a pineapple and orange slice onto my fork and scrolled through my phone. No messages from James, nothing, as if I no longer existed in his orbit. I reminded myself to give him time.

There was a message from Judy asking if I needed anything. I texted back quickly that everything was going great. I'd have the check by the end of the week for my saliva donation and would be able to pay Anora back. I didn't mention any of that to Judy. The next message was from Ealon. An invite for a real date.

My heart pounded and I instantly thought of all the schoolwork I'd have to complete today to make that date happen as I texted back a yes. I stabbed another couple orange slices and chewed as he texted back: *I'll pick you up at the University entrance about 11 am. Dress sexy but casual* with a winking emoji.

What was sexy but casual? Shoving another bite of pineapple in my mouth I sent him a smiling emoji then gathered my stuff. I had homework to complete and no time to waste. The dorm was empty as Kit was probably studying at the library. I closed the curtains to mute out the rainbow that spread across the room and took a seat on my bed as I opened my computer and got to work.

I put my phone on silent to avoid any disturbances and spent the rest of the day buried in my books and on my computer typing. When Kit returned with a small pizza my eyes widened as large as the empty hole in my stomach due to not eating since breakfast.

By midnight I put the final period on the last paper I had due and closed my computer. My mind thinking 'sexy but casual' and Ealon's face etched in my thoughts. His scent and the warmth of his breath on my skin, the touch of his hand on mine and sliding down my side. It sent tingles through me as I fell into a deep sleep.

The next morning, I popped out of bed with an extra spring in my step as I rummaged through my small closet area. My brain on a sexy but casual repeat. I finally settled on a light blouse that I called my hippy shirt. Its colorful, lightweight cloth made it airy and it fell nicely over my small breasts. I followed that up with a pair of capri length leggings and sandals.

He was in the parking lot by the time I got there and had an iced coffee and cinnamon roll waiting for me. "I hope this isn't the date," I joked as I happily accepted the coffee and roll.

A playful smile crossed his lips. "That's it. Eat and enjoy." His smile said he was only joking. "I hope you don't mind a drive."

"As long as the prize at the end is worth it," I responded in my most flirtatious voice.

He pulled sunglasses over his eyes and shifted the transmission into drive. "I'm going to show you a North Carolina secret." His voice cryptic.

"You're not going to tell me, are you?"

"Nope, my lips are sealed." He pulled onto the main road.

The drive was beautiful, whatever this secret place was. I couldn't imagine, but it was a large enough state and contained a very colorful history, so it was even more difficult to guess. Instead, I enjoyed his company and more than once admired his profile. My heart fluttered uncontrollably every time I caught him sneaking a glance my way.

Leaving the desolate country road behind us, we rolled into a small town. It was the sort of town that tested the limits of time. With large store fronts downtown, I expected to see men in their trousers hung by suspenders and women in floor length dresses, horse drawn carriages, and dirt roads.

Its panoramic views made it romantic as we strolled along main street. It was a true one main street, southern town. We stopped for lunch at a cozy restaurant positioned between a river and a creek surrounded by elm, walnut, dogwood and cedar. We chose outdoor seating to take in the views.

The place was casual. The server, dressed in jeans and a Country Grub T-shirt, placed two yellow baskets on the table along with our drinks. I ordered a chicken sandwich and steak fries, which were ginormous and super crunchy on the outside.

"What do you think?" he asked between sips of his soda.

I swallowed my bite of sandwich. "Like we drove into a time capsule. How do you think a town like this stays in business?" There was literally nothing but a handful of shops and three restaurants, historical museum, and a church.

He chuckled as his eyes glanced towards the older couple sitting to our right. "I think everyone is retired."

I laughed as I was about to swallow lemonade and it flew out of my mouth.

He handed me a napkin as he chuckled then crooned, "Young people today," in a shaky voice, holding up a finger easing my tensions.

The older couple flashed their attention our way for a second and I fought hard to squelch the urge to laugh again. When the urge subsided, I took another sip.

"I think they have rules on how many people can live here and their ages. They haven't built a house in decades."

"You've got to stop or I'll never be able to finish my food," I urged.

He smiled. "I'm serious as a dog hiding his bone. My grandparents lived here.

We used to come visit until…" He stopped and grew silent. His eyes shifted away from me.

Now I was curious. "Until?"

He let out a breath. "I had a brother. He was nine months older than me. Our parents would drop us off for two weeks every summer until he passed away."

The jovial conversation did a solid one eighty. "I'm sorry."

He shrugged, his green eyes meeting mine. "It was a long time ago."

The pain of loss in his words matched the pain in my own heart of not knowing my family and so the words fell from my mouth without hindrance. "I never knew my parents. A foster family raised me."

"Why don't we go for a walk?" he asked. I didn't know if it was to change the subject because he was uncomfortable or if he had more to show me, but it brightened the souring conversation.

He circled my hand in his as we strolled the dirt path along the river then he stopped and pointed. "See that house through the trees? "That was my grandparents' home. Summers weren't the same after and my parents stopped dropping me off for the summer, then they got divorced and my grandparents died. I miss my brother Chad but I also miss that I didn't know them better. That's why I come here, so I can be close to them."

Empathy raced through my bloodstream. I'd never known my family to understand what I was missing. Maybe they weren't even good people. I didn't respond and we continued our stroll back to his car. The sunny sky was filling with gray clouds as we left the small town behind us.

"You're really good," I said, thinking back to Saturday at Flashers.

He glanced at me. His eyes showing his confusion.

"DJ-ing. I was impressed." I'd left in a hurry that night without even a goodbye, just a glance at the door, and I wanted him to understand that night was special.

"Thanks. What about you? What's your hidden talent?"

I had to think about that one. I didn't really have any. "I can roll my tongue," I said, sticking out my tongue.

He chuckled. "I'm jealous. I've never been able to do that." He stuck his tongue out but no roll.

I giggled, then a loud boom filled my ears and my heart jumped as I grabbed the dashboard.

He coasted the car to the side of the road. "It's just a flat, but I don't think I'm going to be able to change it before the rain hits." The first large drop hit the front window as the words left his mouth. He glanced around. "There's a house back there, unless you'd rather sit by the road in the car."

Another drop of rain hit the windshield then a couple hit the roof, sounding more like hail than rain. I opened the car door, pushed it closed and ran towards the house, Ealon by my side. Rain falling steady as we reached the porch.

Darkness Within

Heavy rain pouring over my head, I hadn't noticed the place until I reached the porch. I was more worried about getting struck by lightning. The creaking of floorboards under our feet and the peeling white paint made me feel as though the floor would give way beneath my feet. The door wasn't locked as Ealon pushed it open and it moaned at our entry. A shiver climbed up my spine as I grabbed his hand, unconscious at first that I done it until the warmth of it filled my own.

Ealon flipped a switch but nothing happened. "Maybe there're some candles."

I pulled out my phone, turning on the flashlight. The beam caught the dust in the air as the entire house seemed to complain about our presence. We followed the beam, the floor groaning with each of our steps.

"These old houses have good bones," he stated. His voice unsure, as if he'd said it to comfort himself as much as me.

The long, slender entryway opened to a sitting room of sorts. Years of dust covered everything.

Our eyes met as we crept into the room. "I expected trash and mattresses," Ealon stated as he studied the room. The jovial tone in his voice hinged with uncertainty. He meant it to ease both our tensions.

Rain pounded the windows, reminding me we were stuck, at least for now. I let go of his hand and strolled towards the shelves on the wall holding books covered in years of dust.

The floor lamented under his steps, telling me exactly where in the room he was. I turned to see his backside as he flashed his light over pictures on the wall. Maroon wallpaper peeled at its corners displaying each individual strip.

The furniture, yellowed and sun-bleached, showed signs of petite blue flowers in the fabric. "How long do you think it's been since someone lived here or even… visited?"

Ealon shrugged as he ambled towards the shelves. He pulled a book off a shelf, blowing dust from the cover. My luck, the ball of dust went straight up my nostril causing me to sneeze and cough.

"I'm sorry," he said as he rubbed my back. Not that it really helped, but his fingers over my back felt good.

"Look." I took a glance inside the book, an autographed copy of A Wrinkle in

Time. The signature in the closed book safe from the effects of years of sun damage.

He laid the book on a dusty table. "I wonder what other treasures are in this place?"

I sighed. "I'm not sure I want to know."

"Me either, but we're here, might as well explore." He smiled, strolling toward an opening to another room.

What little spirit of adventure I had, had been tested the last few weeks. *What could it hurt? At least these weren't my family secrets.* I followed, unwilling to stay in that creepy room alone. The entire house gave me chills and a sense that our invasion wasn't without someone's or something's notice. A crunch under my foot made me pause and step backwards. A small, yellow metal car.

It seemed such an odd thing in the house that was probably haunted and could easily be a museum or a Halloween money maker. I collected the out of place car and turned the corner into a short hallway. At the end was an arched entryway. The floor creaked under my feet in anguish as I paused by open doors searching for Ealon.

He called, "Chelsea, you have to see this."

I followed his voice into the room at the end of the hallway. Unfinished and finished canvases lay against each wall and an unfinished one was perched on an easel with a pellet of dried paint. A dusty leather bag rested on the floor beneath the easel. The scene reminiscent of an artist that left for a break, meaning to return but, for some reason, never did.

I pushed the dust off one of the paintings, a dark forest scene with a face melted into a tree trunk and an eye staring downward at something unseen. One look and a peculiar feeling wiggled like a worm into my subconscious. I couldn't peel my eyes away.

Ealon stepped and paused beside me. "I wonder what kind of drugs this guy was on."

He kneeled and pushed the extra dust off the name revealing it in full. "Talbot," he read.

A jab stabbed at my recent memory. Tyrus mentioned the name Talbot. It was impossible and ridiculous to think this creepy house filled with disturbing paintings had anything to do with me or him yet how common was the name Talbot? I shushed the thought away, stuffing it into a mental cobwebbed corner of my mind.

The rain pounded away, tiny pings hitting the glass windows. I drew the little car out of my pocket. "Look what else I found." Not that a tiny yellow race car was as interesting as a twisted painting but it meant there had at least been a child in the house. A family of sorts had lived here.

He took the car and rolled it between his fingers nostalgically. "We used to have one of those crazy racetracks that took cars in loops."

I assumed he meant him and his brother. "Can you tell me about him?"

"I will sometime," he said as he snaked his arms around my waist. "Right now, I want to be alone with you in this sinister castle," he said in a sexy, maniacal voice.

That description was right on. A sinister castle that housed an evil artist. I lifted my chin below his and grabbed his jeans by the belt loops.

He pulled away and held out his elbow for me to loop my arm through. "Shall we explore more?" Taken aback, we were alone. *Did he not want to be close to me?* A crack in the distance between us formed. Confidence wasn't something I had a lot of; in fact I had very little.

I could think of many other things to do like eat snake venom, swallow someone else's spit, jump off a bridge, and all sounded more appealing than exploring the sinister castle. However, I wasn't alone and if I could break into Charice's office with James I could investigate the creepy house with Ealon.

I held on tight to the banister as we climbed the grumbling narrow staircase which

I expected to crumble beneath each step. The house had to be a hundred years old, maybe more. Possibly I was over projecting. It did have light switches, just no electricity.

Each room appeared left as if the owners simply vacated or vanished... The beds were made, curtains pulled back, sun-bleaching everything over time. The patter of rain continued. I opened a wooden jewelry box revealing several expensive looking pieces. That was odd, even in the middle of nowhere. Wouldn't the owners have had a beneficiary, children, someone who would have preserved the treasures?

I didn't touch the jewelry as I didn't want to disturb any unwelcomed spirits. "This is really weird. I think we should go," I stated, ready to chance the rain.

Typing something into his phone he said, "I have an idea." He scrolled then clicked on something. His adorable mouth twisting as he read.

A scraping sound above us was the last straw. My heart skipped a beat and I rushed towards the stairs not thinking about anything else but getting out of the sinister house. Hurriedly, I ran down the stairs not as careful going down as I had going up and my leg fell straight through a weak floorboard. I didn't hear the scream that escaped my mouth until Ealon rushed towards me.

His eyes wide as he took the stairs two at a time. "Don't move," he said as he stepped over the weak step. "I'm going to lean down. I want you to grab my back and I'll get you down the stairs where we can look at your leg."

I nodded as I reached my arms around his chest and let him guide me. I barely noted the burning pain as his scent in my nostrils took my mind to other places. Warm liquid dribbled down my leg and the wound sent sharp pains through it. When we reached the bottom floor, I relief stomped on my apprehensions and I attempted to put pressure on my leg but it already burned.

"Don't walk. When we reach the couch, sit down and prop your leg on the table." Concern filling his voice.

We made it to the couch and he cupped my leg and gently helped pull it over onto the table. The huge rip in my capris mingled with red caught my eye before the abrasion. He pulled his shirt off, displaying his chest and distracting my hormonal mind. I studied the edges of his muscles as he padded my leg.

"I don't think it's as bad as it looks. I have a first aid kit in the car. Stay here—"

I interrupted him as the scraping continued from the top floor. "I can walk." I wanted out of that house, not stuck there while he escaped.

A long scrape brushed across the floor followed by a moan. His eyes widened and he helped me off the couch and towards the door, his arm around my shoulder for support. There was no way I was spending another second in that house, nor did I want to know what caused that scratching.

By the time we made it to the car the rain had eased and the only drops hitting our heads were from the trees. The dark clouds moved off, giving way to the lowering sun. That was a true southern storm. They came and went quickly. I sat in the back seat as he mended the two-inch scrape on my leg, pulling out splinters and wiping it with alcohol before covering it with a patch. All with a gentle, caring hand. I'd live.

A tire still to fix, he went around the car and opened the trunk. That's when I noticed he'd left his phone on the back seat. I reached for it then pulled my hand back. One word – guilt. Squeezing my face and going against my will I picked up his phone until I found what he'd been reading when the awful ghostly scraping blew my mind into a frenzy.

It was an article on Prescott Talbot. He was a famous painter known for depressing, distorted scenes. It was thought that he battled lifelong depression and that his war with the illness was the catalyst for his work. He and his wife, Elzbet, were found dead and his son, twenty at the time, was never found. An invisible fist clutched my heart and squeezed. Their lifeless bodies discovered in their home – Talbot House in North Carolina.

I dropped his phone and covered my mouth. We got lucky, so lucky. I didn't believe in ghosts but I didn't not believe either, and that house felt as though a dark presence hung over it. Ealon peaked in. "Can you stand?"

I nodded confirmation and took the hand he offered me as I slid off the seat and stood by the car while he changed the tire. The trees green and thick with summer foliage and wildflowers blossoming, it wasn't the worst place to have a tire blow out if it wasn't for the rain and the sinister castle. My eyes wandered over the peaks of overgrown bushes, catching a glimpse of metal fencing and a name across the top. Years of dirt and vining plants covered most of it but I was able to make out a-bo-H-us-. *Talbot House.*

Lines and Spit

alf listening to the professor, half doodling spirals in my notes, Anora's text caught my attention. She asked if I was in class and if I could meet her at the lab. I didn't really feel like walking to the lab, my leg was still in pain, but sensed the urgency in her message that was surrounded in a bunch of emojis.

My anxiety grew as I impatiently waited for class to end. I remembered she'd said something about the study having to do with genetic diseases and without knowledge of *any* family history I feared the worst. She'd found some irreversible, deathly illness and I'd be dead by twenty-five. Yeah, my angst was in overdrive and I found myself limp-running to the lab when class dismissed without feeling much pain.

When I arrived, Anora opened the door for me as if she'd been waiting. That didn't settle my nerves but accelerated the worry into full blown panic. The rhythm of my pounding heart was so loud I heard it in my ears and my throat dried up like the desert. Her bugged out eyes made her appear like a mad scientist or one who'd drank too many cups of iced coffee. That was it! I was dead. An incurable rare genetic disease!

Her mouth started running the moment I entered which didn't ease my panic but kept it bottled. "I couldn't sit still so I came in yesterday and started processing the last samples. I ran them through…"

My mind blanked as I waited for the ball to drop. I followed behind her into a cubicle-type office. On the desk was a pile of images with lines across them.

She spread them out. "What do you notice?"

Was that a trick question? Was I not dying? Did she just want someone to talk to? "They all have a bunch of lines on them?"

She giggled, easing my panic mode down to extreme tension. "Yeah, they do. You're looking at a PCR imaging of the mtDNA of three unrelated people. Now." She pushed two of them aside and placed a new one next to the one left on the desk. "What do you notice?"

It wasn't a trick question. She was serious and I was supposed to know. I took the time and studied the series of lines. I was looking at peoples' mtDNA which meant nothing to me, nor did I have the slightest clue what I was looking at. What was she expecting me to say? It was better to put it out there and either reach beyond panic mode to catatonic or ease into nervous mode. It could go either way. "They have the same genetic disease?"

She chuckled out loud. "No, neither of these have genetic disease markers. Look again."

I visibly sighed relief and she lowered her eyebrows in question but didn't say anything. I carefully looked them over and didn't note anything but a bunch of matching lines. "They match?" I asked with a grimace, guessing I said the right thing.

"Precisely!" she announced. "These two have the same mtDNA which means they are related. Well, more than just related by some distant relative." Her hand motions were as excited as her voice as she carried on. "mtDNA passes from mother to child, sons and daughters alike. Both are females so, given they have the same mtDNA, they come from the exact same maternal line."

"They're sisters?" I questioned, still not understanding her excitement or why she was sharing this with me. More importantly I was relieved that I wasn't dying and felt it wasn't trivial at this point. It was more about amusing her.

Her bugged eyes grew even wilder. "Exactly! They are sisters, or first cousins maybe. Probably sisters." She pointed to the first one she'd never removed from the desk.

"This one is mine," pointing to the other one she stated, "this one is yours."

For the first time in her presence, she was silent. I processed her words; sisters, cousins… Full on panic resumed. Her words cycled through my head on repeat and black formed behind my eyes. I clutched the edge of the table and told myself to breathe.

She finally broke the silence while my mind was processing. "Are you OK?"

I nodded, unsure what else to do.

She dragged a chair and set it behind me. The blackness growing thicker, I sat down and placed my head below my knees.

"I get it. I freaked when I first saw this and figured it had to be a mistake. It couldn't be true, I messed up, so I did it again and again and the results were the same each time. I even quadruple checked it with my professor. There is no mistake. We come from the same maternal line. My parents were only children. I don't have any cousins," she stated. I lifted my head slightly and watched as she began pacing, wringing her hands together. "We are—"

"Sisters," we said together. The blackness receded, replaced by a looming question mark. *Holy, f-u-c-k-i-n-g shit, shit, fucking shit.* I swallowed, this was as exciting as it was mind boggling. I had family.

In a matter of seconds my surprise turned to extreme anger, as if I was champagne and someone popped the cork. I completely blew up at her. Standing quickly, the chair scraping the tile floor as I did. "No! You don't get to tell me this! I was left to die by pieces of shit who *pretended* to be my family. I had a *fake* brother that was murdered along with them and burnt to a crisp. A child, a small child. Now you tell me I have family and you're it! No!" I stomped towards the door. In retrospect, that was the first time that part of me showed itself.

"Wait," she pleaded. "My mom vanished when I was four. She went to lunch with friends who saw her walking to her car. The car was found where she parked it, but she was gone. You're younger than me. It proves she wasn't killed that day. She may have even been pregnant with you." Her voice cracked with desperation.

The raging angry monster inside me eased. She wanted answers the same as I did. College was a fresh start, but the sins of those before me, of my past, still haunted me. They wouldn't let me go until I knew the truth I didn't want to know. My past was one of things you learn and can't unlearn. The secrets my cheesecloth memory protected me from. I turned on my heel, her eyes filled with water. "I'm sorry. I shouldn't have yelled at you."

She swallowed. "I didn't think of your pain. Don't apologize. Can we get a coffee and talk about it?"

The pleading in her voice and the pain on her face was unbearable. She was my sister, probably, and I liked her. There were far worse people to find I could be related to than a talkative genius. I nodded.

A smile erupted across her face as she picked up a wallet off the table and met me at the door.

Brain Tickle

We spent the rest of the afternoon and into the evening discussing our lives. I didn't know I had so much to say and share. James knew everything but he was also my accomplice. Anora grew up with her dad who had never remarried. She believed he was still deeply in love with her mom and hoped one day she would return, but the police wrote her off as dead. No body was ever found, nor any clues.

Her story broke my heart as much as my own. It also forced my determination and I thought of Ealon and James's skepticism of him. There was so much I just didn't know and maybe James telling me to be careful had some merit. I placed the shoe box on my bed with memorabilia I brought from Judy and Roy's. James was front and center on my mind as well as the mysteries we uncovered. Opening the graduation program, I searched all the names, twice. There was no Ealon. Further compelled, I went online and searched the school website for pictures. No Ealon anywhere.

All that meant was he came too late to be included in any sports or after school activities. Even the programs could have been printed months ahead of time. But I had to at least give James credit. Grabbing my phone, I texted him: *You were right, he's not in the program.* Closing the box, I pushed it under my bed and set my phone on the charger. It was after midnight, hopefully in the morning I'd have a text.

I sprang out of bed when a soprano scream awakened me. A sharp pain shot up my leg as I landed on my feet. Kit stood in front of me with wide eyes shifting from the floor to me. She gulped. "I'm so sorry. I really hate spiders and there was one on the floor. I think you crushed it with your right foot."

Lifting my leg, sure enough: spider guts. *Great!* I leaned back on my bed, defeated.

"Here," she offered, handing me a wet wipe.

The spider's legs separated from its body as my weight crushed it, making it extra gross to clean up but I got it done then remembered my text to James. No message. I let out a sigh. Twice defeated and the day had only just begun. Pushing my thoughts away, I concentrated on my homework.

A box of cereal and a few hours of steady homework, I set my computer aside, leaned back on the bed and took a long stretch. My legs cramped under me for hours were stiff and I screamed as I forced them straight and twirled my ankles. It felt good to get the kinks out.

A glance at the clock, I noted it was 3:39 and my roommate wasn't back yet. I wondered what she did all day. Was it possible for a college student to spend every waking minute not in class at the library? My thought was interrupted by two short raps on the door. It wasn't her, she had a key.

Still in my long T-shirt and underwear I answered the door, expecting one of my neighbors asking to borrow something. I was pleasantly surprised by James. His hair pulled back with a white powdery residue coating it along with his jeans, T-shirt, and boots. He looked like someone dumped a bucket of flour over him. I was sure my face gave away my surprise. I wanted to hug him despite the filth on his clothes.

Before I could say or do anything he offered an apology, "I was a dick. I've been a real dick to you."

Yup! He sure had been. "That's an understatement." As the words left my mouth, I thought of something else. *How did he know my dorm room?*

"Can we go for a walk?" he asked, stuffing his hands in his front pockets.

I nodded. "One second. I need to change." Awkwardly, I closed the door and slipped into a tank top, denim shorts and flip-flops, after pulling my unbrushed curls into a ponytail. We'd both look like shit.

It was a hot day with little wind. "Did you come here straight from work?" I asked.

"No, I like to wear sheetrock," he said.

I giggled. Smart ass James. It felt so good to see him.

His hands still in his pockets, we strolled past the other dorms. "I gotta be straight with you. I took this job because it's a nice set up. I ride to work with my boss and live in a cottage on his property. I had to get away from my dad but I… mostly took it because I knew you'd be here."

That was deep coming from him. It was almost an admission of something private but he held back. He'd lived a rough life and didn't count on anyone for anything. "I missed you a lot but I have to admit something too. I've been selfish and haven't paid enough attention to your needs. It's not all about me."

The left side of his mouth pulled upwards in a half smile. "You're the only person in my life. The only one that matters."

I stopped and he continued another step then stopped and turned on his heel. I stepped closer and wrapped my arms around him. "You're my blood brother." I didn't care how many white flakes from sheetrock got on my clothes or skin.

He circled his arms around me and we stood under the hot sun, sweat beading on our faces, in a hug outside the library. His scent wasn't fresh like the other night at Flashers but it still smelled like James and reminded me of all the good moments we shared. The library door swung open and Kit exited. Her eyes met mine and she smiled then shyly looked away as I raised my hand in a wave.

James leaned into my ear and whispered, "Let's get high."

Those were the words. Past the library were the woods. We pushed our way through the thick foliage. Once surrounded by trees and off the pavement, the temperature dropped notably. "So how did you know where my dorm was?"

"I followed you home the other night," he said, his voice hesitant. His eyes darting away from me.

I took my hand off the branch I was pushing down and it bounced between us. "You're stalking me now?"

The branch separating us, he pulled it down slightly then with the other hand dug into his left pocket, pulling out a bag filled with fat green buds, a snarky smile on his face. He shook the bag then ran.

Asshole! It was just like him to change uncomfortable subjects. I pushed the branch down again and chased him several yards. By the time I caught up to him his back was against a tree, with one leg pushed against it. I slowed and caught my breath, noting he wasn't breathless at all. That perplexed me about him. How could someone who smoked more pot than he ate food and who never exercised be in such good shape?

He filled the bowl and sucked as he put the lighter to it then handed it to me. I sucked so much I stifled a cough. As he blew out he said, "I felt bad the other night and when I saw you leave I thought I'd follow you to apologize."

I accepted his apology as he accepted mine and no more was said. That's how it was and, for that moment, it felt like old times and the distance between us the last few weeks vaporized. If all I had to do was check the program and admit he may be right, I would have done it weeks ago.

We finished the bowl and left campus to grab food. Pot and the munchies were real and, other than dry cereal, I hadn't eaten a thing all day. We took my car to this little hole-in-the-wall burger joint. The place didn't look like much on the outside or the inside. The chairs didn't match, nor the table cloths on the twelve tables, but the burgers were huge and juicy. I could barely wrap my mouth around mine.

"How do you even find places like this?" I asked.

He swallowed his bite. "We came here for lunch a couple weeks ago. They got the best burgers."

He twisted nervously in his seat and finally came out with a confession that threw me for a loop. "I went to the neighbors, where you lived when… you know."

My eyes narrowed. "You did what?" I wasn't upset, but didn't understand why or how his Gremlin would make it that far without breaking down.

He leaned forward with intent. "I couldn't stop thinking about you, about Charice, about what Tyrus said, about…" He paused there, lowered his eyes for a moment and collected his thoughts. "I figured they should know something." On the edge of his words was a hindrance that I didn't push. In retrospect it probably wouldn't have made a difference if I understood it in that moment.

According to James, the neighbors lived further down the road and had to drive past the house to get to theirs. They first introduced themselves shortly after the Moras moved in and remembered seeing a little girl but not a boy. They invited them to dinner. Living in the sticks was lonely and the neighbors felt the need to watch out for each other. The Moras refused their offer and stuck to themselves.

They never saw children playing outside and were shocked and devastated when they learned a boy was murdered and burned along with them. I imagined the guilt on their shoulders for living so close and knowing so little.

I'd have lost my appetite if he'd told me this before I was finished eating. "We were prisoners."

He nodded; his eyes unable to meet mine. "I don't want to bring all this back up but I thought you should know. I'll leave it alone. It's your story."

That wasn't an epiphany, yet it confirmed the dreadful life my cheesecloth brain protected me from. I knew James, and my instincts said there was something else, unrelated to the story that he wanted to get off his chest. Did my story trigger his mom's disappearance? Anora's mom, our mom, vanished too. I didn't know much about his story, the details anyways. How similar were the circumstances?

My mind pondered telling him about Anora and what the DNA discovered. Twirling a lock of hair, I made the decision. "My story just keeps getting deeper. The other night at Flashers I was with my friend Anora. She's studying genetics and bioengineering, she talked me into this mtDNA study. It turns out me and her, we're related, like closely related. She showed me the diagram things," I couldn't remember what she called them, "and ours are near identical."

I imagined his expression mimicked mine yesterday when Anora told me the news. "Can you trust her?" he asked, narrowing his eyes.

Why was his first reaction distrust? I knew why. His life hadn't afforded him the opportunity to know not everybody had bad motives. He didn't trust Ealon either, thinking the worst without even knowing him. I wasn't positive I trusted Ealon either. Whether it was James's distrust washing off on me, or something Ealon did or said or both, I couldn't place it. My adoration of him was waning. Anora, on the other hand, I trusted. My defenses shackled. "Not everyone is out to get me. What reason would she have to lie? I think it's time to go."

He shrugged without any words.

The drive back to campus was quiet. I didn't want the night to end on that note but I realized something else. It wasn't me making things all about me. It was him too. Instead of being happy that I might have a sister, he was suspicious. He went to the Moras' neighbors on his own without even mentioning it to me. He moved here where I was attending college. The tension between us thick again as my mind couldn't put it together. I pulled my car beside his and shifted into park.

He didn't open the door right away after taking off his seat belt. "I'm sorry." He paused, thinking about his words or building up the nerve to say something else that would shatter my world. Instead of words he leaned towards me, placed his hands on my cheeks as his lips met mine. His tongue was inside my mouth and I was kissing him back before I even knew what was happening.

The Ranch

I no longer understood where James and I stood. I enjoyed the kiss and indulged in his tongue mingling with mine. In his own scruffy way, he was hot. Like Anora said, he had a "bad boy" look and wore it well. OMG! That's what she hinted at the night she saw me with him. She was interested in him! I wasn't sure how I felt about that.

James was like a brother or cousin; however, his lips and tongue felt good. I didn't pull away. I wanted it as much as him. But what did it mean for the future of our friendship? Would we lose each other forever if we got together and it ended badly? He was the yin to my yang. Two troubled kids whose souls found each other, whose arms and words comforted each other and made life more bearable. It was tragedy that brought us together.

My soul ached for an answer. There wasn't one. When Anora invited me to "The Ranch" – her dad's house – for the fourth of July, I committed to it right away. It didn't matter that she explained how every year he threw a company party that day with swimming, fireworks, and a volleyball tournament. I was sold on 'will you come with me'.

I'd given her another spit sample the other day and the contents left in Leandra's drink in my car. I hadn't cleaned it since the day we spent together and stared at it every time I sat down in the driver's seat, promising to toss it the next chance I got. However, I always forgot but maybe the universe had another purpose for it.

Anora glanced at me oddly when I brought it to her and I had no choice but to explain. If there was a chance, any chance, I wanted to know. It could answer the question of why we look so much alike and why someone attacked her in the woods. It would also confirm James's concern for my safety.

First, she scolded me that it wasn't ethical for her to test someone's DNA without their consent but, when I showed her a picture of Leandra with her mom in Australia, she decided to do it as long as we kept it a secret between us. Her curiosity was piqued as much as mine as she gasped at how much we looked alike. There were distinct differences, besides our hair color. Our eyes were slightly different colors and our skin tones were a bit different. I was fairer than her. We also had slightly different earlobes but the same freckles, eye shape, face shape, and similar build.

She wasn't sure the sample would still be good but said since I parked it in the garage that may have saved it from the worst.

Anora looked least like us with her blonde hair and much slimmer nose and more refined facial features but, to look at us side by side, we looked related. I was surprised Anora didn't start processing the DNA right away and was taking a break. She was already a workaholic.

In her jeep, we rolled up to a gated fence. She punched in a code and we started down a tree-lined paved drive. I gasped when I saw the house, expecting a modest home off the beaten path not the grand mansion on what had to be hundreds of acres.

"You lived here?" I asked, getting out of the car.

"Yup, welcome to The Ranch," she said, as if it was no big deal.

"I can't imagine how much money it takes to own a place like this," I said in complete awe.

She grabbed her pack from the backseat. "Dad owns Indigo." Indigo was a monster in the tech world. "We haven't always lived here. We stayed in the same house for years. I think maybe he thought

Mom would come home. He gets broody sometimes, but she never did, and Indigo just got bigger. It was like instead of using his energy on a marriage he spent it on the business. So, yeah, you could say he's married to it and he's only a millionaire, not yet a billionaire," she laughed.

The light brick home was two stories, larger than the dorm, and shaped like an L. A porch wrapped all the way around it. The roof sported layers, peaks, and valleys.

A set of wide double doors interrupted the flow of large windows along the bottom floor. With the curtains wide open I saw right through the house. The furniture flowed from one area to the next.

"Dad," she called as she opened one of the doors.

I was a bit surprised, being a tech mogul, that he left the door unlocked and didn't have high tech security measures in place. Maybe he did, I thought, as I glanced around for hidden people identification cameras or finger pads, maybe eye scans.

"What are you doing?" she asked.

Her words caught me off guard. I hadn't realized I was so obvious. "Did you tell your dad?" To avoid the uncomfortable mention that I was inspecting the house for a security system, I redirected the conversation.

"No, we need to know more first," she said. "Come on, I'll show you around."

Redirect worked, uncomfortable moment avoided.

We dropped our bags in her room. I wasn't shocked that she had a framed copy of the DNA x-ray from Rosalind Franklin hung on her wall. The décor was simple and neutral though, with light yellows and pink. With her blonde hair and pink chunk she blended perfectly. From her window was a view of the back. A massive pool with beautifully manicured blooming bushes. Beyond that were a volleyball court and a cottage close to the tree line.

"That's where Clay and Philipe stay. They take care of the gardens and cook. I think my dad enjoys the company and having men around to do man stuff with. Like football and barbecue. Wait till you see them. Philipe is way hot. Clay too, but those muscles on Philipe, mmm," she groaned. "Clay's a lucky man and why is it all the gay men are hot and taken?"

I didn't think she expected me to answer. It was merely a breather for her between words.

She checked the time on her phone. "I bet they are in the kitchen now, prepping dinner. They should know when Dad is due to be home. I bet there's enough time to take you on a golf cart tour."

She literally bounced out of her room and down the winder staircase with its floating steps. It was a very masculine, sheik home. The décor was comfy couches, no knickknacks and very few, but tasteful, pieces of art.

I followed her into the kitchen with its quartz counters. In the center of the large space was a quartz-topped island that housed a cook top. A man with dark hair, a chest so chiseled it showed through his shirt and was a tight fit around his arms, sat at one end of the island bar. His dark eyes warmed when he spotted Anora. I assumed he was Philipe based on Anora's colorful description.

"Well, look who's here," he said, welcoming her into a hug. Another man came around and joined the hug. He was taller and not as muscled with short, dirty blond hair about the color of James's.

"I like the pink," the dirty blond-haired man said. Going by Anora's descriptions I assumed this was Clay.

She flipped her pink chunk. "It's me, right? Oh my gawd. I brought Chelsea along," she said, switching gears. "You remember I told you about her last weekend on the phone?"

"Hi," I said with a cheeky smile.

"You're Chelsea. Anora talked my ear off last weekend about you," Clay said, swallowing me in his arms. "I'm a hugger, I hope you don't mind."

He smelled fresh like a bar of soap. I could have stayed in his arms longer.

"When's Dad going to be home?" Chelsea asked as she scooted out a bar stool at the edge of the island, lifting her butt and planting it.

Philipe opened the fridge and pulled out an armload of vegetables and dropped it on the counter by the sink while Clay pulled out a cutting board and knife.

"In about an hour," Philipe said as he washed the vegetables.

Anora scooted off the bar stool. "Cool, I'm going to take her around the place. We'll be back by the time Dad's here."

"Enjoy," Clay called.

The pool was more enormous up close, about the size of an Olympic, but square and turned on an angle so it looked like a diamond. On the end, by the water fountain, was a jacuzzi. I hadn't realized upstairs that the bushes were like a maze. At the end of the maze was a golf cart.

She took me by the cottage and around the volleyball court and into the woods. "This place is really amazing. Living here it's easy to forget there's other life on the planet. My dad's a cool guy. I think you'll like him. I didn't say anything to him, but if our DNA proves to match by close to 50% we have to tell, or I have to. That would mean you're his daughter too and he'd need to know."

She was correct. It would be the right thing to do. I was still wrapping my head around having a sister. The idea of having a father too was mind-blowing, but I wasn't getting my hopes up. There are a few years between us and I was born after her mom vanished. It was still possible we were first cousins and her mom had a mystery sister she'd never talked about.

I hadn't said it because it was hard to imagine, but I wondered if her mom – our mom – vanished on purpose. What would it take to build a new identity, never mind why she might do it? My troubled life, it's possible she was running from something or someone. *How did I end up in the hands of child predators or traffickers?* They were all the same scum in my book.

"Why did your dad never remarry?" She's already hinted at one explanation of him being so much in love but after so many years it seems he eventually would have gotten over it.

"Marriage doesn't work so well for him. His first wife was his high school sweetheart. Sometimes best friends aren't meant to be married. They started a business together and after a year or so realized they'd made a mistake. They divorced, she kept the company, and he went to college then started

Indigo. They're still friends." She paused. "I think they're booty calls." She glanced at me and chuckled. Would James and I become that one day?

"She visits once a year and a couple times I spotted her coming out of my dad's room, looking slinky, pulling the robe over her chest. I don't know and I don't care. They've known each other most of their lives and she's single too. It wasn't until about ten years ago they got back in touch. Then there was Mom…" Her voice went from jovial to far-away.

As she reminisced about her dad and his first marriage, I thought of James. Her words rang loud and clear. The entire reason I didn't want more with him. We were friends, best friends. We'd known each other for years and after the kiss it seemed he wanted more and part of me wanted more too but sometimes friends aren't meant to be more.

I didn't want to tell her what I was thinking about her mom's disappearance. As smart as she was, she had to have thought of it before. "What do you think really happened to her?"

"I don't know. I was so little and don't remember much, but I know Dad had nothing to do with it and don't like to think she left. She was happy. But I do know now that she may be alive. mtDNA isn't definitive proof that we share the same mom. We could be close cousins. Dad's always said she had no family, but we don't know that for sure."

She parked the golf cart where she found it and we wound through the waist-high bush maze until we reached the French doors to the kitchen.

She flung the door wide. "Dad."

Family Ties

Anora's father folded his arms around her. I saw a man who could be my dad and searched for resemblances, comparing all our features. His thick chestnut hair, curly like mine; her hair much straighter and blonde. His eyes a darker shade of brown like mine; hers were blue, cerulean blue. Even his ears were attached like mine, hers detached.

No doubt Anora and I looked alike but I shared more features with her father than she did. As enthusiastic as she was about DNA it was a bit shocking that she hadn't said anything about it as if she'd never noticed it. I didn't know what it was like to have parents that donated genetic material to make you so I guessed it was one of those things that wasn't on her mind.

She introduced me to her father. He was cover model hot at fifty; handsome and no freckles but her mom had them. The same freckles I did under my eyes - and Leandra. He insisted I call him Gabe.

There were so many of us and it was such a beautiful evening. The weather was perfect, with a light breeze and colorful sunset that spread over the earth. Clay set the table outside. The colors in the sky vibrant, adding to the ambiance. Her life was so different than mine.

"This place is really amazing," I said, attempting to jump into the conversation.

"That it is," Gabe said. "That sunset is why I bought this land. It's brighter and more colorful here and, on a clear night, you can see the Milky Way."

The conversation lingered a bit then changed direction as wine flowed and bowls were passed around the table. My comfortable level eased with the laughter and jokes. Her father was easy and Philipe and Clay added a little spice. They'd been married for a few years, but swore the honeymoon would never end.

Then Philipe brought up something called the perimeter. I listened, not really understanding what he was talking about. He glanced at me and, seeing my quizzical expression, asked, "Did you feel the body scans when you came in the front door?"

My eyes grew wide. "What?"

He cleared his throat. "Yeah, there are cameras when you enter. They scan your body."

Then I noted a lift in Clay's lip as he tried to keep his poker face. Anora couldn't hide her smile and Gabe looked away so I wouldn't see his. "You're joking," I said, shifting my eyes around the table. "There's no body scans."

Gabe chuckled. "That one always gets people and Philipe is the only one that can say it with a straight face. Everyone that comes here wants to know about my security. I don't have a team or special gadgets. I have the perimeter. It's what keeps us safe."

"You mean the fence?" It wasn't high tech and I imagined anyone could get over it.

"You need more wine," Clay said as he stood and filled my glass.

Gabe wiped his hands on a napkin and cleared his throat as if getting ready to make a speech. "No, the perimeter is a one-of-a-kind system that I designed. It senses pupil dilation, pulse rate, heat signatures, rate of breathing, and it gets to know you and what's normal and knows what's abnormal. The fence is for looks but the perimeter keeps us safe."

Now he was talking. "A program. That's incredible!" This man had to be my father: that would explain my love for coding.

Anora added that my major was computer programming. He was impressed and told me to check with him next summer. He may be able to swing an internship at Indigo. I thanked him, incredibly grateful for the offer. A summer internship at a place like

Indigo would be great experience and look fantastic on a resume.

We stayed under the stars and talked into the night. Clay and Philipe were the first to excuse themselves to clean up the dishes, leaving the three of us. There was a spark between Gabe and me as we talked computer. There was just so much I could learn from him. The more we talked, the more excited I got to spend the weekend with a bunch of computer nerds. It was my world.

Unexpected

Not a cloud dotted the sky and the sun was already beating down on the earth. Over my blue bikini, I wore a T-shirt. I'd swathed my sensitive light skin in plenty of sunscreen. Gingers tended to burn easier than others I'd noticed. We sat under the enclosure to eat our breakfast, a smorgasbord of fruit, muffins, croissants, and juice.

I guessed rich people didn't eat so different than the poor, they just had more. Not that Judy and Roy were poor. They were average. We never ate breakfast outside a mansion though, under a large enclosure with views of the sprawling lawn, waist-high flowery bush maze, and giant swimming pool. We also never had servants who cooked and took care of the grounds. Judy did the cooking and Roy tended to the grass, although the yard was small and what one would expect from a simple suburban home.

Anora talked through breakfast and I learned the caterers would be arriving soon, as well as the guests, who'd mostly be spending the night in the house. The volleyball tournament would start at 2 pm and the fireworks at 9 sharp. She was a bundle of energy, her dad more reserved and, I guessed, pretty generous to his employees. He hadn't come from money and believed that if a person is blessed, they should pass it on.

Shortly after breakfast, people showed in large numbers, then trickled in. Anora talked to just about everyone while I took to the sidelines as an introvert. I made some small talk and even took a dip in the pool. Anora dragged me out, begging me to join her volleyball team. I warned her I was unathletic and she laughed. 'So am I. Science nerd, remember?'. She rolled her eyes.

On her team were a couple guys and girls. I couldn't remember all their names but found myself amused as we played. I was in the company of computer whizzes, not athletes, and they were every bit as bad as me at the game. That's what made it fun. Serves didn't make it over the net, and I wasn't the only one that cowered as the ball rushed towards me. There was no diving into the dirt for it.

When our first game ended, Lee, one of the guys on the team, struck a conversation with me; medium build, short dark hair, possibly Asian. He was attractive, but not striking, although there was something about him that caught my eye even as we'd played the game. I think I'd spent more time watching him than the ball.

"You must be new. I've never seen you before," he said, catching up to me as I strolled back to the enclosure to get out of the sun.

"No, I don't work for the company. I'm a friend of Anora's. We go to college together."

He put his hand under his chin and gave me a quizzical study. "Let me guess. You are not a genetic biology major but," he continued to run his finger along his chin, "a computer whiz, some type of tech major; programmer maybe."

I narrowed my eyes. "You've been talking to Anora, haven't you?"

He shook his head. "Nope. A programmer easily identifies another. Your hair is neatly tied back, you have no athletic skills, are OCD, yet wear a lose T-shirt over your suit because you aren't into flaunting your goodies."

I giggled. "Stereotype much? What makes you think I'm OCD?"

"Your mannerisms. You have to do things a specific way."

I knew I was OCD about certain things but didn't realize how obvious it was to others.

"You're also at a party with some of the world's best techies. You have to be a little off and enjoy tech talk to make it through the day." We reached the enclosure and he pulled out a chair for me. "I'm going to get us refreshments. Don't go away."

He returned with an armload of drinks and set them one by one on the table. "Water to hydrate you after spending time under the sun, and beer or a fruity alcoholic beverage." He brought both. I guessed he'd drink whatever I didn't.

"I'll take the beer," I said.

He slid it my way. "That's my OCD. I have to cover all bases. I couldn't just grab a single drink but make sure I brought all the choices."

I laughed as I unscrewed the water and drank that first. "I'm glad you did because I really wanted water, but the beer sounds good too. So what do you do for Indigo?"

He leaned back in the chair. "Security. I build firewalls, viruses, whatever is needed to keep people out and protect the company; our ideas, plans, programs, products." His eyes lit up as he spoke and I noted phantom code letters move across his pupils.

"That sounds pretty cool."

"It is most days and even has some excitement. Cybersecurity is a real risk in today's world. Take banks, they are pretty secure because they protect people's money and other identity factors, but money is the real motivator, anywhere there is money or the potential for money. I protect ideas that in other hands would make someone else very rich instead of Gabe if they broke into Indigo and any tech company or a large bank is infinitely harder than a public entity. Their systems are old and use tech that hasn't been sold in ten years." He chuckled at his own joke.

"You're saying it's harder to steal money than change your identity?"

"Infinitely, yes." He sat up, shook the fruity drink then placed it on the table. "We lost, we're out of the tournament and won't be missed for a while. You want to go for a walk?"

I couldn't refuse. He was charming in his own attractively geeky way. We strolled towards the woods. Anora had taken me left past the pool yesterday and we returned through the other side. Lee and I moseyed to the right. He continued talking about identity thieving. "Identity theft happens because people's personal information isn't protected enough, but changing an identity, even a birth certificate, is like changing a tire."

I wasn't sure how the conversation ended up there but it made me think of Anora's mom and even myself. She vanished, yet was most likely still alive. If changing one's identity was easy in today's world I guessed it was easier twenty years ago. I was a baby when she gave me up, or whatever happened. *Did she have a choice? Was I a liability? Was Chelsea my birth name?* It was possible she didn't know she was pregnant with me. It was also possible she did and I was the reason she left.

I tried not to get too caught up in that. It was better for science to prove us right or wrong than it was to speculate. Anora and I were like-minded in the sense that we liked order in our worlds and were more prone to using logic.

"So you're Anora's friend, huh? Like daughter, like father. Both brilliant," he said as we reached a walking bridge that I hadn't seen yesterday.

How many acres did he own? Lee was 100% correct about Anora and her dad. When I'd compared traits yesterday, I was looking at the outside, but inside they were both geniuses. *Was intelligence an inherited trait?* Sure, it had to be.

We paused on the bridge and I leaned my arms against the rail. He leaned with me, his body close to mine. A moment of silence ended in his lips pressed against mine. A shock of excitement rushed through me and I kissed him back with fervor.

It could have been unresolved emotions since the kiss with James clouded my judgment or the slow progress with Ealon or distrust, but I think it was desire, lust and nothing more.

Our kiss turned into porn on the bridge when we couldn't get enough of each other. Our lips and hands exploring each other's bodies. His firm manhood pressed against my waist.

Between kisses he said, "I know somewhere we can go."

I followed him as we raced through the woods to a small, literal log cabin. I hadn't seen it when Anora had taken me on the tour. I wondered what other treasures were on the property.

He opened the door and our clothes dropped off before it closed all the way. A trail of my bathing suit, T-shirt, and his trunks and tank ended at the bed. His lips caressed my thighs and tickled my sweet spot.

I wiggled in pleasure as he licked and sucked. No one had ever done that to me. He lifted onto the bed and crawled over me. His manhood rubbing against my labia. I guessed this is what was labeled foreplay and it was driving me nuts.

I kissed his chest and brought my hand to his manhood, stroking it as I grew wetter, anticipating his entrance. When I thought I was about to go mad, he entered me slowly and with precision. My chest heaved and I thought at that moment to warn him through my breathless kisses, "I'm a virgin."

He paused, his voice gentle but hesitant, "I can stop."

"No." I swallowed. "I want this."

"I don't have a condom but there might be one in a drawer." His words breathy as he kissed me, but didn't enter further inside me.

"I'm on birth control." I wiggled my hips to force him further into me.

"Are you sure? It might hurt," he warned, unsure maybe if he wanted to take my virginity that I was willingly giving to him without explanation even to myself. I'd coveted not "giving it up" yet I wanted it now more than anything.

Judging by his size, it might hurt, but I wanted him so badly I didn't care. A little pain sure to be followed with a lot of pleasure.

"I'm sure," I assured him.

His lips parted in a smile as he brought himself into me further. "I'm so glad you said that. From the moment I saw you I wanted this." He pushed further, slowly edging his way and moving in and out. My juices covering him.

I took a deep breath when he broke the barrier. A small sharp pain. He paused. "Are you OK?"

A slight grimace, I nodded. "Keep going."

He did, gentle and easy, until he was all the way in. As a natural movement I squirmed around him, my hips and legs gyrating with his. I never pictured my first time, but couldn't have asked for a better one. He was tender and caring, not like the stories

I heard from girls in high school describing their firsts with high school guys.

It was their stories that scared me from having sex until I was ready. Lee was older than me. Still young, I guessed in his late twenties. He'd probably had a few experiences by now, unlike the young, horny high school guys after only one thing.

His rhythm picked up, making me squeal in pleasure as his entire body shuddered against mine when he came. Warm liquid coating my vaginal walls.

He rolled off me, laying flat on his back. "I wouldn't have guessed you were a virgin. I don't mean that in a bad way. You're very tight and very good. Thank you for letting me be your first." He turned his head to the side and met my gaze. "I mean it."

"When I woke up this morning I had no idea I'd lose my virginity today. My foster mom put me on birth control a year ago." I chuckled. "Thank you for being my first and doing it so perfectly."

There was silence while we caught our breath. The cabin was rustic, with fur covers on the bed that we'd slid off and a simple chest of drawers that looked unfinished and a large, older model rifle on the wall. "What is this place?"

"Gabe's hunting cabin. I helped him design the perimeter." He paused and lifted up on his elbow as I turned my head and rolled to the side to hear the story. "He's told you about it, right?"

"Yeah, after the body scan joke."

He chuckled. "I started that joke. Like to see it's still alive. Anyways, I stayed and worked from the house during the months we designed it. There's a lot in the design he didn't share with me, but that's common. We don't like others to understand enough of our designs to steal them. While I was staying he brought me out here. He calls it his hunting cabin but I don't think any hunting happens here. That gun on the wall isn't even loaded."

To me, the cabin seemed a perfect hiding place for someone off the grid. The story of Anora's mom bothered me like a jigsaw that had to be put together, each piece fitting perfectly inside the other. If her mom was my mom, why did she leave? Was someone after her? Was she here, hiding in the cabin?

I knew that was stupid. She wasn't here. That would make less sense. Nothing I thought of made sense. Why would someone disappear, have a baby, and give it up? If I was a risk factor, why not abort me?

He pushed my loose hair over my head. "You think we should get back? It's getting dark. They might start missing us soon and Gabe will have a spread; meats, seafood. You ever tried shark?"

I hadn't tried shark. "No."

He raised himself up. "You got to try it then."

We dressed and I tied up my messy hair. Our walk back was more hurried than our earlier stroll. When we neared the edge of the tree line he paused and cupped my face in his hands, kissed me again.

When our lips parted he said, "That was one for the road."

On my mind was the guilt factor as if I'd done something wrong even though logically I knew I hadn't. We were both consenting adults and even though we didn't use a condom I was on birth control and responsible. It was more what people might think and Anora's questions as she lived vicariously through me. "Should we space our returns so we don't show up together?"

He wasn't bothered by the question, as if he'd thought of it too. I mean these were his co-workers. "You go ahead first. I'll give it five and follow."

"OK," I said as I pressed my lips against his one more time.

It was weird. All I thought of was how good he felt and how much I wanted him – complete reckless abandon. Now I still felt no guilt. I was sure it would come. The lump in my guts for not thinking once about Ealon or James, but for now I was riding the high.

Beer and Socks

Anora thrust a beer into my hand. "Where have you been?" she said, but not as a true question since she continued talking without giving me a chance to respond. "The fireworks are going to be starting and the best place to watch them is from the hot tub."

She pulled me along and jumped in the water. I guessed the beer was catching up to her. I slipped my T-shirt off and slid in beside her. The warm water bubbled around us as we sat back. I doubted she would have noticed if my hair was messed up or if I'd have returned with Lee.

The display in the sky was spectacular. Large bursts colored the dark sky. The water moved as someone slipped into the hot tub beside me. I glanced at Lee who gave me a wink and a smile. Having him this close, I wanted to do it all over again. My mind reliving the tender, affectionate moments in the cabin more than the display in the sky.

He leaned to my ear and whispered, his warm breath against my cheek exciting me all over again, "I'm three doors down. I'll leave a sock in the door."

I stifled a giggle. He was thinking the same thing I was. I snaked my hand between his legs, his swim shorts flowing upwards from the water, and reached in, grabbing his manhood. He moaned slightly. I didn't understand what came over me and never would. I glanced at Anora who had her eyes to the sky as he reached his hand to my stomach and sunk it under the waist of my bikini bottoms.

I tried not to wiggle and alert Anora then leaned over and whispered in his ear, "We can't do this here."

He whispered back, "I can't leave right now." I stifled another giggle as I knew what he meant. He was hard as a rock. "You pull your hand out and I'll pull mine."

I nodded and together we took our hands back. He brought his other hand into the water and shifted his meat then brought it back as he reached for his beer.

"Chelsea."

I glanced upwards and took in Phoebe and Doug. Even from upside down I knew her face.

"Phoebe." I rose from the hot tub and stepped out, giving her a big hug. I completely forgot she mentioned that Doug worked for Indigo.

Confusion painted on her face. "I didn't expect to see you here."

"I know. This is Anora," I said, pointing to my friend who tilted her head upwards to see what was happening.

Phoebe smiled. "I met her earlier, briefly. She scratched lightly at her forehead.

"We go to college together. That's how we met and she invited me. This place is amazing. You and Doug should join us in the hot tub." I wanted to catch up with her but also needed a distraction from Lee. I guessed he could use a distraction from me too, even though he chose to sit by me.

"Sure." She glanced at Doug who agreed. She got in across from me and Doug beside her and next to Lee. No hanky panky. I started it but we had to end it, at least in front of everyone.

I asked Phoebe about her work and thesis which interested Anora as she too was a science major. Doug and Lee talked computers and tech. I followed their conversation, as if being so close to programmers I'd soak up their knowledge. I asked a few questions but spent most of my time between the conversations.

The finale was a successive blast that decorated the sky in purples, blues and greens, pinks, reds. It was brilliant. Some people had smaller children who carried sparklers, their eyes large with wonder as they explored the fire on a stick in their hand.

I knew I was walking on clouds. Anora wouldn't notice, but Phoebe wasn't drunk so I tried to play it cool. Not that I wouldn't have a problem sharing the loss of my virginity with her and she'd probably say 'good for you, waiting for a decent guy' but the conversation would have to happen another time.

The evening died down and Anora excused herself and headed to bed. I gave Phoebe a hug and followed soon after. That was my clue to Lee. I'd stayed in Anora's room. It was large and so was her king-sized bed with a mountain of puffy yellow and pink pillows. There were so many I stuffed a few between us so if she woke she wouldn't realize I was gone.

When the house settled and the halls were silent, I crept down the hall and found his door. Sure enough, he'd stuffed a sock in the bottom. I gently tugged the sock and waited. His footsteps moved to the door and it opened. He glanced into the hallway then pulled me in. One arm around me, his mouth kissing my lips and neck. The other arm, he closed and locked the door.

He lifted me up and pressed me against the wall. His lips, tongue, and hands all over me as he pushed his boxers down. I slid my underwear to the side, my back against the wall as his firm tool rocked against me.

My own wetness running down my inner thigh as I kissed his face and shoulder. I used the wall and leaned in pushing my entrance closer to his hardness as he teased. I loved it, pleasure and anticipation growing with each heavy breath. My hands in his hair, grabbing as his manhood crested my entrance. I pushed into him wanting him inside me, begging for him.

He carried me away from the wall and lay down on the bed with me on top of him. He held my hands as if to guide me and keep me from pushing him all the way into me. His grasp raised my hips up and down as I circled and worked to bury him into me.

I think he liked the energy I spent to fight him and ease him in. It was foreplay that excited him. I felt it in his firmness and heard it in his breathing.

"I want you so bad," he whispered, sliding his hands across my back. "You are so wet."

I kissed his body and brought my mouth to the trail of fine hair leading to his manhood and licked and kissed and suckled, taking in as much of him as I could in my mouth. He moaned then lifted my head. "You have to stop that. I'm going to explode in your mouth."

I felt sexy and exotic. His words aroused me further as I moved across his chest. "Then you're ready." I rested my entrance over his cock and sunk down.

"Not so fast. I want this to last and I won't if you…Oh…oh…" he moaned as I slid further down.

I wanted it to last too, but I also wanted him all the way inside me. I took it slow and was impressed that he wanted me on top, in control. He swallowed as I buried him further into me. I rose and lowered myself, slow and easy, and it felt so darn good I lost control and moved quicker and quicker. My excitement peaking as I experienced my first orgasm.

He held me tight as his body quivered in our finale. Warmth shooting into me and filling me up.

"Where the hell did you come from?" he asked, his tone serious.

"I could ask the same thing." I climbed off him and snuggled in beside him, pulling the cover up.

He turned his head to face mine. "When we leave tomorrow, will I ever see you again?"

Our eyes met and I read the sincerity in his. "I hope so." I didn't want a one-night stand either and was confused about Ealon. It was still possible he was Leandra's attacker. It was possible he wasn't. The mystery behind him and where he came from didn't sit right with me, even though I really liked him. It was as if my cheesecloth memories were reaching for something, warning me.

We lay together for a few more minutes. I wished the minutes in that moment wouldn't have ended. Eventually, I snuck back to Anora's room and crawled into bed. I couldn't even think at that moment what Lee and I were... only that we were.

Your House or Mine

eet for coffee. Ealon's message to me. I stared at it, unsure what to say. A week ago it would have been a yes but after the past weekend and my dalliance with Lee I felt the guilt like a whale on my back as I expected. My relationship with Ealon was undefined. We enjoyed kissing and spending time together. He made me laugh and I felt comfortable with him – mostly. My misgivings were ridiculous yet they were present. The most real excitement we had was the day we found and explored Talbot House.

At the time, I was freaked out and didn't plan on *ever* making a return trip. At the same time it was a fond memory. He'd never invited me home and a part of me considered he was hiding something. I didn't even know where he lived. *Did he represent something I wanted?* Besides his obvious good looks and charming personality, was there anything more to the relationship? *Was he just taking it slow and being a gentleman?*

My insecurities shined brighter than the fourth of July fireworks. I didn't have boyfriend experience and couldn't go to James. After the kiss last week, and his obvious dislike for Ealon, asking him would be a disaster. I didn't even know where we stood. I wanted to bury my face in a pillow. Three men in my life and the only one I wasn't confused about was the one I knew the least – Lee. I was beating myself up and I shouldn't feel any guilt. I wasn't officially Ealon's girlfriend nor James's. *I'm in the mood to be lazy. How about a movie at your place?* I texted and sent before I could change my mind.

Probably the worst thing to do. I was pushing my limits and if it wasn't for my encounter with Lee I probably wouldn't be. I was a busy college student who didn't have time for a social life. At least I'd convinced myself of that. The devil on my shoulder wanted to know more about Ealon and my mixed feelings for him.

Lee added a new dimension to my life. One that Anora had been trying to get me to see. It's OK to be young and have fun, live my life. Since the weekend, Lee and I had video chatted. Whatever was happening between us, we were doing it backwards. Sex first than getting to know each other. My heart fluttered when he called. *Is it possible to fall for two men? Was I replacing Ealon with Lee because of my apprehensions or was it James I was trying to forget?*

A text from Ealon popped up on my phone's screen: *Come by about 8* and the address. The initial anxiety melted away. I took a deep breath but hadn't exhaled by the next wave of anxiety. Could I make it through the night? Would I feel so guilty over Lee that I ruined everything? Should I feel guilty about Lee or about carrying on with two men at the same time? Anora would say: *You're young and they're both hot. Enjoy.* She was right. She said she lived vicariously through me, but I hadn't told her about Lee.

My emotions and guilt peaked and plummeted while I justified my actions. I wanted to look sexy, but not too sexy. I was flipping through the clothes in my closet when Kit walked in.

"Date tonight?" she asked, glancing at me then the pile of clothes on my bed.

"Is it that obvious?"

She laughed, pointing at the clothes pile. "Yeah, it is." She strolled to the closet and pulled out a butterfly sleeve top and matching shorts. Together they looked like a romper but were two separate pieces. She held it up to me. "I think it'll fit."

I held it in front of me and twisted in the mirror. It was cute, comfortable enough for a night in watching a movie, yet sexy enough to catch the male eye. "Thanks."

"No problem, I like to see someone wearing it. I'm so busy with classes I barely have time to breathe. I don't know how you do it," she said, already on her bed with the computer open.

I took a couple steps towards her. "You need a night off. One night to be free and have fun."

"That will be the two-week break between summer and fall classes. I marked it on my calendar." She pointed her finger towards the calendar hanging beside her bed. The days were filled in with stars.

"That's over two weeks away. Let's go to Flashers this weekend. We won't stay out late. We can't drink, so it'll be a couple hours' break. Something to regenerate your mind. They say if you give your mind a break it thinks better when you need it to," I said, attempting to convince her. Her life was the library and studying. I didn't even know if she had any friends. At least I had Anora.

Her eyes shifted away from the computer screen and met mine. "I know what you're trying to do and I'm grateful, but I can't."

I stood. "OK, if you change your mind you know where to find me," I said with lifted eyebrows.

She managed a smile and a giggle. Her eyes already returned to the computer screen. I had a lot of work too and with a full load of summer classes, so I found it hard to believe she didn't have an hour or two during a weekend to get away from school. *Is it me?* I thought, allowing my insecurities to consume me.

I debated on driving or calling a Ryde and finally chose my car. After all, that was part of the deal for signing up for summer classes. Apprehensions filled my gut too, like butterflies stuck in a cage, and I was unsure what to expect. I'd never really been nervous to see Ealon. No, that wasn't true. I'd been nervous to see him again when he showed up at the coffee shop. My nerves so consumed, I invited Kit. Ended up, things went well. They always did with Ealon.

I noted the manicured bushes along the walkway. Pretty standard, apartment-style, easy to maintain landscaping. There were several units. I guessed eight in his building. He opened the door and I was practically knocked on my ass by the strong tropical scent emanating from his apartment. I chuckled, he'd been nervous to invite me over because he thought it would be too messy or smelly. That eased my tensions a bit.

His green eyes traveled over me as he opened the door, inviting me in. Socks on his feet, wet hair, shorts and a T-shirt. I guessed he'd got out of the shower and threw clothes on.

"Is that a tropical Hawaiian scent I smell?" I teased.

"Um, yeah. Default of a bachelor pad is that it's not fit for anyone else." He raised his arm to his back as if to scratch. "The other thing is that I have beer. You want one?"

I didn't bother to ask how he bought beer. "Sure."

"Sit down. I have a casserole in the oven. I hope you're hungry," he said with a little stutter as if nervous as he reached in the refrigerator for a couple beers.

I noted the casserole box at the top of the trash which he'd forgotten to close. "Maribell's, good choice."

His brows lowered in confusion as he glanced at the trash then moved in front of it. "No, no. I made it from scratch." He popped the beer and handed it to me with a silly grin.

"Uhm hmm, you're multitalented. Intern by day, DJ by weekend, and chef by night," I joked.

"Sit down. I've… I've got a couple streaming channels. There's got to be a movie," he jested as he grabbed something off the back of the couch and stuffed it behind him. It looked like a T-shirt. I chuckled inside. He'd been nervous and simply hadn't invited me because his home was a mess.

I sat on the large maroon couch, noting how soft it was. I guessed it was real leather, not the fake stuff. That's when I took a thorough look around. For an intern, this place was pretty nice. A high-top, walnut finish table for four. A sixty-inch TV, a matching walnut finish table on each side of the couch. Studying them closer, I didn't think it was a finish but solid walnut. "Nice place." *How does an eighteen-year-old afford any of this?*

He sat beside me and flipped on the TV. "Yeah, it's my dad's bachelor condo. He usually rents it out, but since I was interning for the summer he put me up here."

That explained it. Every time I questioned anything about him there was always a simple answer and I couldn't find anything wrong. It was James's words and apprehensions that soured me on Ealon between visits. "I'm impressed. Does he buy your beer too?"

He laughed. "No, that was my neighbor. He, uh, brings beer and leaves it every time he comes over. I have a bigger TV and he likes to, uh, watch sports," he said in a very cheeky voice.

The nervous thing was cute and sexy and weird. We'd hit it off so well, so natural at first at least. Had I been reading him wrong? Was it in my imagination? Here I was, second guessing things as I moved a bit closer. He grabbed my hand as if to offer affection yet keep me at bay while surfing channels.

Fifteen minutes or so into the movie, his body visibly relaxed as his back molded into the couch and his shoulders dropped, eventually putting his arm around the back of the couch and even fondled my hair. The aroma of the casserole filling the entire condo and making my stomach remember it was hungry. I wanted more, yet was acutely aware I didn't lust for him the way I did Lee.

After dinner, he lay on the couch on his side, inviting me over. It felt awkward but, as I molded against him, the white elephant moment dissipated, his warm breath in my hair and his hand rubbing along my side and along the nape of my neck. I turned slightly, my lips brushing against his. I brought my hand over his head and ran it through his thick dark curls as our tongues met. Tingles ran across my spine with his fingertips.

Sliding my hand down the back of his pants, I tested his limits. My bra came over my breasts as his hands slid under and cupped them. There was something I couldn't put my finger on that was off. In the moment he had me on the couch, putty in his hands, and he was still on second base.

It wasn't that I was an expert in the area, but I'd listened to the bathroom gossip at school and how young guys rushed in without any foreplay. *Did I listen to the wrong stories? Did girls with good experiences not talk about it?* James always said guys were walking hormones with one thing on their mind.

The fire in my panties was quickly being put out by the wetness coating them. Pasted against him, I couldn't not feel the firmness in his pants. I wanted badly to grab him, take his cock in my hand and feel its silkiness like I had Lee's in the hot tub. My thoughts drifted to Lee, my panties growing even wetter as I felt his touches instead of Ealon's, his scent and moans in my ear as he came filling me with the wet heat of his cum. *Stop, Chelsea!* I ordered, using every ounce of strength to push him out of my mind.

His image replaced with James's. Pushing any men out of my mind now was useless as I wanted it so desperately, my breath heavy as I pushed my hands beneath the waistband of his shorts. He flinched, momentarily pushing backwards, bringing me back to reality and Ealon.

It was that moment, that tiny recoil, that brought a thought front and center. *Maybe he's a virgin?* It would explain his nervousness, why we hadn't gone further than kissing until today. Would the Chelsea of last week, before Lee, feel the way I did now?

No, the Chelsea of last week wouldn't be pushing for more. Her virginity was too important, yet she'd dropped her pants super quick for Lee and begged him to take her. *What was it about him?*

Ealon's touch against my skin brought me back from whatever universe my mind had wandered off to. It was arousing, his lips enticing, as I pondered my sexuality and pushed the boundaries, leading him on and succumbing to him as if it would answer a mystery. Fill in some of the blanks in my cheesecloth memory.

I glanced away from him, my eyes darting towards the ceiling fan that spun above us, moving my hips against him. His breath heavy. The tip of his cock still in his shorts, pressing against my leg. Our lips locked together, my eyes drifted downward spotting something in the corner of my vision. I focused on it as his hands moved down my stomach. It was a picture.

I hadn't noticed a table there, but now I couldn't look away from the picture. There were two boys, the older one with dark wavy hair and the younger with lighter, straighter hair. They were at the beach, the ocean behind them. The older boy was a younger version of Ealon. His dark, wavy hair blown out of place by the summer breeze and his eyes so vibrant a green even the old picture couldn't dull them. The younger boy. I recognized him too from somewhere in my lost memories. It surfaced for a flash and I fought to hold on.

My mind's eye saw the same boy sitting across from me at a table, but I didn't think I was at the table. I looked down on him. He wore a green T-shirt and his hair was slicked back as if sprayed with water and combed. It was a glimpse of something and chills coursed up my spine and I suddenly felt dirty, as if we were doing something wrong. My mind pressing through the cheesecloth to ignite the memories lost in its folds.

My body jolted and a stream of foreign emotions swallowed me. I pushed away from Ealon and fell onto the floor with a thump. His touch no longer sending sweet sensations but cold prickles.

He stared at me, his green eyes round in surprise as he sat up. "What's wrong?" he pleaded, as if he knew exactly what was wrong. The normal Ealon would make a joke, something like 'Oh, you want to take it to the floor' or 'The floor – kinky'. But he asked 'What's wrong?' as if he felt something too.

I scooted away from him, letting that single, incoherent memory guide my actions and words. Anger rising like bile inside me. "You lied to me! You told me you had a brother, an older brother. You're the older brother and he…" I fought to spit out the words, "he lived with me and…" I screamed, scrambling to my feet.

He rose, sitting on the edge of the couch, his cock no longer tenting his shorts. Remorse drawn on his face as wrinkles lined his forehead and his Adam's apple bobbed as he swallowed. He opened his mouth to speak but words didn't come out at first, as if he had to stop and think about his lie or cover his guilt. "Yes, my brother was stolen from us and we never knew what happened to him until they identified what was left of him."

My head spun with the revelation. James had been right: there was something off about him. I'd felt it and questioned that he was hiding something, but I didn't want to believe it. What an idiot I'd been for his pretty face and hot body. I'd been so stupid at the club, so proud to be seen with him, hoping every horny young woman was green with envy.

My brain had been trying to tell me. The touches that felt not quite right. He betrayed me! Heat flushed my cheeks as everything sunk in like a dropped bomb. His brother was my fake brother. *Did he even like me?*

I stepped backwards as he rose from the couch, reaching for my hands. Did he think he could make me forget, charm me? Of course he did. That's what he'd been doing all along. Not anymore! "You've been using me, to what, what, gain information? I was a baby. You weren't really a student, you didn't just graduate, you probably aren't really doing an internship. You went through all this to… to… what?" I screamed, each word a dagger, sharper than the previous.

No more. I grabbed my purse and thrust it over my shoulder as I ran to the door. Propelling it open, I sprinted into the night, tears streaming from my face. He called after me, running outside in his socks. I slammed my car door shut and locked it.

"Chelsea, let me explain, please." He beat on my window.

The car rolled backwards as I shifted into reverse, nearly knocking him over. It was lucky for him he jumped out of the way. The road blurred through my tears. I wiped them away. He lied to me, pretended to date me knowing he wasn't who he presented himself to be. I blinked my eyes as bright headlights shone from behind. Their brightness made it double hard to see the road. I tilted the rearview mirror to shine the light away from me.

The headlights persisted as if following me, and anxiety took over, washing away the sorrow. The college wasn't far so I stayed on my path, ignoring the headlights, telling myself I was paranoid. We were on a main road. The cars passing on the other side gave me solace until we neared the college. Only students and visitors went this far.

Swallowing my anxiety like a frog in my throat, I turned onto the campus, glancing over my shoulder to see a late model greenish truck illuminated by the street-lights: it stayed on the road. The lump in my throat and twist in my guts didn't diminish as I parked my car in the garage. It was late and I was alone. Most students didn't bother with cars. They went places in groups or called Rydes. The persistent silence was broken by my footsteps as my sandals softly patted against the concrete.

I peered into the night and scanned the outside parking lot. Sure no one was there, I stayed on the sidewalk under the lamps and scurried towards the dorms, taking the shortest path possible. I'd felt safe on the campus until tonight. Now, small tremors rattled my hands and my legs felt rubbery as I ran-walked toward the dorms, feeling eyes on me.

You're being stupid and paranoid, I told myself to calm my nerves. *But was I?* Stupid and paranoid. College campuses were known for rape. Young women roofied at parties, date rape, even assault happened. I just escaped a man who lied to me for no reason. It ate at me. What had he hoped to gain?

A rustle of the leaves caught my ear followed by a flash of light. My heart pounded hard and my rubbery legs made it difficult to move. I inhaled deeply and tried to calm myself as I pushed myself forward. The light surrounded my feet.

"You alright?" asked a deep voice belonging to a man dressed in a security suit. The donut around his middle and receding hairline told me he was middle-aged.

My gut roiling. How did I know he was truly campus security? He could be from the truck that followed me with its bright headlights. I nodded and finally found my feet. The dorms in sight now, I collected my legs and ran without answering his question.

Once inside the dorm, I pressed myself against the wall and caught my breath.

Nature's Cock Block

I decided from that night onward to only leave campus in a group, or with at least one other person. There was a reason we were asked to stick with the buddy system. The campus itself had low incidences of violence and was safe, but I wasn't taking the chance again.

Ealon hadn't left my mind. He lied and carried on with a charade. Why shouldn't he have been honest? There was no rhyme or reason. My anger hadn't subsided, but it had eased. I felt sympathy for him but also felt the sting of treachery. My thoughts were clear enough to understand he was hesitant because he felt my old friend: guilt. That was an emotion people couldn't hide from me. He'd texted me once after that night then gave up when I didn't respond. Nor would I, holding firm to my stance. I didn't need to know why he'd done it. He had, and that was enough.

Water splashed against my ankles as I rushed through the rain. The wind attempting to steal my umbrella. Anora texted me earlier. She had the results from our DNA. Excitement and nerves bubbled inside me as I pushed open the glass door to her dorm building and wound through the other students in the hallway.

Water dripping from each of my steps. One knock and she thrust the door open. Her expression excited and confused.

"Take a seat for this. You won't believe what I found." She ushered me towards an ergonomic computer chair.

Her room was a bit messier than her room at home. I guessed there was a maid who visited The Ranch and kept things in order, but here it was just her. Clothes hung off the ergonomic chair as she grabbed them and tossed them onto the pile already building on the floor. It reminded me of the same move Ealon had made. Balling up the shirt hanging on the back of the couch and stuffing it behind. *He's an ass. Stop, Chelsea. He's not endearing or charming, but a fake like his brother!*

As soon as I thought it, the lump formed in my gut. How could I think such a thing of a young boy who was a victim as much as me? Ealon's brother hadn't asked to be kidnapped and made my fake brother. I spanked myself mentally. It was a horrible thought and my defenses against Ealon were weakening. Both him and his family were victims.

Anora grabbed a tablet from off her bed, refocusing my thoughts on her. Butterflies partied inside me as she moved around me and bent down, pushing the tablet in front of me. I swallowed, heart flutters pushing against my chest, as my eyes shifted to the screen. She explained what I was looking at and how percentages worked in DNA between siblings: "Full siblings with the same parents share approximately 50% the same DNA, half siblings about 25%, identical twins nearly 100%, fraternal twins about 50%, always give or take the percentages are never exact, so between three full siblings one could share 48%, another 52% and the other 47%."

She paused for a second and studied my face as if to make sure I was following, then said the words that made my heart skip a beat. "We share 24%, but you and this other girl share 73%."

Anora had a habit of making others think and I couldn't make any sense of her last words. How does someone share 73%? A horrifying thought dawned on me. Our mother was raped by a blood relative. I swallowed hard to push the vomit down. My words deliberate and ragged, "How is that possible?"

"You're sesquizygotic twins," she responded. Her voice peppy.

The vomit ball receded, as she wouldn't be that upbeat if our mom had been raped by anyone, relative or not. Her happiness demonstrated that the sesqui— whatever that I couldn't even pronounce in my head was a rare gem in the genetic world. The narrowing of her eyes noted my utter confusion. I didn't speak.

In her usual fashion she explained, "Sesquizygotic twins share 50 to 100% the same DNA. In layman's terms we call them semi-identical. It's rare but has become an area of study more recently." She stopped speaking abruptly as if now waiting for me to say something. She never ran out of words and I wondered if she'd been explaining everything all her life, always being smarter than everyone.

I didn't know what to say. My mind wasn't really processing her words anymore. I understood what she was saying, just not how it happens or that it happened to me. Flashing in red like a neon sign was the question I assumed she was waiting for. "How does that happen? A sperm fertilizes an egg, half from mom, half from dad. How does, does…" the words stammered from my mouth. I didn't know much in her world but understood the basics of fertilization. That was high school biology.

She folded her legs and sat crossed legged on the floor. "Yes, so keep thinking about that. The sperm flows towards the fallopian tubes, finds the egg, and the first swimmer goes in. It triggers a shell around the egg to keep the other sperm out. Nature's cock block."

I giggled at that, as I'd never heard sperm fusing with the egg called that before. It was silly, but painted the picture of two wriggling sperms going in for the finish and succeeding together.

She paused for a second as I got my chuckles out, her lips curling in a smile. "I've always thought of it that way. The sperm, like grown men, don't want to share. Only sometimes that shell isn't triggered quick enough, or another swimmer makes it in before the shell finishes, and two swimmers fertilize the egg. The egg begins to divide and differentiate like normal but eventually it splits, the same as it would for identical twins."

That was a biology lesson I probably never needed, as unromantic three-way would replay itself in my mind. To make sure I was understanding the threesome correctly I stated, "Me and her have the same father and two of his frisky sperm fertilized our mom's egg."

She nodded and her face lit up. "Exactly! Like I said it's rare but happens. One of nature's oddities, something that adds overall to diversity and the passing on of traits and evolution."

It wasn't as shocking as I thought. Strange news was becoming the norm and for years people mistook Leandra and me. I hadn't really thought we were related, but could accept we were. Already had one sister, now I had two. I was so absorbed in the relationship between Leandra and me that I missed the connection between Anora and me and what that meant for her.

We shared nearly a quarter of DNA, meaning we were half siblings. Our mom *choosing* to vanish was the only option that made sense. It still wasn't a topic I wanted to talk Anora about. If she didn't get it yet, she would. The only other person I knew possibly as smart as her was Lee.

I didn't want her feelings hurt. Our mom was never a part of my life and the more I was learning the more I began to think that was a good thing. Did she have some secret affair that went sour so she had no choice but to disappear, or was she fearful because she knew we weren't her husband's children? She vanished and gave us up, not being able to support us on her own. Shame, maybe that was it, like the guilt that shrouded me with nearly every thought.

That still didn't answer how Leandra ended up with an amazing family and I ended up with child snatchers. The worst floated across my brain. She sold us, a deal behind closed doors, something shady and illegal for money. I swallowed hard. "If we're halves, but definitely share the same mother, then we have different dads."

"I know. I was so sure we'd be full siblings, but what surprised me more was that you and this other girl share so much DNA. Don't know how that's possible" An edge of desperation in her voice as she grasped at straws.

She definitely wasn't ready to hear what I was thinking. I rolled the chair back and joined her on the floor. "What do you remember about her?"

A tear bubbled from the corner of her eye and threatened to make its descent down her cheek. "Not much. I was little, but I remember happy stuff, moments where she held me or smiled, laughed. I can't remember my parents not being happy." The threatening tear fell, followed by more. She wiped them away with her hands and sniveled to combat crying.

"It's OK. This is a lot for both of us. My world has always been messed up but yours hasn't. Sometimes you have to cry." It wasn't often I wasn't the messed up one but tonight, here, it was Anora and she was my sister. I needed to be there for her.

She pressed her hands over her face and lowered her head. I wrapped my arms around her as if I was the strong one not the completely topsy turvy mess that I was. She brought her arms around me and rested her head on my shoulder.

When her tears finally stopped she sniveled. Collecting herself, she asked, "What do we do next?"

In the Back Door

What do we do next? It wasn't a question I'd ever thought someone would ask me, especially someone who seemed to have all the answers. She had a vulnerability and thought I had something to offer. It gave me confidence, even though I had no idea how to answer the question. My gut said we return to the scene of the crime or vanishing.

In the meantime, I was also a college student with a budding relationship, so when Lee called and asked me to spend the weekend with him I didn't hesitate. He was in town and staying at a luxury hotel. The kind with folded towels in the shape of animals and mints on the bed.

I lay on my back with his naked body beside mine, our hands entwined. "Tell me about your family?" I asked. It was random, but I wanted to know more about him. So far, all I knew is that I was addicted and couldn't get enough.

"Dad is first generation from Japan. He didn't immigrate because he wanted to, but the company he worked for sent him. He grew up in the village of Iwakuni. Most of his family still lives there or close. He met my mom, an American woman, they married and he stayed here. I have two brothers and one sister." He paused. "What about you?"

That was a loaded question. I didn't understand enough about my real family to tell him anything and was a bit ashamed that everything was so screwed up, but he didn't seem the judgmental type. "You met my sister but we're not really sisters – foster sisters. I was put in the system when I was a baby so I never met my parents." I thought of Ealon's lie and decided I wouldn't lie. It wasn't a lie to omit. "My foster family are the people I consider my family though. I don't remember anything before them. It was like my life didn't exist until they took me in."

He rose up on one elbow and smoothed my face with his hand. "That's sad."

"Not when you don't know. They are very good people and they love me like their own." Which was true. I was part of the family, even though I now knew I had biological family. I was still processing being a genetic anomaly twin and having a half-sister. Until I was comfortable with it, I wasn't discussing it with anyone except Anora.

"Then it's happy," he said and kissed my cheek without asking more.

I insisted on Japanese hibachi. He laughed but said he knew of a good place and explained the history of hibachi while the chef fried our rice and stacked the shrimp, doing neat tricks that were obviously more for show. I was intrigued that he had family and culture. I didn't know anything about my parents or the cultures my ancestors came from.

He demonstrated how to use chopsticks properly and we both laughed when I couldn't even secure a single rice grain. He did it with skill and brought a bite to my mouth. I had forgotten for the moment about my troubles, at least until we got into his car – a hybrid sedan. Not a cheap car to buy, even though highly efficient.

I thought of my mother and how she vanished. All the evidence, or lack of it, pointed toward her making an escape and going back to the scene, which also meant securing police records if possible. I returned to the conversation that started our relationship. "You said government agencies are easier to break into than banks or high-profile corporations. How about law enforcement?"

"That's a strange question," he said.

I shrugged. "You're the one that brought it up the day we met."

"That's fair. I did. It's part of my job to keep up with it. We don't want anyone sneaking out trade secrets. Law enforcement depends. The FBI or homeland security are far more difficult than the average small town police station. I can probably easily hack into the city's local PD but that doesn't mean I'd have long before I was detected, maybe long enough to plant a virus, maybe longer. Are you thinking of being naughty?" he said with a sly smile. "I can think of better naughty things to do with you."

I giggled. "No, I was curious. I guess it's a matter of finding their back door," I stated, digging for more information.

"I'd rather sneak in through your back door," he said with a wink.

I liked that he was very upfront. He didn't play games, nor did he lie to me. I got off the topic, not wanting to make it sound like an inquisition even though it was. Anora asking 'what do we do now?' a near constant strain on my brain "You wouldn't be sneaking into my back door if I opened it for you."

I figured I'd picked enough pieces from his brain to give at least an attempt at breaking into the Fall City PD. Where Anora was born and our mother vanished from. Any program had a back door. It was a matter of finding it and a simple system would be easy enough for an amateur like me to sneak into.

His kiss still warm on my lips, I marched to Anora's room with an answer to her question. She answered the door in a long T-shirt and rubbing her eyes.

"What are you doing here?" she asked, her voice groggy.

I hadn't thought of the time and felt stupid as heat rose to my cheeks. "I, um, I know what to do next."

She opened the door, inviting me in, and sat on the edge of her bed.

I sat in the computer chair and rolled it around so I could face her. This time I was the exuberant one. "So far you have done everything, but I have skills too and I think we should hack in to the police station and take a look at her file," I said with determination.

Her squinty sleepy eyes suddenly opened wide and round. "It's a cold case, why don't we just go to the station and ask to see it?"

She was right. I wasn't really thinking. That's what I'd done when I spoke with Sugda, but I didn't ask to see the case file. I didn't need to. I already had a copy when I took pictures of it in Charice's office without her knowledge. "You think that will work?"

"It's a place to start. Why do we need to do anything illegal? We have a break coming up and we'll do this together.

Whether there's anything to be found, good or bad. We'll do it as a team."

I sat on the edge of her bed. "You're right." She was and I didn't bother to bring up how we already did something illegal when she tested Leandra's DNA without her permission or knowledge.

When it's Legal...

alls City was barely large enough to be entertained as a city. I was sure hacking in wouldn't be a problem even with my limited skill set. However, doing illegal things wasn't the answer, at least not if there was a legal way to do it.

The mint painted walls with dirt in the corners of the floorboards wasn't a welcoming sight as we entered the building, but we hadn't been given any problems when we asked to see the file.

The clerk raised a brow. "You can't leave with it but you can sit over there." She pointed to a small table with a couple of uninviting metal chairs.

We each took a seat as we waited in anticipation. The clerk didn't return but an officer in plain clothes. He dropped a thin file on the table between us.

A belt held his jeans onto his thin frame. His light hair even thinner. A toothpick twisted and bobbed between his lips. Pulling it out he glanced at each of us. "Which one of you is the daughter?" he asked, his bushy mustache moving like a squirrel over his mouth.

I gulped and let Anora handle that one.

She took the lead without hesitation. "I am."

He leaned an elbow on his propped leg, twiddling the toothpick between his fingers. "You should know we have to follow all leads and, in the absence of them and statistics, there was no one else but your father. No evidence and no motive and we stopped searching. The file's been here ever since."

"Thank you," Anora said.

He nodded and dropped his foot from the chair. Stuffing the toothpick in his mouth, he left us.

I leaned over. "I think he has more hair over his mouth than on his head," I whispered.

She giggled. "I think you're right."

Once we glanced through the file, I understood the warning. They had researched her father extensively, going as far as hunting down his first wife who he wasn't even in contact with at the time. I guess in the search for a motive they found he had a twenty-thousand-dollar whole life insurance policy on her and she on him. They'd taken them out shortly after they got married. Twenty thousand wasn't really a motive since, financially, he wasn't struggling, had a good job, and was left to care for a child who would obviously cost a lot more than twenty K over a lifetime.

They also interviewed her friends she went to lunch with. None noted anything odd about her or the day. She'd been happy. In fact, one friend said she glowed. That comment struck me. That's what people say to pregnant women. I wasn't positive the birthday on my birth certificate was real. The one the Moras had was a nice passable forgery. However, it was the day we went with. Leandra's birthday was two weeks before mine. It was anyone's guess which date was the real date. Maybe neither. Either way, the timing still placed us as old enough she could have been pregnant; at least, I wasn't ruling it out yet.

She added the names of her mom's friends to her phone book and suggested we talk with them. One of them no longer lived in Falls City. Another died a couple years back. A battle with breast cancer.

The trip down memory lane and learning the specifics of her (our) mother's final whereabouts brought down her usual spirits and she wasn't her over-exuberant, talkative self. "Are you OK? We can go home if it's too much," I suggested.

"No, it's fine," she assured me, but I heard in her voice that it wasn't. "I know dad went back to the restaurant, but I don't think he ever searched for her. No time, he was raising a daughter on his own. I don't think he's ever gotten over it and I was just thinking of him," she reminisced, her voice melancholy. She was finally seeing what I was. Thinking what I was. I'd wait for her to say it.

"I'm sure it was very hard on him but he had you. I think you probably helped him get through it," I said as encouragingly as I could. I'd met her father and he was a good guy and a devoted father.

She nodded. "Let's go," she said as she opened the car door and stepped out.

Flowers grew beneath the trees and beds filled with summer blooms lay beneath the windows. There was a small porch up the steps. We squeezed each other's hands for strength as she rang the doorbell. I felt the tension in her loosen when a middle-aged woman opened the door, as if she had some memory of her.

"Hi, uh, I'm Anora McCarn."

The woman's face immediately lit up. "Wow! What brings you here?" Obviously, the woman remembered the name but I guess you don't easily forget the last name of a friend who vanishes after lunch. "I'm so rude. Come in, girls."

I felt much like a tag along as we took a seat on a sofa. A large window with a view of the street in our vision, white lacy curtains over it.

"Can I get you something, water, tea? I can make coffee," she asked nervously. She hadn't asked the reason for our visit. Was it that obvious?

"Thank you, but no." Anora glanced at me and I confirmed a no response as well.

The woman sat down across from us, a coffee table between us and a cozy fireplace to the right against the wall. "I don't know what's wrong with me today." She turned towards me. "Nancy Pickering."

"Chelsea, Anora's friend."

She chuckled. "It's wonderful to meet you." Turning to Anora, she asked, "How are you? How is your dad?"

"He's good. We moved a few years ago and I'm in college now, starting grad school."

I listened mostly, as they made small talk. I was antsy to get right to the point of our visit, but let Anora handle it. This was a mom she knew, and her dad. I was an outsider looking in. Finally, she asked about that day.

Nancy's eyebrows lowered as she remembered. Her voice distant. She didn't glance into mine or Anora's eyes but stared at the wall above us. "It was a very normal lunch. She talked about you and your dad. We all talked about our families and it… there wasn't anything odd." Her eyes drifted to Anora as she gazed into them. "I have thought of that day so often and sometimes I think maybe there was something odd, but that's my mind searching for answers. I was her best friend," she said, her voice desperate.

I chimed in, "What about her parents? Siblings?" A best friend knows things others don't.

Nancy turned her head my direction and clicked her tongue. "You know she was private about that. Never talked about them. I never wanted to pry. I figured the pain of losing them was too much. And she had such a wonderful life with you," she glanced at Anora, "and your father."

We learned zero about her disappearance, but I did learn some things about my mom, like she was happy with her life and at least appeared to be very much in love with Anora's father. It was different hearing it from someone besides Anora or reading it in a police interview. The experience really changed my thinking that our mom had run off for her own reasons.

I did question her past. She didn't talk about it beyond saying her family was killed. It was possible she left because she was running from her past.

Friends and Memories

We got in with the other woman, who agreed to meet us at the very place Anora's mom vanished. It was touch her idea. I wasn't sure how Anora would handle it but she seemed OK. She was strong and was close with her father. She had him to lean on.

The restaurant wasn't anything spectacular. It was in town, although not a busy area. Inside were booths and square tables along the walls and round tables in the middle. It was well lit and teemed with conversation and chatter that filled the empty spaces. We took a seat at a booth in the back corner.

She seemed willing to get right to the point, impatient even, as we ordered drinks. "When you go to the same place twice monthly, after a while you know everyone. The same faces, and when someone new starts working you notice it right away. Any new face stands out. That morning I woke up with a feeling of dread. And there was no reason. It didn't make sense. I've never told anyone this," she explained, her oval face framed with a short, pageboy-like haircut, recently colored as no gray showed.

It was as if she'd been holding onto a secret for years and was about to burst if she didn't get it out. She tilted her head and glanced to her right as if to point something out. "We always sat at that table over there where the older couple is sitting now. That was our spot. I almost didn't come because of that feeling, thinking maybe I was going to be in a car wreck or somehow in the wrong place at the wrong time, but I convinced myself that was silly thinking and came anyways. I sat across from your mother. She looked so pretty that day, as always. Her hair back, curls falling over her cheeks."

I'd seen pictures of our mother that Anora had shown me. I had her hair and we all had her face shape. She also had haunted eyes like there was something she could never say. A secret she couldn't speak or think of. I had wondered when looking at her photos if I too had her haunted eyes.

She tapped her finger against the glass of water the hostess dropped off. "Everything was so normal, but that feeling persisted. Your mom was radiating from the inside out until a man – a large man – I'd never seen him before - walked past us and tipped his hat. I'd swear your mom flinched. I've played and replayed that moment in my mind. At first, I thought I was just looking for something to ease my tension to make the sinking feeling in my gut go away. Projecting myself onto her."

I understood feelings and anxiety. They were my friend and my enemy, dictating my life and the guilt always creeping into my gut. I asked, "Did you tell this to the police?"

Her brows lowered into a V as her green eyes met mine. "No, I was shocked when they told me what happened and I didn't think about it and when I did I didn't know what to even say. He wasn't a local, but that didn't make him a criminal. Maybe that flinch was my imagination."

Anora folded her hands onto the table and leaned in. "You don't think it was."

"Not anymore. I've had many years to think about it. I did eventually go back to the police while her case was still active but I don't think they ever followed up on it and what was there to follow up on? It was more my conscience that I went back to them."

She was right. It's not a crime for a man to tip his hat to a table of ladies. The flinch probably had nothing to do with him and more to do with her swallowing a bite wrong or a reminder of someone. I did find it odd that nothing was mentioned in the file. But small southern towns weren't known for their record keeping. They probably never made any notation of it.

On the way out, she showed us where she'd been parked and where our mother's car had been on the side of the restaurant. There were no windows from the inside looking out. There was a back door close by and a dumpster. The door I was sure led to the kitchen. "Was it busy that day?" I asked. If she was hiding her past or looking over her shoulder, why wouldn't she park in front, closer to the road?

"I suppose. This place gets a good crowd," she said, her eyes rolling upward as she thought back.

Once we parted, Anora took us by her childhood home. It was nothing impressive, not like The Ranch. A basic house, four walls, a front door, small front yard with a couple trees and a tire swing in one of them along with a fence around the back. She joked, "My dad sold the house so we can't go inside or break in."

I deserved that hit. "What about the hospital? Were you born here?"

"Yeah, Falls City General," she said proudly. It gave me ideas. I wasn't past hacking into the police station or the hospital.

Anora drove us back to The Ranch. It was much closer than going back to campus and we had a three-week break. A few days there would be a nice place to gather our thoughts.

Stay

Her father was away on business for a few days, meaning we were alone in the house. Clay and Philipe not far if we needed anything. My mind raced as it was supposed to be slowing down and resting, but the thoughts kept coming. *She glowed, she radiated*; I believed she was pregnant at the time of her taking. I tossed in bed as I considered searching her dad's room, but I remembered the perimeter. No doubt it detected movement inside the house as well.

The house practically empty, she gave me a room of my own for our short stay. My mind racing with thoughts and curiosity, I crawled out of bed the first night and popped open my computer. Searching her dad's room might not be an option but I wasn't past brushing upon my hacking skills. Falls City General hospital was connected to five OBGYNs from two different practices. Three of the doctors were old enough to have delivered Anora. As I considered how to access patient files I clicked mindlessly on my own computer.

I paused when I came across a folder labeled HB. It was buried in the C drive. "Curious," I said aloud as I clicked it. There was a document and three jpegs. I glanced through the pictures. One was a small house with solar panels on the roof and tall trees on all sides. It was the type of place someone went to when they wanted to hide off the grid. Another was a young man, another was my mother. I paused there, searching her face. *Why was this on my computer?*

Charice gave me the computer. She hid the file on it. I was impressed she knew how to do that. My finger hovered over the touchpad, unsure if I wanted to know what was in the document. My conscience argued back and forth, and my stomach paid the price as it churned from the anxiety. *You can do this, you have to do this.* After several minutes of working on my nerves and building my confidence, I gave in and clicked the touch pad.

It was a letter from Charice and contained information about the only possible connection to my family she found. A man named Hadj Botlat. He was my grandfather. My heart stopped for a second. It just froze as I caught my breath. He was my mother's father.

The door swished lightly behind me. "I couldn't sleep either. What are you doing?"

Blood raced through my veins as I closed the computer and swung around in the chair. "Couldn't sleep," I blurted. Hadj Botlat would be her grandfather too, but I couldn't bring myself to show or tell her. Her words 'We're in this together' played in my head. I was being a horrible sister, but who was this guy? I didn't even know what I was going to do with the information.

"How about a movie and a late-night pizza?" she asked.

"Sure." It was the out I was hoping for and she didn't ask questions. Relieved, I followed her downstairs as we put a pizza in the oven and snuggled onto the pillowy cushions of the sectional.

I woke with my head buried in the soft brown cushions of the couch, my arm hanging off the side, the sun on my back. Anora's foot pushing against my leg as she stretched.

"I was afraid the body snatchers had taken both of you," Clay teased, his voice carrying from the doorway.

After a hearty meal, Anora and I took to the pool. Our floaties bumping, I asked, "How about her doctor?"

"Doctor patient privilege," she said as if she was a lawyer.

Gently, I kicked her floatie with my foot. "I know. That's why I'm thinking of going around it." I didn't know if doctor patient privilege or HIPPA laws applied to missing or *dead* people.

She lowered her sunglasses and tilted her head my way. "The perimeter."

Our eyes met as those words came up again. *What the heck was this perimeter?*

"You're antsy to hack something, but medical files? I'm sure there's prison time involved if you're caught." She raised her sunglasses and tilted her head back.

"Do you think your dad is tight on security because of what happened to our mom?" I asked. I really wanted to understand what this *perimeter* thing was.

"Yeah, I do. Our old house had the beta version of the perimeter. This here is the 2.0 version. I don't know if it was to keep people out or to spy on people inside, like waiting for mom to come back. It would be the first thing to detect her." The edge in her voice said there was more, as if maybe she thought her dad knew more than he said or maybe it was my imagination, like our mom's friend who noted the flinch when the man tipped his hat.

Whatever exactly the perimeter was, I was impressed but also a bit freaked out and feeling claustrophobic even though The Ranch sat on many acres of land and was vast enough to conceal the confinement. I guessed she was pretty used to it.

A week later, I convinced Kit to go to Flashers with me. A part of me kind of hoped to see Ealon even though I wouldn't admit that to myself. *Was I wrong?* He was distraught, searching for answers and clues that might bring him closer to the tragedy his brother and family faced. It wasn't so different really from me. *Was I making excuses for him?*

The night he DJ'd, his hand along my leg, his body close to mine on the dance floor. Maybe I was being too hard on him. His gentle touch as he'd mended my leg at Talbot House forced my heart to long for him. My mind flopping between the tender moments and how maybe they were all fake. Could they all have been an act? Weren't any of them real? I wanted to believe at least some of them were, even when my gut reminded me that he'd lied. There was no way to forget that.

It was possible I should give him the chance to at least say his piece, I considered, thinking how I hadn't been forthcoming with Anora. I hadn't lied, but I hadn't been completely honest either, nor had I said anything to my foster family. Was I doing the same as Ealon? The flexible walls of my heart were caving and it was only time until they collapsed and let Ealon back in.

Choosing Kit over Anora had more to do with the large amounts of time we'd spent together over the past week. We were back to the *'what do we do now?'* question and I was still teasing the idea of hacking into doctor records. There were only three to choose from. It wasn't like everything Anora did with our DNA was legal or authorized. The study was about mtDNA and genetic diseases, not tracing your own family tree and I was sure testing someone's DNA without permission was probably a felony.

A blue V-neck tank and jeans were Kit's nightclub attire, but she wore them well as they hugged her tiny curves. I went casual as well with a red teedie style shirt and a pair of denim shorts. It was comfortable like a T but a little dressier. Heck, it was summer and my feet wanted flat sandals not clunking heels. She was a lot more fun now that the semester was over and she wasn't rushing from one class to the other or spending every other waking minute in the library.

We maneuvered our way through the crowd as we didn't bother to get a seat, instead we hit the dance floor right away. There was no sign of Ealon and my heart dropped a bit as I remembered how sexy he'd been that night. The memories resurfacing. I forced them back and stuffed them into a corner of my mind. If I never saw him again it was my own fault. *No, it was his*, I reminded myself, almost instantly switching my thoughts to Lee.

A set of firm arms grabbed my waist. I spun around expecting a rando guy instead coming face to face with James. He grabbed my hands in his. "I know we need to talk. I haven't known what to say. I—" he blurted before I could get more than his name out.

I followed him off the dance floor to a quieter corner near the restrooms. "I know, me either. I'm sorry. There are things you should know. Can we talk outside?" I asked, my eyes searching his one that wasn't covered with hair.

I figured Kit would be OK for five minutes and probably wouldn't even notice if I stepped outside for a minute, but what I had to say was private and even in the semi-quiet area near the restroom people still came and went.

The air was thick and balmy, and the streetlights were softened by the moisture. His hair more tussled than usual as if he put his head in a fan. His shirt hung loose over his torso as if he'd lost some mass. It wasn't like James was ever a big guy, but he had some definition and now, working construction, he should have more not less.

He stuffed his hands in his pockets the way he always did and shifted on his feet as his eyes darted from me to the ground. "I know I shouldn't talk about this but, that guy, he's been lying to you."

"I know. I haven't seen him."

He lifted his eyes, meeting mine and, bringing a hand out of his pocket, he raked his hair back. "His name is Miles Maverick and he's not doing an internship at a law firm. He works for a law firm. He's an investigator. A year ago, when my boss went through his divorce, he was the one who dug up dirt on my boss's wife." He brought his hand from his head to his ear and rubbed it like maybe he was nervous.

I hadn't known Ealon lied about his name and, although I had suspicions, I wasn't positive he'd lied about the internship. How stupid could I be? I'd come to Flashers hoping to see him, maybe give him a chance to explain, but his lies weren't the innocent white lies I'd convinced myself they were. Even comparing his situation to mine. No, he didn't deserve my pity. "Seriously! I knew he lied but his name isn't even Ealon! He's also the brother of the boy who… who was posed as my brother."

James's eyes narrowed at that statement. "What?"

A cool breeze pushed through the muggy air and with it a sour scent I couldn't place. *Was it James?* My attention switching back to James's appearance, studying his face; sunken cheeks, hollow eyes. I'd been so surprised to see him and so happy at the same time I hadn't gone beyond his frumpled clothing and hair. Acutely aware now, as James was always clean and showered except when he came to my dorm after work, my stomach tightened. "What's really going on James?"

He shrugged and stepped back. "Nothing," he said in defense. "Go enjoy your night." He turned on his heel and plodded away, leaving me confused.

Hack or Not to Hack

I should have chased after him that night instead of standing in place watching him walk away from me. Something beyond my problems was happening with him. Who cares about Ealon or whoever he is? James was more important and now he wasn't responding to my messages or answering the phone.

My thoughts and inner workings a frenzy of confusion. *Where did James live now? Who was this boss of his and why did he look so horrible? Was he lying to me about his job and was he really living on the streets?* I thought the worst and my body felt heavy. I was a horrible friend. A horrible girlfriend. Sure, Ealon lied, but I had sex with Lee. That is what really bothered me the most about the situation with him. I hadn't been transparent and was a complete hypocrite. Now I was abandoning James. I let him walk away. It was no wonder he didn't respond to my messages.

That conversation with James was the final straw. I didn't care anymore about breaking laws. I knew enough to scramble my IP address and find a back door. There were three doctors to choose from. I'd start with one and work my way to the others. Phantom pains arose in the finger I pricked in the blood pact I made with James. Each stroke forcing me back to that night at Flashers.

I wanted James to come knocking on my door again the way he did the day of the... kiss. We got high, junked out, and laughed. It was almost like old times until our lips met and our tongues found each other's. Nothing had been the same since, not him, not me.

Every footfall outside the door made my heart stop and flutter then drop like a rocket falling back to earth as they always moved on past my door.

I pulled my hair back and got to work, hoping to ease my thoughts and anxieties about him. Doctor two, I found records for McCarn. It was her. I scrolled through seven years of appointments. Other than prenatal care for Anora the appointments were spaced out once a year. I knew I couldn't stay in long so I continued scrolling for something that stood out, assuming the yearly visits were pap smears. The last date was five months after her yearly on Sept. 13th. Eight months before I was born and 10 days after she went missing.

She never made it to her last appointment. I wondered if Anora's dad even knew. The only answer I came up with was that she was pregnant. I clicked on the last yearly appointment. She went in for a pap and was given a prescription for birth control. I went back to her first appointment. Seven months before Anora was born. *What do I do with that? What did it mean?*

My thoughts were interrupted when the doorknob turned. I thought maybe my wish came true, but blew out a sigh as Kit appeared.

"What are you working on?" she asked as she mulled through her clothes hanging in the closet. The hangers sliding across the metal bar. "It's break." She glanced over her shoulder at me.

"Stuff. Not schoolwork or anything, but other stuff." My words so flimsy I didn't even convince myself.

She pulled a shirt off a hanger, barely noting my words. "There's a BBQ in the food court tonight. I guess it's like a "blast" for us summer students still here. You should come with me."

"Thanks, but I'm not feeling so well." My stomach was in knots between James and what I learned about my biological mother.

Once Kit left, I opened the letter from Charice, reading it again. There was a number for Hadj and coordinates. I didn't have the nerve to call him. Typing in the latitude and longitude, the location was north along the Virginia border buried in the trees and mountains. *What kind of man was he? He didn't even have an address.*

I jumped out of my chair and skin when someone knocked on the door, rushing to answer it. Every part of me hoping it was James and a little let down when it was Anora.

Looped around each arm was a bag. "I saw Kit. She looks like she's having a good time. They do this every year. When you've been to one you've been to them all. I grabbed us each a burger." She let a bag drop into her hand and set it on my desk. "I also brought us this." She opened the other bag, displaying a six pack of beer.

My eyes lit up. All the tension and overwhelming anxiety, I needed something to temper my nerves. "Just what I need."

She smiled, handing me a styrofoam box and opened a beer for me, placing it on the desk. Taking the other styrofoam box and a beer, she sat on the edge of my bed. "I hope you're not doing anything illegal," she said in jest, but I think she was genuinely curious. Her teeth sank into her burger.

I avoided the statement, as I didn't want to lie. I wasn't ready to share it with Anora. She'd probably be mad that I hacked in, or disappointed. "I was thinking about our mom. It's like she didn't exist before marrying your dad." I paused as I grabbed my burger then, before taking a bite, I said the thing I'd been avoiding. The thing she had to know.

Her intelligence was never anything to question. "I think she was running from something."

She swallowed her bite, her eyes drifting to the wall in front of her. "I know... I thought that too." She heaved in a deep breath. "I talked to my dad after we met with mom's friend. He doesn't know anything. He always knew she was running from something or someone, but she never confided in him."

She turned her head and met my gaze. "I know I shouldn't have, but I've always known he knew more. That's why he built the perimeter. He confided that she had night terrors. She'd wake in the night sweating, curled in a ball, or screaming. She wouldn't see a doctor over them and came up with the idea of the perimeter. It was her idea. Dad gave her everything." A tear trailed her cheek, then another.

She wasn't ready. A ball of guilt rolled in my stomach. I changed the subject. "We need to drink this beer," I said, pushing mine towards hers. "Cheers to finding each other."

It was avoidance. I had no idea what to possibly say but none of it shocked me. I had plenty of issues of my own. Nightmares not one of them, but anxiety, and a constant state of doom lingering over my head and around me. These problems of hers passed to me whether genetic or side effects of abuse. Since Anora and Leandra were normal, I figured it was psychologically induced mental illness. Kit had mentioned that one evening as she was watching something on her phone about siblings. They'd been given up at birth, one went into a good home. The other was abused. The mother had been raped, triggering PTSD and other mental illness. Sometimes everything was normal in people until that moment when enough was enough. 'Nature vs. Nurture' she called it.

Anora pushed her beer against mine. "You're right. We have each other and, don't worry, I haven't mentioned that to my dad yet."

I took a swallow of the beer as she brought hers towards her lips then paused. "When will Leandra be here?"

Sister Tree

Leandra: the other sister. Anora was anxious to meet her even though we couldn't let her in on the secret, at least not yet. Anora hoped maybe she could involve her in the mtDNA study. I agreed; it worked on me. Of course, neither of us knew at the time that we were related. This time we'd have to act surprised, which would be more difficult done than said.

I spent the final weekend of break with Lee. Internally, I knew it was in avoidance of spending time with Judy and Roy. I wanted to see them but figured I'd crumble and tell them everything. Biological parents or not, they were my nuclear family. I couldn't hide anything from them, especially not something as big as having sisters and even now a grandfather that lived off the grid. I might even spill my guy problems with Ealon and James as well as my interest in Lee.

Lee showed me things. We were computer nerds and it was almost foreplay to learn as he taught. I'd say we were equally turned on by it. I didn't have ties to him either. He was someone on the outside who understood nothing about the inside. With him, I could lose myself and be completely free.

Registered for my classes and books already purchased, I waited with Anora by the river. Leandra made it to campus late yesterday and was meeting us today. We figured we'd give her our tour of campus and take her to the Coffee Bean.

A breeze was always present at the river. In the summer it was the only place on campus bearable in the heat and humidity.

"That's her," Anora stated as I glanced upwards, our backs to the river. "Even in the buggy glasses she looks like you. Same size, same shape, even her hair. It's much darker but caked on her head, she has the same bouncy curls. She carries her shoulders back. You sometimes slouch," she said, pointing out my insecurity and Leandra's confidence with her shoulder comment. As usual though, her talk was nonstop and the comparison was something I'd done myself, only silently.

I stood to greet her. Anora followed my lead and we met her partway. Anora introducing herself before I even had the chance. She effervesced with excitement and I hoped she didn't accidentally let the cat out of the bag. Her intelligence aside, she didn't have much of a filter.

Dressed in shorts and a light blouse Leandra responded, "Anora. I like that. It's different, pretty. Leandra." She gave me a quick hug, which I hadn't expected. "How was summer?"

"It was OK. Stayed busy with work. How was Australia?" I asked, genuinely interested, but also wanted her to lead the conversation for now.

We strolled along the river as she described her experience. I was more than a tad jealous. At the same time I was happy she was able to travel and do things I'd have to wait years to do. After meeting Lee and his talk about Japan, I put it on the top of my list of places to visit. One day, when I had a career and the money to do so.

Anora was the tour guide, pointing out the stadium, swimming pool, and each college, admissions, the food court. She even gave her the same speech about food passes and warning about the coffee. We all giggled with her exaggerated hand movements and speech.

Dark clouds moved in, pushing out the heat and bringing in a chill. It was definitely rain weather so we took that opportunity to grab a Ryde and head for coffee and a dry seat.

Leandra's eyes round as she pulled her sunglasses over her head. "This place is so cute and this coffee is amazing. No joke," she said, swallowing a sip as we took to the comfy couches in the back. I was surprised it wasn't busier with all the students back on campus, but figured some were still unpacking and getting their schedules and textbooks.

"No kidding. Nobody drinks the stuff on campus. Give it another week and this place will be standing room only about this time," Anora stated, not taking her eyes off Leandra.

Leandra turned her head as she took in the cozy corners and welcoming décor. "I bet. Thanks for the tour. The campus map is horrible." She giggled. "What are the bookstore lines like?"

I thought of my incident over the summer. I'd got my fall books early. "Expect it to take all day. If you have a computer though, I found a website where you can buy the PDFs."

"I prefer the actual text. Easier to highlight and bookmark pages."

Anora rejoined the conversation, "What's your major?"

Leandra sighed as if that was a sore subject. "I'm not sure. I had to declare one but really I'm not so sure. I know I want to do something in the medical field, but I'm not sure what. The core classes are the same. In two years I'll figure it out. Either a physician assistant so I can work in an online telemedicine practice or medical research and development."

Her words excited Anora. I was sitting between two science junkies. "Tele and online medicine are the way of the future. Why sit in a doctor's office for an ear infection? I was reading how they are working to diagnose more through online tools. It's incredible. I'm a biotech major, so keep up on the latest developments."

The spark that ignited a conversation a bit over my head. By the conversation, you'd think they were the sesquizygotic anomalic twins sharing 73% the same DNA. I left them to their science talk and went to the counter to order us each a piece of the pie of the day – apple.

A few steps from the counter and the door opened. The dark tussled hair framing his face with its sharp male edges, and his emerald eyes meeting mine, I stopped in my tracks. Ealon.

Panic clutched me as my psyche divided in three. I considered turning around and returning to Anora and Leandra. Another part of me, the guilty part, wanted to apologize and give him the chance to explain himself. The last part, the brave part, wanted to face him. Tell him what I knew, call him out. That part of me never won.

The distance between us filled with tension as we stared at each other, neither of us moving until someone came in behind him and he scooted out of their way. It was my moment to bolt and I heavily weighed in on it but, like always, the guilty part of me won the battle and I stayed put as he walked towards me.

My mouth dried like Death Valley and my heart pumped quicker with each of his steps. *Thump-thump, thump-thump-thump.* I tried to muster spit and swallow but my throat felt closed in. The air thickening and losing oxygen. Our gazes locked.

"Chelsea, I, uh. Can we maybe talk?" he asked. The tone of his voice belying the confidence in his stance.

I nodded like an idiot, unable to form words. Sometimes I hated my cowardice. The most backbone I'd ever shown was the day I told him off, but still took the spineless way out and ran away.

We sat at an open table by the door with a view of the street. I focused on the parade of cars to avoid locking gazes again and, from the corner of my eye, he seemed unsure what to do with his hands as he tented them on the table then pulled them down and rubbed his palms along his shorts. "I'm really sorry. You have a right to be upset at me."

The truth was, I really wasn't upset at him anymore, even after James revealed more about him. I didn't interrupt, as I was unsure at all what or even if I wanted to say anything.

He kept his voice low and his words deliberate, as if thinking carefully about each one. "You must think horrible things about me but I never meant to lead you on. There's more you should know. I'm not interning, but work for a lawyer. I'm an investigator. That's how I learned about you. I have access to information most people don't. Your name was never released in any paper," he said, as if this should assure me of something, or I didn't already know that.

He let out a breath, relieved he'd got the hard part over with. "I was desperate to understand more about my brother's senseless death and I forgot you were a victim too. The youngest victim, who wouldn't have known or remembered anything."

My head still turned slightly towards the window, I shifted my gaze to him. His head hung as if staring at his hands. The moment stretched between us in silence.

"I'm a piece of shit." He glanced up. "I know my actions don't say it, but I have to. I really like you, that's why I didn't push for more. I didn't expect I'd fall for you. I thought we'd maybe just be friends, but there's chemistry between us. I know you felt it too… We can't start over, but maybe you can forgive me."

My words finally found themselves and even I was surprised by them, "I'm sorry I went off on you. My early life is a black stain in my head, and I don't remember it. That picture triggered one of those protected memories and I couldn't face it. It's not a path I want to travel down with you or anyone. My mind has found a way to unsee things… horrible things that are better left unknown. Whatever your brother and I went through it's better you don't know."

My admission that I didn't want to know was unexpected. Recently, my actions might say otherwise; the search for my mom, conversation with Tyrus, visiting Chief Sugda. These were things that appeased my curiosity. Tricked the memory side of my brain into thinking I wanted answers but, when push came to shove, I didn't. I feared what might happen, how I might change if I knew the truth.

He nodded and twisted his lips in an awkward fashion as we again experienced a cumbersome silence as if there was more to say but neither of us could formulate the words. I glanced over my shoulder, remembering Anora and Leandra were still there. Deep in conversation, I wasn't sure they noticed I was missing.

This time I broke the silence. "There's one more thing. Why did you lie about your name?"

His eyes narrowed in suspicion. "I didn't. Why would you think I did?"

"Isn't it Miles?"

"Who told you that?"

Why couldn't I just walk away with us, maybe not friends, but not on bad terms? With James's recent behavior, was it even true? Was he really a Miles and not Ealon? "I have my sources, Miles Maverick."

The corner of his lip turned upwards in a partial smile. "Miles Ealon Maverick. I go by Ealon. Miles is a stuffy white name."

Now that was the Ealon I liked. The one I fell for.

Crash and Smash

Ealon and I didn't continue any type of relationship, but at least it ended on a good note. Anora and Leandra became thick as jelly and I teased Anora in private that she needs to recheck our DNA samples to be sure she isn't the twin. She convinced Leandra to give a spit sample but, with our fall schedules and Anora's work focused on her masters, she didn't have the time she'd had over the summer and Leandra had yet to give it.

The weather gave way to a chilly fall and the leaves changed into bright colors. My classes far more interesting than my summer courses, as I was learning material I'd use. Enjoying the last bit of sunshine from the day and music blasting in my ear, I hammered my keyboard trying to smash out the project for my computer organization and systems class. The hot coffee from the food court was much better than their iced. I never thought I'd be a coffee drinker, period, but Anora and college had convinced me otherwise.

A shadow moved over me and I turned to see a familiar set of eyes and shaggy bangs beneath a hoodie. I leaped off the bench and wrapped my arms around James. No matter the distance and time between us. He was always a face I wanted to see. Memories of our last meeting over the summer at Flashers, he'd been unkempt and nervous. His behavior and appearance odd. My body close to his now, he smelled like a bar of soap and felt good in my arms.

I pulled away and tugged the earbuds out, letting them hang over my shoulders. "Where have you been? You haven't answered a single text."

He pulled me into another hug and whispered in my ear, "I know. I've been avoiding you."

I rested my forehead on his. "Why?"

His hands caught mine as he curled my fingers in his. "I can't see you, but I can't stop either, so I gotta be honest with you. I'm in love with you, Chelsea Mora, and I can't get you out of my mind. I try. I've been on a destructive path trying to avoid thinking about you but it doesn't work and I feel like shit the next day. You are my everything."

My breath caught and my voice dropped off the planet. What was he saying? He couldn't be in love with me, could he? I loved him more than anyone, but I wasn't in love with him, was I? I struggled to find words to say and a voice to say them.

"You don't have to love me back, but I had to say it so I can get on with my life."

His words choked, and he stepped away. Letting go of my hands, he turned on his heel.

My eyes couldn't believe I was watching him walk away again. *Feet: work, move, chase him.* I urged my body to do something. I couldn't let him walk out of my life forever but I wasn't in love with him. Was it better for him to be free of me? I stared at the tiny scar on my finger and water filled my eyes as I squeezed them shut.

My nose burning and body shaking, as I couldn't fend off the tears of losing my best friend. In the forest the day of graduation, I thought I heard him say 'I love you' but didn't acknowledge it. His strange behavior towards Ealon. The kiss in the parking lot. I pulled my lips in as my mind relived the feeling of his lips against mine. "James!" I hollered, chasing after him.

I barely noted other students as James's back grew further from me, but one face stood out – Kit. She'd never asked about James, even when I'd disappeared for a few minutes at Flashers or the time she saw us outside the campus library. I felt her eyes on me now as I rushed past her, gaining ground. Each step closer until I was only a few steps from him. "James."

He paused but didn't turn around.

With no idea what to say or do, my body went on autopilot, grabbing his hand and walking beside him. Words streamed from my mouth between deep breaths from running and crying. "I love you very much, more than anyone. You are the most important person in my life and I don't want to live without you." I sucked in another deep breath and squeezed my eyes as I felt myself fall apart. "But I'm not in love with you."

He wiggled his hand free of mine and wiped the tears beneath my left eye then kissed the spot on my cheek. His warm, minty breath lingered as he walked away and tears streamed my face. From the earbuds resting against my chest Fallen Angel by TIX played. The words filling the holes of my cheesecloth brain with James front and center.

A hand on my shoulder caught my attention and I spun around. Kit took me in her arms. I rested my head against her shoulder and bawled like a baby. She pressed her head over mine, her long dark hair falling over my cheek.

Part 3

Barely Breathing

Twinsies

Kit thought James was my boyfriend. It was easier to let her believe that than explain the truth. I spent most waking moments thinking about him. Construction was everywhere, yet he had to take a job here. If he'd have gone somewhere, anywhere, but here we'd still be friends. Everything would be the way it was supposed to be. Me and James together. Here I was, mourning the loss of my friend. He might as well have been dead. I'd never see him again. I'd let him go. Each day became a tiny bit easier without James but he never left my thoughts.

Colorful leaves sprinkled the path. The river current pushed an amber-colored mid-sized leaf until it stopped against a rock. More leaves piled up until there were enough they pushed around the rock. I was like that amber-colored leaf, floating with no purpose.

"Hey," Leandra said as she came jogging up behind me then in front. She turned on her heel and jogged backwards to face me. "I went by your dorm but it was empty," she said. "I've hardly seen you in weeks."

I didn't respond but met her hopeful gaze.

She twisted her face and wrinkled her nose. "Sooo, I was invited to this party on campus and I think you should come." Her wide smile and expectant eyes were hard to refuse.

I sighed. "I don't know. Maybe."

She stopped in front of me. "Please. It's a costume party and I thought we could go as twins. Not just school twins but party twins." She opened the large denim bag around her shoulder and pulled out a box with a lady on the cover. The color read Summer Copper. "Look, I even have the hair dye." She held it next to her cheek. "But that's not all. If you'd rather go brown, I have that too."

Twins. If only she knew it wasn't just pretend. *How could I refuse her?* "Sure."

Her eyes widened." Ahh!" she hugged me. "Let's go do our hair!" She didn't hide the excitement in her voice. Like Anora, she was exuberant and expressive.

Her dorm was set up similar to mine except she had two slim windows instead of a single large one and the beds were horizontal to the window instead of vertical. There was more room between the beds but less room in front of the closet. A young woman on the bed closest to the windows lifted her head from a book. A strip of royal blue went through the center of her dark hair along the part line. Her skin white and pasty.

She glared at us with steely eyes that matched the steel nose ring and matching ear gauges. She tucked the book under her arm. "Do your thing. I'm out."

Leandra ignored her and turned to me when the door shut. "Ignore her. She's always like that. I ignore her, she ignores me, and most of the time everything is good."

I guessed I was lucky to get Kit. She wasn't so bad. We didn't have much in common but she didn't look like something from the depths of hell. "Most of the time?"

Leandra shrugged. "She brings the boyfriend over sometimes and I… leave, since I woke up one night to her moans. Anyways, my hair or yours?"

I covered my mouth. "Seriously? They just had sex with you here, sleeping?"

She pursed her lips and bypassed my question, holding up the boxes of hair color. She put the brown – Havana Roast – next to my face and the Summer Copper next to hers. "Let's look in the mirror."

I followed her into the restroom, and we started at the colors. I liked my color, it wasn't common, but I didn't want to hurt her feelings.

She tilted her head and lifted the curls off her neck. The box of hair color next to her face. "I think I should. I want to be a ginger. I've always loved your color." She laid the box on the counter, let her hair down, then turned to me, lifted mine gently around my ears. "Yeah, I need to go ginger."

It was solved. I was keeping my color. I let out a silent sigh. Her hair was so thick it took two boxes to cover it completely but, when it was done, I washed it out and blow dried it. Side by side in the mirror, we gave a collective gasp. Neither of us ever saw the resemblance all through high school but now, staring at each other… Her hair the same color as mine, we looked like the true twins we were.

"We could switch classes tomorrow and nobody would know. I can't believe this." Her eyes fixed on us side by side in the mirror.

There were no words unless I confessed that our half-sister Anora, who she didn't know was her half-sister, tested her DNA from the milkshake she left in my car over the summer. That wasn't happening. Nope. No way! "What are we going to wear?"

"There's this guy – Darian, and he's so yummy. He's going to be there so we have to look tantalizing." The words rolled off her tongue. We didn't have the same taste in clothes and I certainly didn't have anything tantalizing. We did put together some fun retro outfits at the thrift shop over the summer though, so there was hope we'd agree on something. I remembered the first night I went to Flashers with Anora. She let me borrow a sequined black dress that hugged my small curves in hopes Ealon would notice me. Those butterflies moved into Leandra's belly now.

"OK, but no bunny costumes."

She giggled. "I don't know. With this fiery red hair we might look good as bunnies." She leaned her head onto my shoulder.

Two days later, we ended up at the mall and agreed on a teal baby doll dress and ankle buckle embroidered heels. At least we didn't look like Playmates or street walkers and the color brought out the red in our hair without making us look too pasty. The plan was for her to come to my dorm and do our make-up so we didn't disturb her roommate with a one-way ticket from hell.

Bug-Eyed Boogaloo

*N*o *class until Monday,* the sign on the door read. I checked in the online classroom for an announcement, and it seems Dr. Alexander's wife was in the hospital delivering their first child. Congratulations to them. It left me with a free day. Sometimes karma has a strange way of working out.

I woke up in a sweat this morning after having a dream I barely remembered. The part that stuck and left an impression was Charice lying on white satin in a casket made of walnut with roses sprinkled around her head. She looked peaceful until her round eyes popped open and her mouth moved. The words didn't make a sound. I stumbled backwards and that's it. All I remember, anyways.

She'd left me with information about my biological grandfather. No one else had touched that computer before me. It had to have been her. I'd ignored it, mostly, scared of what it might mean or what I might learn. Now it was time. That's what my dream meant to me. She was trying to tell me to visit him. Why else would she leave that information buried in a hidden file on the computer? She knew I'd find it, yet it would be safe from others.

I couldn't help but wonder if that's why she *suddenly* had a heart attack. The thought of murder was preposterous, but it could be so. The Moras weren't the best people and were tied up in a child smuggling ring. Maybe my grandfather had some answers. It was time to take control and throw caution to the wind and be *brave*.

Courage and bravery weren't in my repertoire, but today I felt the burn of determination and strength instead of helplessness. My nerves and stomach roiled the entire drive but I couldn't ignore the information Charice had left for me or the dream. This man, Hadj Botlat, could be my grandfather and I deserved to know one way or another.

A bumpy dirt road cut through the woods and ended at a small literal log cabin. It was so far away from everything, I couldn't imagine living somewhere like this. I know most people would have called first and I considered that maybe I should have as my throat dried and hands sweated from anxiety. *Deep breaths,* I told myself as I opened the car door.

I stepped towards the cabin. Its narrow porch boasted a wooden rocking chair and several wind chimes that tinkled in the breeze. Leaves crunched under my feet and I considered I should have told someone, Anora, Leandra, or even James. Thinking his name sent an overwhelming wave of sadness through every cell of my being.

Deep breaths, I reminded myself again as panic clutched my gut. The thought this man, grandfather or not, could be a horrible person. It was obvious already that my mom didn't stay in touch with him. She'd told Anora's dad she had no family. Why would someone say that unless they wanted to forget them?

The cabin appeared friendly but was so far in the middle of nowhere a person could get murdered and no one would ever know. *Deep breaths, deep breaths.* I stepped onto the porch and knocked once on the door. *What if he didn't answer? Would I go home?* As the thoughts surfaced, the door opened.

I wiped sweaty palms against my jeans. An older man, thin and muscular with a balding head and unbrushed brown-gray beard and mustache stared at me. He grabbed my arm and pulled me inside. I screamed in surprise as much as in horror. The force in his arms sent me stumbling and I almost fell over.

He ran his hand through his non-existent hair. "Sit, sit, sit, sit." His eyes bugged out as they planted on my face. He then ran to the window and pulled back the curtain a tad and peeked out. "Did anyone follow you?"

I folded my arms across my chest and stood. That was a weird question. "No."

He turned around and faced me. "Good. Why are you here?"

His inhospitality angered me. I wasn't scared anymore but upset, disgusted. *Did he treat everyone this way?* "You should be nicer to people. I may be your granddaughter." I smiled inside as I didn't know I had the strength to stand up to someone that way.

He continued to rake a hand over his bald head as if there was still hair on it. "I knew it, I knew it. You look just like her."

"My mother?"

He nodded. "Sit, sit. I will tell you, then you must go."

I sat on the red, white, and black plaid tattered couch. I wanted to know, but was still angry, leaving my arms folded across my chest and my brows lowered.

"I was married, we were very young. She had a daughter Kandyssa Rae. I called her Kandy. She was a sweet girl. I traveled on my job and didn't see them much, not as much as I wanted to, but I supported them, took good care of them. When Kandy was sixteen, she ran away. It broke my heart in pieces. Lyn and I never had children of our own. She couldn't, she'd had Kandy very young and it was hard on her body."

He continued the story with the same choppy sentence fashion. Kandy's disappearance was hard on him and he was shocked when Lyn showed no remorse. Sure, she made a show for the police and others but when they were alone she never shed a tear. She packed Kandy's stuff right away and set up a craft room. It upset him and he put his foot down. They got in a big fight and she threatened him.

His father was abusive to him and his mother. Shortly after they got engaged, she insisted on meeting his parents, even against his better instincts. He was in love with her and she was an alpha woman so he gave in and they went. Kandy was about three at the time and his father was enraged at how stupid he was to marry an unwed mother who was nothing more than a tramp.

Lyn took it better than he expected and calmed his father down. Once things were rather pleasant, she offered to bring them all lemonade. She'd made it fresh that morning and handed out the glasses to everyone with a smile on her face. Within minutes, his parents were dead.

"She convinced me she did it for me, for us. He was an evil man and my mother was complacent. It was her fault too, because she never stood up to my father, never protected me the way a parent should. I agreed with her. Everything she said I thought of a million times myself. My father, he'd lived through the depression and didn't believe in banks. He kept all his money in cash at the house. We cleaned it out and changed our names, married, and started a life together," he said. His words less choppy and his eyes less buggy.

"That's how she blackmailed you?" I asked, my arms now unfolded and almost in disbelief.

"Yes, and all those years she was always so happy when I was home. Kandy became difficult as a teenager. What teen doesn't have drama or hate their parents? I know she abused her. I didn't know until I saw the same lack of remorse for the loss of her child that she'd had the day she killed my parents. I was an accomplice. I couldn't come back from that and wasn't sure she hadn't killed her daughter. I went back to work, left town, and never returned. I changed my name again and moved out here."

"You don't know what happened to Kandy?"

He finally stopped pacing and stared at me. His eyes tired and mournful. "No, but you're here, so she didn't kill her."

"No, she married and had a daughter, then vanished and had me and another daughter, but I never knew her." The heavy weight hanging on my back went away and I sighed internally after admitting so much to a perfect stranger who was my step-grandfather.

He sat on the couch opposite me. "I knew about you. I contacted a woman many years ago when I read about what happened to you in the paper. I wasn't sure you were hers, but once I saw you I knew for sure. I couldn't allow Kandy's fate to happen to you and begged her not to contact Lyn."

"Charice?"

He raked his bald head again and rolled his eyes. "Yes, I think so."

"She's dead." The vision of her lying in the casket mouthing silent words to me flashed. It was still hard to believe I'd never see her again.

He didn't look surprised. "Did she die of an unexpected heart attack?"

I nodded. His question confirmed she was murdered. My heart cracked, as she lost her life, her family lost her, because of me. *It was all because of me.*

"There's something else… After Kandy ran away, Lyn started leaving at odd hours in the middle of the night. I didn't let on that I knew, but I thought maybe she'd done something to Kandy. I followed her one night to my parents' house and there she met with a couple – a man and a woman. He was thin with dark hair and she was about his size but carried herself in a way that showed dominance. I couldn't hear them and left before them to make it home before her. But I went back on my own. Kandy wasn't there and I didn't find anything."

A couple? The Moras? I'd seen their pictures. Were these her co-conspirators or is he making all this up and the one I should truly be worried about? I didn't feel any warmth from him but I didn't feel as though he planned on harming me either. I'd continued spinning his name around in my head. Botlat. My brain arranged the letters T-a-l-b-o-t.

The familiar knot of anxiety twisted my guts, the rhythm of my heart picked up pace. *Could he be talking about Talbot House? Was his father Prescott Talbot and his mother Elzbet? Be brave, breathe, you can do this.* I swallowed the knot forming in my throat and carefully constructed my words. "Pres…cott Talbot and Talbot House."

His brows lowered and connected like a caterpillar. "How would you know that?"

"That's a yes."

His eyes now shadowed with suspicion, but heck, I'd listened to his crazy, far-fetched story so he could listen to mine. I explained the short version of my story and his face grew soft for the first time. He apologized and for the life of me I'd never understand why people always apologized for circumstances out of their control. The sun was setting by the time we finished talking and he invited me to stay the night instead of drive.

I really wanted to leave, but he was far out in the boonies. There were no lights and I was likely to spend the night lost and sleeping in my car. I felt staying at his house might be safer and I didn't think he was someone I needed to worry about.

I don't know what woke me first, the smell of eggs and pancakes or the sun streaming through the window.

"Morning, sunshine," he said in a chipper voice.

I opened an eye and peeked. His back was to me as he flipped a pancake in the air. *How did he even know I was awake?* "Morning, Hadj." Yesterday he struck me as a crazy man. Today, his beard and mustache still a mess, his eyes and behavior were normal and it was hard to believe this guy was the same guy that pulled me into his log cabin yesterday. If Lyn did that to him she wasn't a person I wanted to meet.

"I hope you got a good appetite. Plenty of pancakes."

My stomach was at the table before my body, as it smelled delicious. After breakfast, I said my goodbye. He asked me to never return, not because he didn't ever want to see me or get to know me, but because he was afraid of her and didn't want me followed. He'd eluded her for over twenty years.

I felt more comfortable once I turned onto the paved road. It was weird how anything that appeared more civilized gave me a false sense of security. There was still a long way to go before I'd be close to home.

My gas tank running on fumes, I pulled into a gas station over the state line. A chill hit me when I opened the door. I pulled my jacket over my shoulders and pumped the gas when a man on the opposite pump, standing beside an older model green truck with a fair share of dings and dents, leaned backwards and glanced at me. His face tilted downward, the bill on his camouflage hat covered his eyes and shadowed his face. But I could tell he was studying me by the position of his body and the slow raise of his head. My arm hairs shackled when I noted how hairy his arms were and my breath caught when his head raised high enough his eyes met mine.

Curled in a Turtle Shell

My thoughts coalesced into fear. Panic seized my body and my limbs and feet were frozen in place. The man from Edisto Beach. It wasn't a coincidence. I hadn't noticed, out of fear, how hairy his arms were that day but now I did and didn't doubt he was also Leandra's attacker.

He lifted his hat and pasted a cocky smile on his face. "You look like you need some help." His words not a friendly gesture as they carried a mocking tone. He might as well have said *you knew I'd find you, right?*

I shifted my gaze, searching the gas station for others. We were still well in the country and not many cars passed the gas station, even fewer were parked close. There was a large, newer model red truck and it was gun country. I reminded myself to breathe. Gun-toters wouldn't take kindly to someone kidnapping a defenseless woman. That calmed my panic a notch, enough my hands unfroze.

My door open and the only thing between me and him, I lifted the nozzle and placed it back on the pump. I prided myself on the first step and moved backwards slowly, an eye on him, then dropped onto my seat and lifted my legs inside the car.

His gaze hadn't left me as he watched every move, bathing in my fear. A cocky smile painted on his face. I grasped the door handle and pulled but it was stuck. His hand held the edge, stopping it from closing completely. From the corner of my eye, another truck pulled into the gas station. That gave me the strength to say, "Let go or I'll scream."

His cocky smile turned into straight lips. "No need to be nasty. I was only offering to help." He took his hand off the door and I slammed it shut and immediately hit the lock button. I felt his eyes on me as I turned onto the road.

Flustered and wanting to get away, I hadn't noticed I was heading the wrong way. Going back from the direction I came. Too scared to turn around, I kept going until I spotted a dirt road. Checking my mirrors, and noting no other cars behind me or in front of me, I safely slipped onto the dirt road to get my bearings and find an alternate path that wouldn't take me past the gas station where the man might still be waiting.

Too flustered to even find a new route on my GPS, I took several deep breaths. Once my hands stopped shaking I was able to reprogram my route. It would take longer, but I found one that kept me on country roads for at least the next couple hours. I hoped that would be long enough to get far away from him and I hoped it would be dark enough not to be seen on the freeway.

My anxiety now minimal, I turned the car around and got back on the main road, but only for a couple miles until the GPS directed me onto another country road then another. After about an hour of not seeing his truck, I felt almost home free. As expected, the road kept me close to double wides and ranch-style homes on large plots of land and they gave me a false sense of security.

After a few hours, I couldn't sit still. My bladder was full but I was too scared to get back on the main road and find a gas station. I did what country girls do. I pulled off on another dirt road and ran into the woods, dropped my pants and released the contents of my bladder.

The rhythmic humming of a motor and crunch of rocks told me someone else was turning onto the dirt road. I picked up my feet and ran towards my car, peering through the trees. A green truck. *His* green truck, as noted by its shabby appearance. The man from the gas station. *How did he find me?*

There was no time to waste. I ran to my car and flung the door open, jumped in, and started the engine. I hit the gas hard and closed my door simultaneously. A cloud of dirt and rocks kicked up behind my car as it bounced over potholes.

The clanks and thumps against my car concerned me and I worried I wouldn't have a car if I didn't slow down. I turned quickly onto another dirt road or driveway, my GPS repeating to make a U-turn. Ignoring it, I crept slowly down the road and turned into the trees, hoping he wouldn't see me.

After several breathless minutes, the truck didn't pass. I stayed put for several more and when nearly thirty minutes went by, I backed my car out of the trees and turned it around. The Kia was small and maneuverable. I crept towards the road I came from, figuring I'd lost him. When I reached the end of the road, two trucks, one on each side, sat in the middle of the road, engines running.

One the beat-up green truck and I clearly noted the driver. The man from the gas station still wearing the camouflage ball cap. I pictured the cocky smile back on his face, seeing it again now even though he wasn't close enough to actually see it. The other, the red truck parked at the gas station. There was nowhere to go. My single thought was to go any direction they weren't. I shifted my car in reverse and hit the gas.

The Kia bumped and thumped backwards. I kept my eyes on the road and didn't glance to see if they were following. The road was narrow and tree-lined. They wouldn't be able to pass me. My only hope was that the road led to another and not a dead end.

Time didn't seem to move as I bulldozed backwards over the potted road. My tires crunching rock and bouncing over holes, tossing my body up and down. It was on one of the ups that I noted pavement ahead. I kept on my course, hoping they hadn't turned around and thought about what I would do when I got to the paved road. I wasn't a race car driver but hoped I had enough skill to pull a 180 and escape them.

My palms grew wet with sweat as I contemplated the 180, picturing it over and over in my mind. When my tires hit the pavement, it was time for action. I turned the car and hit the brakes then left off the brakes and hit the wheel the other direction, flinging the car.

It happened so fast I didn't see a thing until I heard the crunch. My head flew forward, my nose smashing into the steering wheel. Crunching metal filling my eardrums and everything went black.

Duct Tape Fixes Everything

Oil and gas fumes filled my nostrils as I regained consciousness. My head throbbed as if someone had hit it with a shovel or stuck an ax in it. Pain radiated as I opened my eyes a sliver. Green, silver, and shades of red blurred in front of them.

I couldn't scream or breathe from my mouth. It was taped shut. My wrists tingled but I couldn't move them. They were stuck together, and my feet. I was beyond panic, fight or flight had taken over on the dirt road when I flung my car into, I guessed, a tree. My head and nose ached but my mind was clear now, no panic, fear eluded me. I had to find a way out of the mess.

The green paint mixed with scratches revealing the metal beneath, some rusty, and the firm metal against my back told me I was in the bed of the truck, hog tied like livestock. It was night and we were in the country. The stars bright and clear. I was on my own as I hadn't told anyone, not even Anora or James, where I was going. *Why would I tell James?* He walked away and I let him because I couldn't say what he wanted to hear. How had I been so stubborn and stupid?

Ignoring the pain in my head, I wiggled my body, pulling my torso then legs along toward the edge of the truck bed. I needed to sit up and see what else was around.

I moved my legs further toward the edge and found the wiggle worked better, putting them first then sliding my torso along until I reached the wheel well and caught my legs beside it. Using that for leverage, I pulled my torso upwards until the upper half of my body was vertical. Mindful of the rear window and not wanting the driver to see me, I slid downward and took in my surroundings.

The truck bed was empty except for me. No tools, loose wood, or anything. Nothing. I didn't have many options. The tape was tight around my feet and ankles. Behind me, all I felt was the cold metal of the truck. I lay back down with no current alternative and watched the scenery pass, counting the turns. I wondered if this is what happened to our mother. Had they kidnapped her in broad daylight and tossed her into a truck bed?

The tires rolled to a stop and the engine cut off. The hum of another motor persisted for a few seconds until it, too, cut off. The driver's side door creaked open as if it needed a healthy dose of oil. I closed my eyes and painted a picture in my mind. Footfalls moving around the vehicle paused. I felt their eyes on me.

"She knocked herself out good," a male voice said. It wasn't the man from the gas station. I guessed it was the other truck man.

Footfalls moved away from the truck. "What are you doing? Aren't we bringing her in?" said the same voice.

"She ain't goin' nowhere," said Green Truck Guy. I recognized his voice from the park and the gas station.

Their footfalls receded and a door opened and shut. They'd left me out here and I was going to use the opportunity. I wriggled back to the wheel well, used it as a brace and pulled myself up again. I was able to lift my shoulders onto the edge of the truck and bend my knees enough to pull my legs over the side. They hit the ground and I dropped on my butt, pain from the fall barely registering as I scooted in the dirt towards the woods, fearing for my life.

Then I worried I'd leave them a trail in the dirt, so I lowered on my side and rolled the rest of the way. I didn't know how long they planned on leaving me there so I hadn't a second to waste. When I hit the woods, I sat up and searched for rocks, something big and sharp enough to break through the tape on my ankles and wrists. Scooting deeper into the woods I managed to find a large boulder with a sharp edge. I lifted my legs, placing the sharp edge of the rock between my ankles, and rubbed back and forth. Desperate, I barely noted the pain in my legs. The tape loosening with each scrape, giving me strength to keep going.

The tape nearly destroyed, I gulped and stiffened when I heard Other Truck Guy's voice. "What the hell? Hey, hey," he hollered. His feet rustling the fallen leaves with each step as he ran toward the house.

I hurried and, nearly there, pulled my ankles apart using every bit of strength in my legs. I didn't have time to get my hands free. Soon enough they'd be looking for me. I scooted towards the closest tree and used it to guide my body upward, then picked up my feet and ran.

I heard their voices and heavy steps on the broken branches and leaf clutter, which meant they heard mine too. "You should have put a tracker on her, meathead," called Green Truck guy as I nimbly moved away from the sound of his voice.

"If you'd have injected her like I said she wouldn't have gotten away," responded Other Truck Guy.

Tracker, injection. That was how they found me. Green Truck Guy wanted to scare me but, more importantly, he'd stuck some kind of tracker on my car when he clutched the door. I felt stupid. How didn't I think of that? *You were scared*, I answered my own mental question.

I couldn't change the past, but right now I had an advantage. The woods were large. I had no flashlight, only the moonlight to guide my way. I slipped into a large evergreen bush, its spiky leaves scraping my skin, and curled into a ball, hoping they wouldn't see me.

Each grueling second that passed, I expected the leaves over my head to be pulled apart and Green Truck Guy to peer down at me, but from the sounds echoing through the empty forest they went the other direction.

I woke in the morning to the sun streaming through the hibernating, leafless trees. No sign of the men. Wasting no time, I scrambled out of the bush and found another rock which I used to free my hands and pull the tape from my mouth.

My body ached, my head and nose throbbed, and my stomach complained. I hadn't eaten in twenty-four hours, but I was free. I wandered through the forest, listening for sounds, any sounds, all sounds. By mid-day, I heard what sounded like a stream. Every part of my body wanted to run and dip my mouth into it and drink like a deer but I was more than aware the men may come looking again. They may even already be searching. Crunching leaves echoed and my mind thought every sound was them.

Watching my steps, trying to be stealthy, my ears followed the sound of rushing water until I found it. Noting I was alone, I cupped my hands into it and sucked up the water. It was the most refreshing thing I'd ever drunk. Rocks dotted the stream, meaning it wasn't deep. On the other side were more woods.

I decided to use the water to get them off my trail. No doubt I'd left footprints along the way. Pulling leaves over my trail from the woods to the stream, I stepped into the water. It was ankle-deep and I walked further towards the middle. My body shivered as it reached waist high, hitting my sensitive belly. I pushed forward until reaching the other side.

Shivering, I dragged my soggy feet and legs onto the shore, giving one last scan to the other side. I felt as if I'd put some actual distance between me and them, but didn't want to be spotted in the open. They could have a gun and be able to spot me from miles away.

Hours of walking, the sun readying to set, my body ragged and tired. I didn't feel I could take another step when I heard a familiar sound that was music to my ears. *A car*. The hum of its engine told me a road was close.

Angel in a Sea of Demons

My body screaming in pain as I pushed it to its limit, I wouldn't give up as I pressed towards the road. It wasn't a busy. The purring motors of the cars and swoosh of their tires spaced out. When the pavement came into view, I convinced myself if I could just get there I'd get a ride. Stumbling to keep myself upright, I fell to my hands. My arms gave out and I face planted in the leaves. A sharp pain cut through my body, radiating from my already aching nose.

I pressed onward, crawling to the road. The cars I'd heard long gone but there would be more. One arm and one leg at a time, I forced myself toward the edge.

"Oh my, miss," a female voice moved through the darkness. An oval face with short, bobbed white hair swam above me.

My arm heavy as lead, I raised it before gravity pulled it back down.

"Oh dear, can you move?"

Thin wrinkles webbed around her blue eyes with skin bags below, I noted as she came into focus. Her lips straight and pink. She moved around me, staring as if I was a wounded animal.

I opened my mouth but the noise that came out was scratchy and didn't sound like me. "I think so."

Finally getting my bearings, I realized I'd passed out roadside. A small silver car was running just a few feet from us. I assumed it was hers. She was the angel I was hoping for. The person who could take me to a police station or a hospital. At this point, I'd be happy with anywhere the men in the trucks weren't and a phone.

I'd dropped onto the ground, my head to the side. She wasn't above me at all but staring down at me to the side. I pressed my palms against the ground and pushed as she helped me sit upright.

"My, my, you've been through something. Hold on." She walked to her car and grabbed an item from inside it. Upon her return, it was a water bottle. "Here, drink this."

She lifted the bottle to my lips for me to drink. More ran down my face than in my mouth but it was refreshing. "Thank you."

"Let's get you up. You need a meal."

I shook my head. "No, I need the police."

"You need a hospital, but it's late and we are far away from either a hospital or the police. Let me take you home. You can get a good meal, a bath, and rest. Tomorrow I'll take you to town." Her words soothed me, yet they weren't warm and cozy.

For the moment she was right. It was late and I had no idea where I was. Food and rest would be good. Tomorrow was a new day and the men looking for me hadn't found me. I was safe for now.

A soft light shined on a long porch. My legs ached and I gingerly followed behind her and dragged myself up the steps. The accident, lack of food and water, along with my injuries, my legs felt like weights and pain shrieked at me with each step. I cringed and took deep breaths as she held the door open for me.

Small blue flowers dotted the wallpaper, and a large blue throw rug was soft beneath my shoes. I followed her from the foyer into the kitchen where I collapsed onto a wooden chair with a flowery blue seat cushion. She hadn't said much, didn't even introduce herself as she opened a can, poured it into a pot and turned on the stove.

She brought me a glass and sat opposite me at the table. "You're lucky I came along. That head, you have a baseball on your forehead and that nose of yours matches – all black and blue. I don't think ice will do much for it now. Probably rest, but you are covered in leaves. We'll have to get you bathed."

I took the glass and lifted it toward my mouth. It felt so heavy in my weary arms, but the lemonade was sweet and wetted my thirst. "Thank you."

"I was doing what any good citizen would do. My late husband had a soft spot for helping people." Her straight lips curled into a quirky smile as she rose then headed to the stove. She stirred the pot, her back to me.

There was a window above the sink, the curtains drawn open. The moon shone enough light the trees were visible. It felt like I'd walked to the edge of the world but, staring outside, I realized I'd probably only traveled a few miles. We were still deep in the woods.

She carried a steaming bowl and placed it on the table before me. Slipping the potholders off her hands she dropped them on the table and sat across from me.

I thanked her and lifted the spoon, her eyes on me as I ate. Her pink lips straight as if a smile might crack her face. I guessed she wasn't used to finding young women passed out by the side of the road, but she hadn't asked any questions. If I were her I'm sure I'd be full of them. Correction —I'd have called the police.

After the soup, which helped squelch the hunger I'd felt for the past twenty-four hours or so, I followed her down a long hallway with the same blue flowered wallpaper. The wooden floor below my feet not as soft as the area rug. She stuck her hand into a room and flipped the light switch.

"I'll start the bath then I'll get you a night gown," she said as she turned the water on, putting her hand beneath it as if testing to make sure it was the right temperature and poured something in it, I guessed it was bubble bath.

Once she left the room, I peeled my clothes off and dropped them to a pile on the floor. Bruises covered my body and she was right: I had a baseball on my forehead and my nose was swollen and dark. I was sure that was from the car crash. The body bruises I could only imagine. I stepped into the tub but the water was steaming hot.

I pulled my leg out and turned the hot water knob off, letting the cold only run. Foot falls told me she was returning. A quick knock on the door she asked, "Are you decent?"

What did she mean by decent? I was naked, that's what people do when they bathe. I pushed my foot into the water, cold on top but burning underneath, then pushed myself under the coat of bubbles. "I'm in the tub," I said as I turned the water off.

The door moaned as she opened it. "I found a gown that I'm sure will fit you," she lingered beside the tub. "You should let me scrub you. Sit up."

I did as she asked, too tired to put much effort in myself. She scrubbed my back, each bristle felt it was taking skin with it. I cringed and tightened up. Not sure what to do or say and not sure that my body would allow me to make any sudden movements. I doubted she did it on purpose. My body was in such bad shape anything would have made it ache and hurt worse.

"Your hair is such a mess," she said, picking at my curly mop as if searching for lice. "Look at this." She held her hand out in front of my face. A bundle of leaves and twigs in her palm.

Without warning, she dumped hot water on my head. My eyes shot open wide as I screamed.

She sat back. "I'm sorry dear. I'm just trying to help."

It wasn't that I wasn't grateful but, after ripping up my back with a brush made of what felt like needles and dumping near scalding water on my head, I'd had about enough from this woman who was looking less like an angel, but my guilty conscience kicked in. "It's OK, my head is tender."

She nodded and stood, wiping her palms on her pants. "You finish up." Her figure wasn't full as much as it was thick and large-boned, I noted as she walked, heavy-footed, towards the door.

Tonight, I would accept her hospitality and tomorrow I would leave, even if she wasn't willing to drive me into town. I needed the rest and wasn't going to fool myself that I didn't.

I slipped the gown on that she'd brought me. A near perfect fit and it was warm and soft. The pillow cradled my head and I sank into the mattress and slept soundly.

When my eyes popped open the next day, panic hit me first, then I remembered where I was. The old lady and the blue flowered wallpapered. Sunlight streamed through the crack in the curtain, lighting a line of dust across the room. No blue flowered wallpaper here but something equally as gaudy – busy blue and cream paisley that made my head hurt to look at it.

The baseball on my forehead throbbed when I stood and it was nearly as big today as I remembered it last night. The gown hung on me as it was the right size. It hadn't struck me last night as I was tired, woozy, disoriented, but it couldn't be hers. Her body was much thicker than mine. Not even in her younger days did I imagine it fit her so whose was it? *A daughter, maybe?*

She hadn't looked old enough for a great granddaughter that was anywhere close to my age. Picturing her face, I figured her to be around sixty-ish, give or take. About Hadj's age.

My clothes weren't in the room and the drawers in the single chest were empty. I hoped that meant she'd been nice enough to wash them. The wooden floor was cold against my feet as I padded down the hallway, making a pit stop at the restroom across the hall.

A kettle whistled from the kitchen and I guessed that's where she was. I hadn't remembered her name or if she even told me. Last night was fuzzy. The past two days were fuzzy. I stood in the doorway of the kitchen, her back to me. She turned as if listening to my footsteps.

"There you are. I made breakfast but you were still sleeping. I was just having tea. Would you like a cup?" She dipped a bag into steaming water in a mug.

"Yes, thank you."

Her straight lips lifted into a kind of smile, not a full one but a half. More an upward curve. She placed a steamy mug of tea in front of me and a plate of scrambled eggs and toast.

"There you are. I don't have a microwave to warm it up so you'll have to eat it cold." There was that weird smile again.

Cold eggs were gross, but I didn't complain. I needed nutrition to build up my energy and ate with a smile on my face. "Did you put my clothes somewhere?"

"In the trash. You can't wear those again. I'm sure I have something else that will fit you."

It wasn't that I was extra partial to those clothes, but they were mine and I preferred to take them with me. "If you don't mind, I'd like to keep them."

"I mind." She took a sip of her tea. "They're filthy and ripped to shreds," she said followed with the upward lip curl again.

Cold eggs on a near empty stomach weren't as bad as I'd expected and I was grateful for her help even if she was unnerving and threw my clothes away.

"Can I use your phone?"

"There's no service out here." She stood and exited the room, only to return a few minutes later. "I laid clothes on the bed. Get dressed and I'll drive you into town."

That was more like it! I felt bad, she'd been kind, but I couldn't stay in that house with her one more minute. The clothes she laid out for me, a pair of red sweatpants and un-matching green T-shirt. I slipped them on and stuffed my feet into my shoes which, surprisingly, she hadn't thrown away.

Tires on gravel and the purr of an engine told me someone was coming down the road. I pulled the curtains back and the familiar, gut-wrenching panic twisted inside me. Ignoring the pain in each step, the ache that crippled my bones. I flew down the hallway and into the kitchen.

"We have to go. Now. We have to go! There are men coming down the road. They did this to my head!" I urged, pointing to the black and blue baseball on my forehead.

"I've got this," she said, then strolled to the pantry and grabbed something large – a shot gun.

I felt my eyes double in size. "No, we can go!"

The truck tires rolled closer and the engine cut off. Hefty footfalls moved towards the house.

Time was running out. I urged her again, but not soon enough. The door opened and she cocked the gun and pointed it towards the men entering the house.

I scooted backwards towards the hallway when she turned the shot gun on me. Her straight lips curling into a real smile. I swallowed. This was the end of the line for me. She knew them!

Creepy Crawly Panic

She ordered them around, grumbling at them as they bound my hands behind my back and my feet to the chair legs. Blaming them for losing me and how she always has to clean up the mess. My ears didn't want to hear. I thought I'd gotten away. Thought I'd lost them. No, I went full circle.

The woman, her oval face and light blue eyes no longer helpful, and certainly not angelic. Her true colors were demonic. I was trapped in some kind of redneck nightmare. Other Truck Guy pulled a small stream of more duct tape and ripped it with his teeth then flattened it over my mouth.

She waved them off and pulled a wooden kitchen chair closer to me and sat. Her arms across her chest, her blue eyes stared at me, filled with disgust. Her straight, thin, pink lips tight. There was only one person she could be, but why all this? They followed me to Hadj's. It wasn't coincidence seeing Green Truck Guy at the gas station so he could plant the tracker on my car.

In hindsight, I should have stayed on the freeway. I got myself in trouble by taking the country roads. Mentally, I kicked myself then reminded myself it didn't matter. They were tracking me and eventually would have caught up with me, if not on the road then at the college.

She leaned back, her eyes studying me closely. "She wasn't my daughter. I stole her right out of her stroller while she was sleeping. Mom was too busy with the other child to notice," she said in a mocking tone.

"She was exactly what the couple wanted and they were paying big money. All I had to do was take care of her for a couple days, but they backed out. I was about to leave her in an alley when I met Judah. He fell in love with her. He married me because he loved her. Always showering her with gifts."

If I could open my mouth, I would spit on her. What a horrible waste of a human.

She continued: "His travels allowed me to start my own business. A highly successful one. Men like little girls and when Kandy was old enough, had come of age, she had the potential to be a bigger money maker. Babies are a lucrative business."

She whored her out? That was my mother she was talking about. Her words made me ill and vomit threatened my esophagus. If I had any doubts when Hadj told me the story, I didn't now. Lyn was every bit as nasty and vile in person as she was in the story. I worked to swallow the vomit rising inside me to avoid choking on it as duct tape covered my mouth.

She pulled her legs out in front of her and crossed her feet. "The sneaky bitch. She must have ground up sleeping pills in my tea," she seethed.

The horrible story was coming together. My mom ran away from home because she was pregnant. The father was anyone's guess. The child was meant to be sold, so it didn't matter. She was livestock. The bile threatened again. Anora's father wasn't her biological father and that explains why she shared less DNA than Leandra and me. We had the same father – Anora's father. She didn't know that and I wondered if he did.

"She could run but she couldn't hide from me forever either. That's how I knew we'd find you. The boys found her, in a quiet little town and wouldn't you know it she was pregnant with twins. Two for the price of one." She clucked her tongue. "She fought for you and your sister. I guess you want to hear that, but it wasn't enough. I'll never understand why people will look the other way when it comes to getting a child. They will pay and do anything without asking a single question. Your sister got lucky." Her words sick and depraved and her tone like business as usual. She was the worst kind of person.

"I see it in your eyes. You want to know about the boy and the Moras. They were special and the backbone of my operation with her ruthless nature and his nursing skills. He was a nurse practitioner who specialized in OBGYN. He delivered you and your sister." She paused to let that sink in.

"Oh, the silly boy. He was something the Moras did on their own. I guess they thought you needed a playmate." She laughed hysterically, like it was a big joke. I thought of Ealon. He wanted answers, now I had them. This was more than he needed to know. Sometimes not knowing was better.

Once her laughter subsided she spoke again, "They liked small children and the woods are probably full of the Moras' dirty deeds."

Vomit rose in my throat again. I pushed it down, knowing the next time I wouldn't be able to stop it. Leandra's parents were so cool. They took her to Australia. It was hard to believe they paid for her illegally. They were intelligent and educated. It would be stupid and naive to think they didn't know. I didn't want to hear any more.

"You were such a horrible little thing, always crying and screaming. That's why I let the Moras keep you. I couldn't stand the sight of you," she sneered.

The feeling was mutual. I couldn't stand her either. Tears bubbled in the corners of my eyes. My poor mother. The vomit rising again.

She stood and walked behind me, her hand against my face. She pulled up the tape and ripped it off. Vomit gurgled from my mouth as I screamed in pain.

"You nasty child." The soles of her shoes sounded toward the door. Then she paused. "I'm sure you'd like to meet your mother. Don't worry, you will. In fact, you'll spend eternity beside her," she drawled and cackled.

Cold Eggs

They left me in the kitchen in a puddle of my own vomit until the sun lowered in the sky, then Other Truck Guy and Green Truck Guy ripped the tape off. Instantly, I felt the welts forming on my skin with the burn. They locked me in a room with nothing. The walls covered in a horrible green and pink paisley wallpaper and bars over the window. I wondered if this is where she kept my mother. No doubt the clothes I was wearing were hers.

I grabbed the bottom of the shirt and brought it to my face and snuggled. This was the closest I'd ever get to her. It smelled of fabric softener. There was nothing left of her. My mind shifted to Leandra. She was my hope that someone would notice something was amiss. She was supposed to meet me at the dorm to do our makeup, get dressed up, and head to the party.

What day was it? I left Friday after Dr. Alexander cancelled class. Saturday was the party and the day I was chased, Sunday I wandered in the woods until she found me last night. Yes, it was only Monday. If I survived, would it be right to tell both Anora and Leandra what I knew?

They had beautiful, perfect families. This would shatter them and Leandra didn't even know yet she was our sister or that Anora was our half-sister. No, they didn't need to know any of this. Anora not being her father's biological child and Leandra being sold to her parents. That was not something that someone casually shared. There was no way to tell them without destroying them.

Only I knew the truth and they were better without knowing unless it became life or death for them... It wouldn't. There were reasons Lyn hadn't gone after them. Anora had protection and the perimeter, something her mom – our mom – thought of, yet it didn't keep her safe once away from the home. Her daddy a millionaire and owner of Indigo, it would make front page on every paper and every social media site – millionaire and owner of Indigo, daughter kidnapped.

Leandra. That situation was different. Her parents were well-off but not a household name. Lyn was cruel and horrible, but not stupid. She wouldn't go after her. I was nothing. A child raised in the system and, by admission of her own words, she dealt with the nobodies. People who wouldn't be missed.

Lyn mentioned how the Moras loved kids and had dirty little secrets in the woods around their home. The words gave her pleasure. How many children? A barrage of children's faces marched behind my eyes. I couldn't unsee them.

Silence pervaded the house and my soul. I had to find a way out. The window was clamped shut as if super glued. It didn't budge and the bars were spaced too closely for me to slip through. If I broke the window, surely she would hear it and I'd still have to find a way to remove the bars.

I felt along the walls and the baseboard, even tried every wooden slat in the floor. I was locked in. There was no way out. At some point, my body gave in to exhaustion and I woke up with the sun shining on my face. My back stiff from the floor and achy still. My wrists and ankles burned and my face continued to feel like it hit a brick wall.

A paper plate sat near the door with a styrofoam cup beside it. More cold eggs and toast. I picked them up and ate, ignoring how they felt in my hands. I needed my strength. I gulped down the lemonade, then remembered Hadj's story of how she poisoned his parents through the lemonade.

At this point, I'd welcome it. For my life to end. There was no way out and whatever she had in store for me I wasn't going to like. Was she planning on using me the way she did my mother? I felt sick to my stomach thinking about what she'd put her through. I needed the nutrition in the food and fought the waves of nausea threatening to expel it.

Judah, she called him Judah. That was his real name: Judah Talbot. My mom escaped, he escaped. I'd also escape and not get caught again like my mom did.

Time passed and the house remained deadly silent. *Was I alone?* The doorknob in my hand, I twisted it, then banged on the door. The sound echoed through the house but wasn't followed with any footsteps or nasty words.

After studying the room again, I came to the same conclusion as the night before. There was nothing. I studied the window once more. *I wasn't giving up!* The bars looked tight. The heat kicked on. That was it. Somewhere in the room was a vent!

I walked around. A steady flow of warmth heated my ankles from the wall with the door. I carefully peeled back the ugly wallpaper to reveal a vent. The screen taken off, it was a square hole in the wall. I certainly couldn't fit inside it and there were no screws. My mom. She locked her up too, and learned as she'd taken the screws out, possibly to use them to loosen the bars on the window. A smile crossed my lips.

There were no screws now, just an empty hole, but maybe my mom had left something in the hole. I ran my fingers along the edges. A cold blast pushed my hand toward the back. Warm air had steadily been flowing from the vent and the sudden brush of cold caught me off guard. *Did she schedule the thermostat to blow out cold air at certain times of the day?* The tip of my finger rolled over a small object. As a reaction I pulled my hand back. Whatever it was pricked it and dribbles of blood flowed from the small wound. I didn't care and thrust my hand back into the hole until I found it again and pulled it out. A screw. "Thank you, Mom," I said aloud as if she was with me, the cold blast of air that guided my hand.

It was small enough to fit into the old worn-out lock on the door. I twisted it in various directions, trying to find the sweet spot that would click the door open.

The purr of an engine and the gravelly sound of tires on the rocky dirt road told me someone was coming. I didn't know where the road ended or if there were other homes along it. I ran to the window and peered out. A small silver car – her car. The first night had been fuzzy but I remembered a silver car. It was a chariot whisking me away from hell, I thought. Instead, it dropped into its eternal fires.

I tucked the screw back into the empty vent and pushed the wallpaper back then sat against the wall, beneath the window. Medium footfalls told me she was alone.

Hours passed and I scooted along the wall, listening for sounds of her movements that would tell me something useful. All I heard was a creak and moan here and there when a door was opened or she stepped on a loose floorboard.

At first, it was the movements of an older lady and the grumbling of an imperfect house. As if my mother was whispering in my ear, I stared at the floor. Could there be a basement? It wouldn't be strange or unheard of for a mountain home to have one and it wouldn't be strange for a basement to have its own door or window. Stepping across each floorboard in the room I searched for ones that creaked and wasted no time in collecting the screw to pry the floorboards.

Creaks and footsteps in the hallway told me she was heading my way. I stashed the screw between the floor and baseboard trim. Pulling my legs between my hands, I sat on my butt and waited. Sure enough, the door rattled and opened. Her large-boned figure framed by the doorway and she peered down at me with her demon eyes.

A tray in her hand. She didn't say anything but lowered the tray and set a foam bowl on the ground and another foam cup. Glancing at me with disdain she put a hand on her hip and held out the tray. "Pick up your plate and cup from earlier, put them on the tray."

I did as she asked, wondering if I could take her on. Did I have the strength? I chose against it. The knot on my head still gave me dizzy spells, most likely a concussion, and my body still ached, but it was better each day. I was getting stronger and would wait her out, take her on when my full strength returned.

"The boys will be here soon to take you to the restroom." With that, she closed the door.

Why did the boys have to do it? Was she afraid? Did my mom get away on her watch? I imagined a woman my size taking Lyn down, stealing the keys and running far away. "If you did it so can I," I whispered to the air.

The boys came. It took both to take me to the restroom which was, incidentally, a left into the hallway and on the opposite side. About ten steps. Green Truck Guy opened the door and watched me march down the hallway and Other Truck Guy watched from the open doorway. It was really unnerving to have his filthy eyes watching me pee, but I had to go so bad that it didn't matter.

"What are your names?" I asked as I washed my hands.

No response.

I walked toward Other Truck Guy and paused in front of him. "I should call you something; Batman and Robin, Storm Troopers, Flotsam and Jetsam?" I was pushing it, but at this point what did I have to lose? Death would be welcome over Lyn's horrid plans for me.

He narrowed his eyes and pushed me out the door. I stumbled into the hallway.

"Bubba and Bubs," called Green Truck Guy. "That's what you can call us."

Feeling snarky, I didn't let up. "Which of you is Bubba and which is Bubs?"

"You decide." His face didn't show any sign he thought me humorous.

I ambled down the hallway. "OK, I'm calling you Bubba and him Bubs."

Bubs grabbed my shirt from the back and pushed me into the room. The force sent me stumbling into the wall on the other side. The door slammed and was locked before I turned around.

The Doldrums

How quickly the days ran together. Cold eggs and toast in the morning, steaming soup in the evening, and always lemonade and a single potty break. It was enough to keep me alive and I wondered what the end game was. *To break me?* I was already broken. The longer I was stuck in that tacky, horrible little room the more alert my senses and the more driven my desire to be free.

When I wasn't contemplating my escape or death, I thought of James. His lips, messy hair that always fell over his eyes. How sexy he looked caked in white dust. A hard-working, blue-collar man. He'd escaped a hard life and was starting on his own and that made the white dust a sexy look. I thought of Anora's interest in him and chuckled when I realized she liked him, was possibly interested in dating him. That made me a tad jealous. It shouldn't have, but it did.

The night in the car when he kissed me. I hadn't complained or pushed him back. I welcomed it. I feared being in love and commitment, but I did love James with all of my being, not just as a friend. I was in love with him too. I passed the time daydreaming of escaping and finding James. I'd wrap my arms around him, confess my love, and kiss him passionately like the moment in the car. That was the moment my heart knew I loved him. It was my brain that refused. It wouldn't allow him to walk away again.

Each night, I chipped away between the floorboards until, finally, I loosened one enough to lift it up. The planks were solid and thick, not like a modern wood floor. Carefully, I slid the loosened plank off and stared into the darkness below. The moon was a sliver and didn't provide enough light but it was enough to see more wood. *What a waste.* I'd spent countless amounts of time chipping away to find what felt like plywood.

It wasn't a waste. It did bring me to the conclusion the only way out was the door. I slid the plank back into its place until it rested evenly with the others and returned the screw to its home in the vent. When I turned around, my heart thumped like a marching band. On the opposite wall to me sat a boy, his soulful dark eyes stared beyond my flesh. They dug at my essence. The equivalent of spiders moving through my veins and arteries. His knees rose to his neck and he was thick. I guessed about eleven. Straight, dark hair framed his face.

I swallowed. How did he get in here? Were my eyes playing tricks on me? On my hands and knees I crawled towards him. Knots tightening in my guts, my breathing heavy, I repeated, *It's your imagination.* All I'd eaten for days was eggs, toast, and soup. I had a large knot on my head and probably a concussion. All the logical explanations I thought of didn't answer how the boy was there. I wasn't imagining him. He was as there as the shadow behind him.

"Hello," I whispered, my voice shaking.

He didn't respond. His eyes moving through me as if he was seeing my memories. The ones lost in the cheesecloth in my brain. Almost at his feet, I sucked in a deep breath and squeaked, "Can you help me?"

His straight lips curved into a smile and he vanished. *You are seeing things!* I glanced at the spot he vacated and my eyes were drawn to the slender gap between the floor and baseboard. White glowed from the darkness moving towards my knees.

My hand followed the glowing light where the boy had sat. I stuck my pinky finger into the gap. The tip touching something that felt soft, like paper. I needed something long and slender – the screw! It wasn't meant to unlock the door, pry open the windows, or loosen the floorboards to find a non-existent basement. It was meant to slide into the gap and retrieve whatever was there.

I hooked the screw in the middle of the paper and edged it closer and closer until it peeked out of the gap. I pressed my finger over it and edged it the rest of the way.

Excitement jittered through me as I scrambled to the window where the moon's light was the strongest. Something dropped from the middle and plunked to the ground. I reached down and picked up two keys. One appeared to be a house key and the other a small key, like for a mailbox or deposit box.

My heart thumped as I placed the keys gently on the windowsill and read the note.

Take the keys. One will open the door. The other, my father's safe deposit box.

There was no name. Hard to tell if it was my mom, or some other young crafty girl who was locked away. Had I seen a ghost or did the energy of the dead leave imprints in the future? I didn't think even Anora knew the answer. Whatever it was, the boy guided me to the note and the keys. He was also probably the cold blast that pushed my hand to the screw in the vent. It struck me oddly, as it was a boy. Lyn mentioned the Moras liked children and the woods were littered with them. They were vile humans and I was sure that boy was one of theirs. "I'm sorry," I whispered into the air as if his energy was still there. A splash of water landed on my hand and I realized I was crying for him, for me, for all of us.

The sun would be up soon and Lyn would wake, cook the eggs and toast and, in about an hour, she'd bring them to me, making sure they were nice and cold. I folded the note with the keys inside and placed it back into the back of the vent near the screw.

I lay on the floor and planned. Bubba and Bubs would show late in the afternoon. I'd get my bathroom break, then dinner. They'd leave and I'd be alone with Lyn. Once I heard her go to bed and close the door I'd give it a little time for her to fall asleep, then I'd make my move.

My plotting gave way to a soothing night's sleep. When I awoke, the sun was high, meaning it was about noon. The woods filled with naked trees. I saw right through them and didn't see any homes, but I'd been in those woods and hadn't come across a single cabin. I'd learned not to drink the lemonade until the sun was lowering so I wouldn't have to hold my bladder for long.

I tried to remember the house. I knew the hallway led to the kitchen and there was a door just off the kitchen with the blue area rug. My eyes closed as I drew a mental picture of the kitchen. In the pantry was a shotgun. I hoped the shells were there too. I'd take it with me as a precaution. The first night was fuzzy, but I thought I remembered Lyn hanging her keys on a hook near the door.

Bubba and Bubs arrived on time for my usual bathroom break and I was returned for the usual steamy soup. It wasn't always the same soup, but was always canned not homemade. Some days chicken, other times vegetable. After dinner I lay on my back and conserved energy as I felt the vibrations of the house, feeling and listening to where they were at each moment.

The day happened as they all had, in the never ending doldrums of this pathetic world. The sun disappeared beyond the horizon and the moon displayed little to no light. I dropped away from the window and sat beneath it as the front door closed and heavy footfalls plodded across the gravel – one set only. I jumped up and raised my eyes over the window as Bubs pulled the truck door closed. That wasn't good. They hadn't broken their routine since I'd been here. All the more reason I had to leave tonight.

I ran the plan through my head, over and over, attempting to find a solution for any problems that might come up. Lyn made her usual walk to bed, followed by Bubba's heavy steps behind her. He went into a room across the hall and next to the bathroom, she went to the end of the hall as usual. Why hadn't he left? He always left and went who knows where. Were they planning something?

I hadn't seen the room next to the bathroom but there was a door. A closet maybe, I thought, as his heavy steps sounded towards the kitchen then disappeared.

Everything was fuzzy, as I was out of it the first night. I kicked myself now for not paying better attention to the layout of the house. As soon as chirping crickets filled my ears and silence permeated the house, I stuck the key in the lock. Whatever they were planning I assumed would happen in the morning since they'd gone to bed. The lock turned easy. "Thank you," I whispered to my guardian angel whoever *she* or *he* was, my mother or some other young woman and, of course, the boy.

Careful not to make a noise, I closed the door behind me and took gentle footsteps. I'd listened for days and knew where each creaky floorboard was. In order to be extra stealthy, I held my shoes and walked barefoot. The hallway felt as if it would never end and I fought the urge to rush. Once I reached the kitchen, I opened the pantry in slow motion to catch or avoid any creaks that might wake Bubba. I couldn't see, but felt along the wall until my hands found the large, bulky shotgun. Finding the shot was harder to do. With no light from the moon, I stood on my tiptoes and pressed my hand along the top shelf. All I felt was more cans of what I guessed was soup. How long had they planned on keeping me prisoner?

Sliding my hand along each shelf and feeling each object, I found the shot on the chest level shelf. I should have known they weren't worried about keeping it safe from anyone, but keeping it handy. I didn't have anything to carry the shot in, so I loaded them into the barrel, as many would fit – five. I didn't know how many were already in there or if the shotgun could hold that many shells. Before grabbing the gun, I slipped my shoes on, the keys inside my left one. Loaded and ready, I held the weapon in front of me, barrel pointed ahead.

Not knowing Bubba's exact location, I didn't want to chance waking him. Tiptoeing across the kitchen and sliding along the wall of the entryway, I found a doorway. Peering around the corner, grateful for the clear, starry night that allowed enough light, I spotted Bubba asleep on what appeared to be a couch. Relief washed over me when I glanced ahead, towards the door – a set of keys shone against the wall, hanging from a peg.

A partial wall separated the entryway from the other room where Bubba slept. No wonder I hadn't remembered. There was nothing to remember because I hadn't seen it. I grabbed the keys and a creak sounded on the other side. I wasn't home free yet. My breath caught and I froze. Keys in hand and finger close to the trigger. I pictured how Lyn held the shot gun and brought it upwards. I pushed my upper body forward a slight bit with the butt against my shoulder.

The floor creaked again, closer then closer. I'd never fired any kind of gun. When his large form appeared, he stopped. "Don't move," I said, barely above a whisper.

He froze in his tracks then, as if dismissing me, said, "Put that dang thing down. You cain't even shoot it."

Did he want to put money on that? I wasn't joking and pulled the trigger but nothing happened. Then I remembered Lyn had slid something on the side. He moved closer, my heart pumped fast and steady as my fingers fumbled, searching for the lever. "I said don't move," I threatened. I had the weapon and wasn't scared to use it once I figured out how to work it.

When my fingers found the slide on the side of the shotgun and pulled it. The gun recoiled into my shoulder sending a wave of energy to my waist and nearly sending me backwards into the wall. I stumbled to catch my balance.

Through the darkness, I barely made out Bubba. It happened so quick I hadn't understood I shot him. His body thrown backwards into the wall with the force of the shot. In the darkness, I watched his shadowy form slide downwards, sending a shockwave through the house as he hit the floor.

I swallowed, then set the gun alongside the wall, keeping it close. I had one chance to gain my freedom before Lyn turned the corner and I had to shoot her too. My palms and fingers sweaty, the doorknob wouldn't open. I dried them on my shirt and grabbed for the knob again when I realized it wasn't my sweaty hands – the door was deadbolted. Clicking it over, I reached for the knob again when I heard Lyn.

"What the hell you shooting at Bubba?!" Her voice worse than nails on a chalkboard, more like a group of female cats in heat.

I collected the shotgun, my throat dry with nerves, and stepped into the kitchen, pointing it towards the entryway from the hall. Light swept over the room as Lyn flipped the switch, illuminating all of her in a blue, long-sleeved nightgown and worn fuzzy slippers. Her lips tight but her eyes round with shock seeing me in the kitchen with her shotgun.

"Stay there or I'll shoot you too," I threatened as I stepped backwards towards the door. It wasn't that I wanted to kill her and splatter her guts across the kitchen like I had Bubba, but I would.

Her eyebrows shot up. "You shot him. Why, you little bitch." Anger and hate filling each word as they streamed from her mouth. Her fat hands on her hips, like she had authority over me.

Heat rose in my face. *Me? The bitch?* All I wanted was freedom! To return to my life and James. I fought the urge to shoot, knowing full well there were four more shots but I wasn't a murderer. My eyes narrowed as I held the gun steady with one hand and reached backwards with the other for the knob. Twisting it open, I felt the fresh, chilly autumn air on my back. It felt good after days of being locked away and caged like an animal. In my excitement, I made one grave mistake.

Hate is a Four Letter Word

I'd forgotten to listen. Large, hairy arms wrapped around my neck. As a reaction, I pulled my arm and hit the trigger again. A shell released and splintered blowing Lyn backwards. She stumbled sideways and slid along the wall.

The arms let go and I was kicked forward a few feet into the sink. My abdomen hitting the counter and the gun shattering the window and exiting. I reached for it, catching glass in my hands instead. Bubs came at me. His large form moved quick. Heavy steps shook the floor beneath me. Before I could move, he grabbed my arm and flung me, cracking my head against the table. My body hit the floor with a crash.

A chunk of my hair felt as though it was being torn from my head as Bubs grabbed it and dragged me across the floor to the pantry, put a foot against my back putting pressure on the spot that hit the counter moments ago. At this point, my body was beyond pain as I kicked and grabbed for anything. His large hand and fat fingers grabbed my wrist and twisted. Unable to budge, I launched a futile attempt to twist my body under his weight. A firm grasp formed around my free wrist as it was forced alongside my other and sticky duct tape was wrapped around them.

My feet free, I pushed upwards for leverage but soon enough he grabbed my ankles and wrapped the sticky duct tape around them too. A fist in my hair again, he dragged me upwards, bending my back in a direction it wasn't meant to bend.

Lyn was slumped along the wall, a chunk of her shoulder blown off. "You see that. That's all you!"

"It's too bad it didn't hit her chest," I frothed.

His heavy boot was thrust into my ribs, causing me to cough and lose my breath. My scalp lifted off my head as he grabbed the same chunk of hair. He pushed my head into the floor, smashing my freshly healed nose and forehead baseball, then a sharp pain wrung through my head and everything went black.

Icy water streamed over my head, shivering me awake. Through the rivulets, Lyn and Bubs swam into view. Her arm tied in a makeshift sling around her neck. My only regret is that I hadn't killed the bitch.

Lyn's eyes stared at me, frosted over in hate. "You are just like your mother, fighting everything I do for you. I fed you and took care of you and this is what I get."

Everything she did! Bullshit! How delusional was she? I cocked my head back. "You deserve worse."

My cheek stung as her hand slapped it. A cringe on her face and I knew that hurt her worse than it did me.

I couldn't stop the vengeful smile erupting on my face, followed by a deep chuckle.

Bubs moved into view, a wooden bat in his hand. He swung and cracked it on my thigh. No doubt what caused the sharp pain that knocked me out earlier.

I laughed harder, then stopped abruptly, "Are you going to kill me, sell me, breed me?!"

"You are worthless!" Lyn hollered, her eyes narrowing and face pinching as it must have caused her pain. Good!

The bat cracked against my thigh again. I didn't feel pain. I hadn't felt pain for a while. I'd been broken all my life. My mind and body were focused on getting out, making my next escape a permanent one, and if that meant they both died, then so be it. It was my pleasure to save the world from them. There was only one way out. For the first time since the icy water poured over my head, I scanned my surroundings, the bookcase, sun-bleached wallpaper, and dusty furniture. They'd taken me to Talbot House.

I thought back to that day Ealon and I ran in here to get away from the rain. A scratching from above frightened me out of the house. *Was it a message from the otherworld or was Lyn or one of the boys in the house?* Tyrus mentioned Talbot. I thought the connection was Hadj and I was so wrong. The abandoned house was where they trafficked kids, at least I assumed it was based on Hadj's recollection of seeing the Moras here and the little car I found belonging to one of the children.

Their methods were stagnant and unoriginal as they had me propped and duct taped in a chair. Hadn't they learned I would stop at nothing? Couldn't they think of something better? My mind envisioned all the ways I could torment Lyn, making me happy she wasn't dead yet.

Bubs grabbed hold of me and slung my body over his shoulder. There wasn't much I could do to fight him, but the time would come. I counted the slats in the floor as he carried me out of the house and into the chilly evening. Not quite dark, but not light, the sun was setting. How long had I been out? The cold water they'd thrown on me froze to my skin. He dropped my body into the trunk of the silver car and slammed it shut.

Closing me in with the darkness, my legs and arms bound, I bounced up and down with the ruts in the road. It felt like we were driving into the woods. After a few minutes, the car stopped and the trunk opened. Bubs grabbed me, tossing me over his shoulder again as he marched. Finally dropping me onto the ground, my body hit with a thud. No pain. *There is only one way out, only one way out,* repeated in my head.

My chin in my chest, Lyn stood in front of me. I noted her shoes and Bubs walked around behind me. "We're cutting you lose, don't bother running because I'll shoot you before you get to the tree line," she snarled as a threat.

I wasn't running any more, there was only one way out. The duct tape sliced away, I assumed he used a box cutter, although, I didn't see it. He freed my feet as well. I glanced upwards to Lyn who had a handgun wrapped in the pudgy fingers of her hand with the good arm, poised on my face. She wasn't going to shoot me. They had something else planned.

I sat upright as Bubs ordered, taking in more of my surroundings. Beyond Lyn were gravestones and woods surrounded by a small clearing. I assumed we were in the woods behind the house, a family plot.

"Take the shovel," she ordered as Bubs thrust it at me. "It's time to meet your mother." I'd never heard more cold or callous words.

Buying my time, I grabbed the shovel before it hit and followed Bubs, the gun in Lyn's hand no doubt perched at my back. He stopped and pointed to the dirt. Beside it, a patch of slightly raised earth with a rock on it, no doubt to mark my mother's grave. "Dig," he ordered.

Giving them each a torrid glance, I plunged the shovel into the ground. This wouldn't be my grave. I would play along. *There's only one way out.* I dug deeper and deeper. There was something cathartic about it. Loose dirt piled up around the edges of the hole until I was standing at least four-foot deep.

I hadn't even glanced at either of them, instead my mind ran through the scenario of being buried alive which was the best-case scenario. The worst case, being shot first or tortured, then dumped in the hole. Lyn wasn't in good shape, mean and hateful, but also in agony. Pain that made me smile in satisfaction.

"That's enough," Lyn ordered, her voice less forceful than even before I started digging. Hate still punctuating each word.

I stopped as they ordered, shovel in hand. Absorbed in the digging, I hadn't noticed it was night. Darkness washed over us, but a fresh new moon lit the sky.

"Hand the shovel up and lay down with your hands by your sides," she demanded.

In an effort to keep a poker face, I fought the urge from the tug at the corners of my lips to smile. I did as she asked, staring into the earth. Dirt clods flew over my body and I listened and welcomed the vibrations from their movements, focusing on that rather than the pressure mounting from the earth over me. Lyn was restless and in pain, her familiar footsteps receded while Bubs continued to toss dirt over my body. A clump, then another.

The rhythm of the dirt clods dropping over my body told me he was in a hurry. They came faster, sloppier. I used the space beneath my nose to breathe and slowly raised my ass upwards so the dirt would fall on either side. That didn't work as well as I'd hoped and made breathing even more a task as dirt fell into the space. Another dirt load fell over my body. I moved an arm while I still could, another dirt load, I moved the other arm, cupping them under my nose and mouth then raised my butt more.

Bubs was too busy shoveling to worry about me. A muffled conversation took place between them and vibrations moved away from me. I waited, taking careful breaths in the small air pocket I created. When no more dirt clods fell from above, muffled voices and vibrations were gone, I lifted my torso with determination. Loose dirt slid down my back and over my head as I pushed and crawled backwards until my shoes hit the wall of earth, then braced my feet and pushed my body upwards. My scrapes and bruises freed from the pressure of the earth's weight. Dirt fell around my head as I gasped the fresh air.

Taking several deep breaths, I regained my strength, forced the dirt from my eyes by forcing tears and stayed low. I crawled to the tree line then stood, following it to the house. I pushed the rugged overgrowth of bushes surrounding Talbot House aside and noted the silver car was parked alongside the house. My lips curled in a smile as I hoped that meant Lyn was in such bad shape they wouldn't be leaving too soon. *There was one way out.*

In a matter of a couple weeks, I'd become someone I didn't know. The someone I feared and warned Ealon of – the monster I feared. Anxiety hid this part of me, always nervous and scared, but Lyn brought it to the surface. Using the brush as cover, I stayed on my feet but lowered my body and crept towards the vehicle. There were plenty of rocks, pointy rocks, I felt beneath the soles of my shoes. Grabbing one that appeared sharper than others, I plunged it into the driver's side back tire then crept into the woods and waited.

James circled in my head as I remembered the many moments we shared together and my letting him go. Was it to spare him from this monster side of me…? He hadn't left my thoughts, ever. All I wanted now was to get back to him, smell the soapy scent on his skin after a shower, find his eyes hidden beneath his shaggy hair, feel his arms around my back and his lips pressed against mine.

"Watch your step, I've got you," Bubs said with concern, interrupting my thoughts of James and freedom. *Only one way out.*

Lyn ordered him around. *What did she have on him? Was Bubs a kidnapped child too?* That was the first time the thought occurred to me. I'd heard of Stockholm Syndrome. *Was I witnessing it?*

I didn't care much to kill Bubs and hadn't wanted to kill Bubba. She was the one I wanted dead and buried, but I hadn't the nerve to shoot her when I had the chance. He carefully guided her to the car and opened the door, even helped her in. There was love in his actions. For an instant I felt sad for him, but the moment faded and my disgust returned.

Closing the passenger door once she was safe inside, he went around the back of the vehicle, coming around the driver's side he threw out a few explicatives when he saw the tire. My lips curled in a maniacal smile.

The kind someone makes when they know they've won. There was no spare in the trunk or I'd have noted it when I was pushed inside. My satisfaction didn't last long when I had another thought, *He may have taken it out to put me in.*

He opened her door and spoke too low for me to hear, then walked away. Damnit! But his leaving gave me an opening. In her weakened state, I could wrap my hands around her neck and choke the breath out of her.

Only one way out.

Patience, I reminded myself as I crawled to the front of the car and reached underneath, digging another sharp rock into the front tire, surely he didn't have two spares lying around.

I dug deep into the rubber, until I heard the hiss of air and felt it on my hand, then crawled to my spot and waited. When Bubs returned he had a spare donut tire. He yelled, "Fuck," when he spotted the front tire.

My smile of satisfaction returned. He dropped the donut, blew out a breath, and opened her door. His voice raised and upset he said, "We shouldn't have taken the car, the front tire is flat too."

Her labored words were music to my ears. "Then we'll spend… the night… here."

Patience my friend and darkness my cover, I watched as their shadows moved behind the curtains, keeping an eye on my prey. They thought I was dead and that was my advantage. It was a strange house with outside steps reaching a second-floor balcony with a door.

When there was no more movement inside the house, I carefully made my way up the balcony steps, remembering how I'd fallen through the ones inside the house. The fact I'd been there was to my advantage. I tested each step before putting my weight on it. The door, damaged from the weather and lack of care, opened with a few tugs.

Instead of going directly downstairs I checked out the rooms upstairs – bedrooms and a spiral staircase that went to the next floor. The bedrooms, like the rooms downstairs, were as if nothing had touched them in many years, dusty with an odor of mildew. Hadj or Judah or whatever his name was mentioned money in the house. I wondered if there was still any stashed. Was that what the key was for? That would come later. I had work to do.

Heading downstairs, one cautious step at a time, the way I'd come up the balcony stairs, I paused when I reached the step I'd fallen through. It was hard to see through the dark, but there appeared to be nothing beneath the steps. Maybe a storage closet or something.

Moving on, I reached the bottom and stalked towards the sitting room where I'd last seen them. Bubs's large form was in the chair and Lyn's full but shorter frame was on the couch. I slid along the wall and bookcase, then around the corner into what appeared to be a kitchen. I really hadn't a plan driving me. Hate and disgust urged me and the mantra repeating in my brain: *only one way out.*

Enough light from the moon and many stars, I spotted a set of knives on the counter, probably dull from wear. I reached for them when I noticed the gun. It was lying alongside the duct tape and a box cutter. As I suspected, that's how he made the clean cuts in the tape. *What idiots!* Even the shovel rested beside the front door. They really thought I was dead.

Maybe the gun wasn't loaded. I'd take my chances. Looping my hand through the duct tape roll, stuffing the box cutter into the waistband of the sweats hanging from my waist, I picked up the gun. I first had to subdue Bubs, quickly and quietly. Slinking back into the sitting room, family room, or whatever it was, I focused on Bubs, wrapping the duct tape around his ankles a few times. He didn't budge, as if worn out from burying me. I stifled a chuckle and considered what to do with his hands that were flailed on each side of the chair.

A wooden lever on the side gave me the idea. I wrapped the tape around his left wrist then around the lever. He wiggled but didn't wake. Crawling around the chair, there was another lever on the other side. I did the same with his right wrist. Cutting another strip, I considered putting it across his mouth but wasn't ready for him to wake yet. Hanging the strip of tape from my arm I pointed the gun at him, square at his face.

I clicked the trigger but nothing. It didn't budge. The safety. I felt along the side and found the lever, clicking it over. The barrel still pointed at his head, I rethought it. Blowing out his brains was quick and painless. I wanted to watch him suffer at least a little. His boot on my back, hand grasping my hair, and kicks to my side all fresh in my head, not to mention the dirt stuck in my hair and every crevice of my body.

I lowered the gun to his heart, it would take him a little while to bleed out. *The knees?* No, that would take two shots and too long for him to die, so I pointed for the throat. He could choke on his own blood.

The decision made, I fired and the shot cracked through the air. At such close range I hadn't missed. From the corner of my eye, Lyn startled upright. Her face distorted and twisted in pain from the quick rise.

I chuckled out loud. "I wouldn't move again if I were you or I'll blow off your other shoulder and it would give me great pleasure," I said with satisfaction.

Bubs gargled and bounced in the chair. "Now Bubs, you're not complete," I said. Keeping an eye and the gun on Lyn, with one hand I tore the duct tape hanging from my arm and smoothed it over his mouth. "Much better."

With Bubs out of the way, I sauntered towards Lyn who sat frozen. Her eyes wide, with fear in the icy cold blue of her irises. There were so many questions I could ask, but what good would it do? We stared into the hate in each others' eyes for several long minutes.

She broke the silence. "Are you… going to kill… me?" she said, pain filling each word.

I'd never taken pleasure in another's pain, but she wasn't human. At least, she had no humanity. I pulled the trigger and shot at her other shoulder, hitting just above the armpit instead. "I told you not to move!"

She gasped in pain as she reflexively moved the arm of her previously blown out shoulder to her new wound to cover the new bullet hole. A wail soaked in agony let loose from inside her.

Patience is my friend. I waited for her howl to subside before speaking. "You are the worst kind of person. One that takes small children, babies, away from their families and sells them into slavery or pimps them out herself, selling those children like cattle. Livestock is treated better. They aren't raped or tortured and they aren't fed cold eggs!" I didn't know how much of my words she was hearing as agony gripped her body. I knew the burn and the pain. "Let's walk."

She sneered, anguish saturating each of her movements, evidenced in the twisted expression on her face. I had the gun and no time for her pain. "A little quicker."

Her movements labored, she rose from the couch. The gun pointed towards her in one hand. The other I pointed toward the door and took great pleasure in watching each of her arduous steps. "Open the door, will ya," I ordered.

She heaved in pain as she turned the knob. I grabbed the shovel resting near the door and dragged it, letting it scrape along the earth for dramatic effect. We marched around the back of the house toward the family graves. Her march was more of a drag as her feet shuffled along the ground.

She dropped to her knees.

"Get up!" I ordered, digging the head of the shovel into her back.

"No, kill me here," she said in a shaky voice.

Only one way out.

I was convinced someone as mean and vile as her had the will to keep moving.

To test that, I whacked her blown off shoulder with the shovel and her lungs erupted in a shriek of horror. "No one will hear you," I said with a shrug, not sure she heard me above her wailing.

I walked in front of her, keeping some distance, the gun stuck in the waistband of the sweats around my waist, and brought the shovel beneath her chin. Lifting it upwards, I raised it so her eyes met mine. "Get up or I'll keep torturing you as long as there is breath in your lungs." For a moment, I didn't recognize the malevolence in my own voice. It was like someone else was inhabiting my body. No pain, no fear, no guilt, no remorse, only vengeance.

She sputtered and stood, dragging her feet toward the graves. Once we reached them, I pushed her into the mound that was mine. "Next time you bury someone alive, make sure they are dead first," I mocked.

Her body shuddered as I imagined she was fuming inside for her stupidity.

"Dig with your hands," I ordered, dropping the shovel and walking behind her, but not before I caught the glimpse of hate in her face.

Shudders and jolty movements from the pain racked her body as she dug and the hole grew bigger. She didn't dare pause. The pain in her arms and shoulders worse than the pain I had yet to inflict on her. I wondered if she was planning an exit strategy too. There was only one exit for her. *Only one way out.*

When I was satisfied the hole was large enough for her body, I forced the shovel into her back pushing her into it. Her face eating dirt. She spit and spluttered. While she dug, I considered my next move. Torture was a bitch.

I held the shovel high, her eyes widened in horror as she groaned a plea, "Stop, you can't do this. I've watched you all your life and this isn't you."

How the fuck did she think she knew me? Her pitiful words angered me more. "You fucked up my life you stupid, ugly bitch!" Years of pain and anger rushed to the surface and seethed from my pores as I brought the pointed end down hard on her thigh until it hit the bone. Her screech echoed through the empty woods and her body went limp. Blood bubbled from her leg. I didn't trust that she was dead. No, she could be knocked out from the pain. My old friend patience joined me.

Her body twitched, then twitched again. Her eyes didn't open and I didn't know if she was dead or alive. I assumed alive but unconscious. I waited longer, until her eyelids fluttered, then smashed the shovel, pointy side down into her throat until it came out the other side. I continued smashing her head with it until it was nothing but a bloody, mushy mess.

In Endings are Beginnings

A lake not far from the graves. I washed the dirt from my body. The chilly water releasing the hate inside me. As if it wasn't my own but someone else's. I didn't smile at the fresh remains of Lyn's body or Bubs's blood-soaked form. I even left him in the chair but peeled off the duct tape and bagged everything that might have my fingerprints on it and tossed it with several heavy rocks in the lake. It gurgled and sank.

Light streamed over the horizon as the sun rose. A wet, soaking, freezing mess, I walked toward the town Ealon and I visited. Something sharp pushed against my foot with each step and I remembered the keys.

I paused, removed them, and ran-walked back to the house. My instincts said I didn't need to search the entire home but beneath the stairs. Kicking against the broken steps, I lowered myself into the hole. Through the broken step, light streamed from the upstairs windows onto a lock box. The key fit nicely into the lock. Inside were ten bundles of hundreds. Thinking decisively, I remembered a bag in the artist's room, beneath the easel. I stood on the lock box, tossed the money onto the stairs then grabbed the steps and pulled upwards. Once out of the hole, I ran to the room and, as I remembered it, a dusty leather bag lay beneath the easel.

Pleased, I strolled toward the town, the leather bag filled with money over my shoulder. The hum of a motor close, I moved off the road. It pulled alongside me and the passenger window unrolled. A woman, platinum ringlets draping her cheeks and falling across her chest, asked me if I wanted a ride. I wasn't sure if she was old or just had naturally light hair.

The old me would have said no in fear, but the new me didn't have that fear anymore. "Thanks," I said, opening the door on the sporty silver convertible with its top on.

"Where are you heading?" she asked.

I turned and took a good look at her. She had a friendly face with fine wrinkles that showed she wasn't a young woman but what stood out more than anything was her eyes. One eye was amber, the other an emerald green. Peace rested on me, as if this woman was someone I'd waited for. I felt light as air as a chill moved from inside me. Her eyes quickly shifted upwards then down and rested on mine.

"There's a town not far," I responded. *What just happened?*

The car moved forward. The drive silent. Yet something had happened. I thought of the boy, the keys, the screw, how I hadn't felt myself, and the odd something about the woman. Unsure what my mind was piecing together, I asked, "What happened back there?"

She responded, her voice calm. As the words left her mouth I knew them to be true. "I was there, trying to stop him, but was side-tracked by the spirits of several boys. One was different and refused to go the *peaceful beyond*. I didn't understand then, but he was attached to you. Whatever happened, he helped it happen. Somehow, he was inside you. Now he's gone. His spirit finally released."

I should have considered that crazy talk, the words of someone ranting and raving, but they weren't. She was right. I'd seen him and felt him inside me. The rage and vengeance wasn't only my own but his too. Together we destroyed evil.

"There's one more thing. You can't return home. Everything has changed." She pulled a newspaper out from between the gear shift and seat and handed it to me.

The words splintered my heart, heat rushed into my cheeks, and water filled my eyes. James was dead. According to the paper he killed me, but it wasn't me. Leandra. It was

Leandra. The plan was to meet at my dorm. Her death wasn't a case of mistaken identity. Bubba or Bubs killed her. It wasn't James. He was blamed, as it stated my roommate had seen us arguing. I thought to the day James admitted his love for me and I watched him walk away. Kit was there, she comforted me. They tied up loose ends. *What about Anora?*

Sobs choked my throat as I croaked, "How do you know any of this?"

She explained in a soothing voice, "I have a connection to the spirit world. Think of it as a ghost radar. I knew that girl wasn't you. She's your twin. You're almost identical but the hair. She's in the *peaceful beyond* and so is James."

Did that mean they were in heaven? There was solace in knowing they weren't trapped here like the boy for their anger to grow. I'd never be able to tell James I was in love with him. That remorse I would carry in my heart forever.

Epilogue

I had no life to return to, but I did have ten grand. I was dead and a ghost can do anything. Finding the house that was my prison for days, I destroyed. The shotgun lying on the ground outside the window I wiped clean with bleach and placed it in Bubba's stiff and bloated hand, then set the house on fire.

I worried someone might find the hidden files on my computer, so I took care of that too. Computer viruses are nasty bugs that can be planted remotely. Remembering and using what Lee taught me, I made a new identity and found a job as an entry level programmer. The benefit was it was a work from home position in Japan, even the interview was virtual, and moving expenses were paid for.

I visited Iwakuni where Lee grew up. It was a beautiful village, but I wasn't there as a tourist. Curiosity drove me. It was a long shot I'd ever see Lee again. What happened between him and me wasn't love. It was common interest and lust. Destiny is a strange thing. Mostly, I live in obscurity.

In my spare time, I built my own program that sorted through newspaper articles during a specific time frame and criteria. After three months, two weeks, and four days, I found what I was looking for. My mother's abduction.

In 1967 Germany, Ingrid Shwartz married Herb Solly, a US soldier. A year after their wedding, a daughter was born. Two years later they moved to the US. In 1970 my mother was born, Lina Solly. Two months later, Lina was stolen from her stroller in a park, just as Lyn had said. A month later, Herb died in a car crash and within six months Ingrid and the oldest daughter, Martha, returned to Germany. I imagined it was hard for her, being a single mother in a foreign land.

Six years later, she remarried a German man, Luther Kohl. They never had children but he was a widower like her, with two sons. They are still married.

I watch them in silence. Torn between the desire to know my biological grandmother and keep my anonymity. Sometimes the past is meant to be the past. I didn't want to anguish her. I wanted to hold the tiny woman in my arms. But I couldn't. It's better that I'm dead.

It's better Leandra's parents never know the full truth. They saved her from something horrible. Anora has a great life and a loving father, even though he isn't a DNA father. No need for her to ever know she is the product of something ugly. She has issues with her mom's disappearance, but I'd rather that than the knowledge her father isn't the man she thinks. As for my foster family, they buried me.

It's my story and I choose my path.

Felicia

Evan's Girls Volume 5

Chapter One

eat flushed my cheeks as Shyanne flipped her blonde locks over her shoulder while leaning towards Cam in her low-cut blouse that showed everything but nipple. The school hoe, who would end up like her mom, working at the gentlemen's club, wasn't getting her gel nails into my boyfriend. I pushed through the crowded high school gymnasium and marched up the bleachers.

"Hi, Cam," I announced in my approach.

The left side of his lip curled upward in a partial smile, making his dimple pop. "Hi, Angel."

I scooted in beside him, his eyes now on me and not the bimbo. I glanced her way, throwing daggers at her with my eyes. She got the message and moved on to someone else. It was well-known at Palm Village High School in south-western Florida that she was good for a quickie or blowjob. There were stories she even did lap dances at parties. Whether these were rumors or not, she lived up to them, always sweetening up and flirting with guys; taken or single.

Cam handed me a bottle. "You thirsty?" He winked.

That wink meant he spiked it. His mom was an alcoholic, not a wino, but a true alcoholic who drank the hard stuff. I collected the bottle from him and took a swallow. He spiked it hard today. I choked as the fizzy, sour liquid puckered my lips and burned my esophagus on its downward path.

Cam chuckled. "Easy. Don't drink it all at once."

It tasted something like rotten lemonade. I kissed his cheek, drawing my lips close to his ear and whispered, "What the hell is in that?"

He whispered, "Carbonated lemon drink, cheap tequila, and a little orange juice."

I visibly shuddered and we both laughed.

He took my hand. "Let's get out of here while we can."

Our hands entwined, we snuck out the back door and ran to the outside bleachers. It wasn't often Poppy let me off the leash and our clock was ticking as he'd be in the parking lot, waiting, at nine sharp. He was OCD punctual.

Under the stars, our lips met, his hands pushing under my blouse to cup my breasts. His finger wiggling the nipple as I grabbed his shirt and lowered myself onto the bench.

"Should we go beneath?" he asked, inquiring whether we should go under the bleachers. That was our usual spot, and I could tell by the rock in his pants he was feeling extra horny.

I nodded. No one would say I didn't indulge my boyfriend. We'd been each other's first and had been dating nearly seven months, since right after my sixteenth birthday.

He pushed me against the wall beneath the bleachers, his lips suckling my nipples as I pulled the condom out of his pocket then unwrapped his package, letting his pants fall. I'd been sure not to wear any underwear to give him easy access, and less to put on after meant it would take less time. He pulled my skirt up and I rolled the glove over his rock. Poppy would kill me if I got pregnant or I'd have to finish school pregnant and homeless.

Moans escaped my lips as he pushed hard inside me. My bare back rubbing the concrete wall. The barely healed concrete burns would be replaced with a fresh set. I couldn't wait until I could have sex in a bed.

He pumped harder and faster, his breathing heavy and hot on my face. One last firm pump and he groaned in release. His cum fillin' the glove.

Sex with Cam didn't last more than a few minutes, which saved my back a lot of pain and agony. The worst part was I couldn't reach my back to put aloe on it. Things would be better if I had a different guardian. Poppy was strict, barely let me out of his sight except school and the occasional school activity so long as my grades stayed at least a B and I wasn't late when he picked me up. Other kids had cell phones, went to parties, group dated, and stayed at each other's houses. I had to put out extra since I couldn't do all those things with Cam. It was important he understood how much I loved him and wouldn't take advantage of hoes like Shyanne in his moments of male need. For love, I endured the burn on my back. One day...

We went topside with about an hour left to burn and drank the sour lemonade.

"With better ingredients I could be a bar tender," he said after swallowing a gulp and handing it to me.

"You sure could. This stuff is pretty nasty, but if you had the real stuff to make it I bet you could make it taste real good." I swallowed a smaller sip this time then handed it back. I found it was a positive to massage his ego.

The sky was clear enough the stars twinkled like Christmas lights. Palm Village was a small town between Bradenton and Arcadia. When I say small, I mean mostly retired folks and mobile home parks. The rich people owned houses. I lived with Poppy at Twin Palms mobile home park in a single wide. That's why I couldn't even sneak out. The walls were paper thin and every noise carried.

Cam gave me his old cell phone and put me on his plan. He kept the new phone for himself but he pays for it out of his own money that he makes at Dalby's Motor Shop. Poppy doesn't know and it's probably better the phone doesn't make calls anymore either. When he dropped it the screen cracked and it stopped making calls but we text. Texting is safer anyways.

The bottle finished and fifteen minutes left we strolled to the gym, kissed behind the building and went in. I had to be sure I knew who won, as Poppy'd ask and he'd know if I was lyin'. Like I said, Palm Village is a small town. The scoreboard flashed 50 to 48 and everybody was jumping up and down. We won. That was good.

I pressed my lips against Cam's one last time for the night.

"Text me later," he said.

"Of course, and don't be talkin' with girls before you go home. You make me look bad, like I don't take care of my man and you know I do," I said in warning. I had a tad of a jealous streak and he knew it.

He pulled me closer for one more kiss. "Of course, you're my Angel. What do I need any other girl for?"

Light flashed over the potholed parking lot. A lone moth fluttered past my eyes and the scent of the freshly mowed weeds tickled my nose. I'd say grass, but I didn't think the school ever had any, mostly we had dollar weed and dandelions. Now we had stems of dandelions.

Poppy's truck pulled into a space. The light continued to blink and flash then went out as I opened the passenger door.

"When they gonna fix those damn lights? Two weeks ago it was the other one and I see it still ain't fixed. As much taxes as we pay, that school should be a castle," Poppy harumphed. He complained about just about everything or anything he could conjure up.

"Poppy, it ain't that big a deal."

"To hell it ain't!"

There wasn't much use in saying anything more. It would just make him lose more of his wiry gray hair or add new wrinkles below his eyes or on his forehead.

I glanced towards the school. The gym doors were opened. Cam stepped out and gave me a wink as he strolled alone to his Harley. He'd picked it up cheap and rebuilt it. He was proud of the machine, even taken me on a ride once during a football game in the fall. A smile crept over my lips as he was alone. To make sure, I looked over my shoulder as Poppy pulled onto the road.

Chapter Two

stepped out of the shower onto the rug after dryin' most myself. Poppy was picky about water on the floor, so I tried to be careful. I flipped my head down and wrapped the towel around it then stepped off the rug. My foot caught a wet patch and I tumbled forward, catching myself on the counter. I flipped the light off. Distracted by the slip, I nearly forgot to grab a second towel for my middle. Flipping the light back on, it clicked and went out. *Damn it, stupid bulb!* I grabbed the towel in the dark and wrapped it.

I slid the rug over the wet spot so Poppy wouldn't yell later and went across the hall to my room. I dropped the towel around my middle. At twelve my monthly visits started, and I hated so much that women had to bleed monthly. Men didn't have any of that to deal with. They didn't even have to sit on a toilet or squat to pee. It wasn't fair. However, I did like my breasts. They'd grown full and round. Heck, men didn't have that – not without hormone therapy anyways. I squeezed them, enjoying their fullness. Cam enjoyed them too.

I slipped into jeans and a cute lavender top that I'd pull down a tad when I got to school, slipped sandals on, then brushed my chestnut hair. In the summer, it lightened in places, giving me natural highlights people paid a lot of money at salons for. My cheeks had a natural flushness and that was good, since Poppy wouldn't allow me to wear make-up.

I rolled a band over my arm for later. By noon it would be ninety degrees and the wet air would get heavy and my hair would be my enemy. Cam loved my hair. He said it was perfect. It was mostly straight, but the ends had a little wave to them.

"Felicia, it's 7:05," Poppy shouted from the living room. We left at 7:10 every day. Like I said, OCD punctual.

"Coming, Poppy," I hollered and grabbed my backpack.

Life hadn't been so bad when Gam Gam was still around. Her brown eyes smiled as much as her lips. Poppy was much happier when she was around before cancer took her. My family died when I was a baby and Poppy and Gam Gam took me in. The only other relative I knew was Uncle Trev. Poppy said he was a no account who never held a real job and sponged off others. He'd let him visit, but never stay more than two nights. I guessed my mom's family were all dead since I'd never met any of them. My dad, Martin, was Poppy and Gam Gam's only child.

We rolled into parent drop off and I'd nearly forgotten the light bulb. He'd be angry as a hornet if I didn't tell him now and he had to find out on his own. Poppy was particular about maintaining the trailer. We even had a carport. "The light bulb burned out in the bathroom," I said as I opened the door. I slung my book bag over my shoulder once my feet hit the pavement.

He nodded. I closed the door and he drove off. My usual path was around the old brick building. It housed a few classrooms, the media center, cafeteria, and gym. Everything else was in portables. Black dirt stuck into the grooves of the brick. The mortar was barely distinguishable. The rutted sidewalk curved a path to my first period. I watched my step, as a root growing beneath the sidewalk broke it and I'd tripped several times over the past year.

The portables weren't much better than the building. The siding peeling on a few and the ramps sagging. My third period, Mr. Trucher, had a bucket under the leak from the roof. What I did like about the portables was the air conditioning. In the buildings, the rooms were too hot or too cold, depending on which side of the building you were on when the sun hit the windows. Most of the blinds were broken so there was no way to keep the light from heatin' up the glass.

Cam waited for me outside my first period. That was our usual routine. "Hi, Angel." He handed me a caramel whipped coffee. Another luxury Poppy wouldn't allow me. He said 'coffee's not healthy for growing girls'. But, in one year and two and half months, I'd be an adult. I couldn't wait.

I took the icy caffeinated beverage. "Thank you."

Cam was a few inches taller than me and. standing close enough even with his hat on. I glanced up into his golden eyes. There was rarely a time he didn't wear a cap. even during sex. The bell rang and our lips met for a morning kiss to start the day. I watched him walk off, his ass filling out his jeans nicely. I enjoyed the view. Once he rounded the corner and I couldn't see him anymore I walked up the saggy ramp.

After meeting Cam behind the building and making out for a minute, I walked to parent pick up where Poppy was always waiting as soon as the bell rang. It was shocking not to see Poppy's truck. He was never, ever late. I thought to run after Cam, maybe have him take me home, and he would 'cept I thought of how angry Poppy'd be if a boy dropped me off. Double that if I was caught on the back of a motorcycle.

When all the cars were gone, sweat bubbled in my cleavage, and Poppy still wasn't there I considered my options. I could keep waiting or I could walk home. Cam would be on his way to work if he wasn't there already.

The school was on main street and only a couple miles from the trailer park. The humidity moved out as dark, looming clouds moved in, bringing a refreshing breeze. Every afternoon in the summer, the rains came. The air cooled off long enough to dump their excess water then the sultry heat came back. I made use of the dark sky and walked home quickly, hoping to get there before the storm.

I stayed on Main St. in case Poppy was late one time in his life, instead of taking a few side streets that would get me home quicker. Half-way home, a motor rumbled beside me. I glanced over at a late model Ford pickup, recognizing the driver, Gillian, right away. A girl in my third period. "You wanna ride?" she asked.

A ride would be nice, but it'd be even nice if Poppy'd let me get my driver's license, a job, and my own car. I finished driver's ed last year and had my learners but Poppy insisted I'd have to wait till I was eighteen and living on my own. 'Not under my roof' he'd say. I guess there was some weird Florida law that he'd have to add me to his insurance policy and teenagers cost too much money.

The sky complained something awful, meaning the storm was moving in quick. "Yeah, thanks," I said. The truck rolled to a stop and I slid onto the bench seat.

A car went around us and she let her foot off the brake, checking behind her before continuing. "It's gonna be a bad one today. Look," she said, pointing to the sky.

A bolt of electricity shot from the sky, not more than a mile or so up the road. Lightning and thunder coming that close to each other was never a good sign. She pulled into the trailer park and I directed her to mine and Poppy's. His silver truck still in the driveway under the carport.

"Thanks," I offered as I got out. It didn't make any sense. Did he take a nap? It wasn't like Poppy had friends, male or female. Other than church, the once-a-week trip to the grocery store and occasional trip to Bradenton for home repair materials that he couldn't find in town, he was always home.

I took in a deep breath after walking onto the small deck. I swung the door open and was hit in the face with an eerie quiet that nearly knocked me over. Poppy didn't like electronics, but he did like the TV and had shows he watched like clockwork. I peeked into the empty kitchen. His morning coffee mug still by the sink and no dishes in the drainer, which was weird. He always ate lunch and the clean dishes waited for me to put away when I got home.

My arm hairs shackled and I grabbed a kitchen knife, just in case. "Poppy," I called with no response. The knife firm in my grasp, I stepped easy into the hallway, pushing my bedroom door open. The room looked the way I left it. I glanced at the bathroom door across the hall. It was wide open, light shone from the window onto the carpet. I walked to the doorway and gasped.

Poppy's left leg lay over the side of the tub, and inside the tub was the rest of him. A trail of dried blood curled from his head and had washed down the drain. By the window was a step ladder and resting on the sink counter was a light bulb.

I rushed to his side and laid the knife on the floor. "Poppy, Poppy." I pushed against his chest and tears flooded my eyes. Poppy was hard, but I didn't have anyone else. "Poppy," I urged, through tears and shortened breaths. *No, no, no!*

"Help!" I called with no response. My voice bouncing off the walls of the trailer. It was up to me. My cell phone didn't make calls. Why didn't he like electronics? I could call right away! I rushed to the rotary phone in the kitchen. My hands shaking as I tried to plug my finger into the holes and dial three numbers.

Chapter Three

My butt ached from the hard plastic of the waiting room chair. I wiggled and my foot wouldn't stop tapping. The minutes between my 911 call and the ambulance arriving were an emotional eternity. I blamed myself for Poppy's accident. I pulled the rug over, covering the splash on the floor, but hadn't checked for others. The light bulb burned out while I was in the bathroom.

The first responders allowed me to ride in the ambulance while they continued to try and keep Poppy stable. Once we reached the hospital, he was immediately wheeled into a room and I was left with my own guilt and fear in the waiting room. The white walls, uncomfortable plastic chairs, and pharmaceutical commercials on the big screen didn't ease my conscience. If Poppy died, what would happen to me? Where would I go? Wasn't like I had anyone but my no-account uncle. Maybe, since I was nearly an adult, they'd let me stay in the trailer.

My foot tapped uncontrollably, urging me to get up and move. I paced 'cause I didn't want to leave the room in case the doctors came out and told me I could see Poppy and that everything would be fine. It had to be fine. He had to be fine.

The minutes stretched into hours. Time ticked as slow as it could. The minute hand on the large clock moved forward then backwards before plunging forward again. I pulled out my phone and stared as I contemplated texting Cam.

A woman in scrubs walked into the waiting room. Pink faded gloss covered her lips but still brought out the dark tones in her skin. She glanced at me and walked closer. "Felicia Chickle?"

I swallowed hard. "Yes."

Her oval face wore a solemn expression "Your grandfather is stable for now. He's being taken to the ICU where he's likely to stay for a while."

He was alive. My heart perked up and the guilt started to fade. "Can I see him?"

She nodded. "Follow me."

We went up the elevator to the second floor. "Wait there and I'll talk with the nurse."

After their discussion, she directed me to a small room. My grandfather lay quiet and peaceful. Seeing him so helpless brought tears to my eyes. He was never a weak man nor someone who wanted anything to do with someone else takin' care a' him. He was proud and independent. Now he lay in a hospital bed with machines hooked to him. Tubes came out of him everywhere, beeps and blinks assaulted my senses.

"The doctor will be in soon." She left but was soon replaced with another nurse.

Her yellow scrubs cheerier, along with the white shoes on her feet with happy face emojis on the toe. "I'm Kirsta," she said as she pressed buttons on one of the machines. "I'll be your grandfather's nurse tonight."

I wiped my tears and squeezed my eyes to alleviate the burn in my nose. "What's wrong?"

She stopped pressing buttons and turned to me. "He had a nasty fall. He's not out of the woods, but we're going to take extra good care of him. Do you have anyone at home?" she inquired. It wasn't her business and all she told me was the obvious. I'd found him. He was changing the light bulb, the ladder slipped on a slick spot and he fell backwards, hit his head on the faucet, before hitting the cold porcelain of the tub.

Taken aback and irritated with her I lied, "Yeah, I can call my uncle." Even if I knew his phone number, my phone didn't make calls.

She nodded in confirmation, but I saw the doubt on her face. "The doctor will be in soon." She padded out of the room, her feet barely makin' a sound. From the corner of my eye, I watched her talk with another nurse, or maybe a doctor of sorts. They all looked alike. My uneasiness over Poppy turned into anxiety over my future. Was she talkin' with that other person about me? Were they calling the department that snatches children from their homes? There was a story a couple months ago in Florida. A twelve-year-old girl was sent to live in a foster home and they sexually molested her. That wasn't happening to me! I had to get out of there before they hauled me into foster care. I wasn't having that. I pulled out my phone and sent a text to Cam. *Poppy's had an accident. Can you come to the hospital?*

He responded almost immediately. *Closing up the shop. Be there in 30. Wait for me outside the ER.* I put the phone to my ear and pretended to talk. The emoji shoe nurse, Kirsta, glanced my way. I pretended to hang up and stuffed the phone in my back pocket. Poppy's hand felt colder and fragile in mine. I leaned over him and whispered, "I have to go Poppy, because they're gonna take me away from you. My friend Cam is picking me up. I know you'd like him if you gave him a chance. He's a real upstanding guy and he loves me. They'll take care of you here. You'll be home before you know it."

I glanced over my shoulder and didn't see emoji shoe nurse. She wasn't as cheery as I'd thought she'd be. There wasn't time to wait for the doctor. I had to get out now. Nobody was taking me anywhere 'cept Cam.

We could go back to my house, pick up a few belongings. I knew where Poppy kept cash. He didn't like banks and hid a stash in the kitchen in an old coffee can beneath the sink. I didn't doubt he had a sock hidden somewhere in his bedroom stuffed with cash too. It was time for me to be on my own and independent.

I turned on my heel, coming face to face with a woman in a white lab coat. Her dark hair tied in a bun and a name tag that read Dr. Randen.

She introduced herself and explained Poppy's condition. "Your grandfather hit his head hard. We've stopped the bleeding but it'll be touch and go for a while. He's breathing on his own and his organs are functioning, but I'm concerned about the swelling in his head."

His head looked the same size. What was she talking about?

"Do you have somewhere to go? One of the nurses will help you with that call," she said this as if I needed their help. I was sixteen years old. I knew how to make a phone call. She said this to be nosy. That was it. She was gonna call and I'd be sent to foster care.

"I called my uncle. He's on his way," I said, matter of fact like. "In fact, he's probably here now, waiting outside the front entrance. I'll be back to check on Poppy tomorrow."

Her face was unreadable. I couldn't tell if she believed me or not. "We can escort you downstairs?"

Hell no! I had two feet and didn't need no help. "I can manage," I said in a snarkier tone than I meant.

Her eyes narrowed and the side of her lip twitched, demonstrating my tone bothered her. "What is your uncle's number?"

Nosy bitch! I gave her the home phone. "Call it. He won't be there cause he's on his way here." I walked around her, held my head high and shoulders back as I made my way to the elevator. My good fortune, it opened before I even pressed the button, revealing a middle-aged man. His jeans and T-shirt weren't the clothes of a social worker. I let out a breath I didn't know I was holding, rushed into the elevator without looking over my shoulder, and pressed the button. I didn't wait to see if anyone else was coming. I needed to get out now.

When the doors opened on the bottom floor, two men stood in front of me. They looked to be orderlies in their plain white clothing and stocked cart, and stopped their conversation when they laid eyes on me. I smiled and exited the elevator. Neither said a thing to me as they pushed the cart into the elevator then restarted their conversation. Maybe they were gossiping.

I went around the circular hall to the ER. A police officer stood near the exit. My heart palpitated, then beat like moths trying to free themselves from my chest. I pulled out my phone and pretended to text as I strolled past him as calm and cool as a lemonade in summertime.

Small puddles from the earlier rain I'd nearly forgotten about filled the ruts. I walked towards the parking lot. I wanted to be where Cam could see me, but hopefully out of sight from hospital personnel. I didn't need them coming for me and dragging me off.

When the rumble of a motorcycle filled my ears, I visibly relaxed. Even with the helmet over Cam's face, I'd recognize his Harley anywhere. He looked sexy as hell on his cycle as he rounded the corner and pulled into a parking spot near me. He pulled his helmet off, his hair dropped above his shoulders.

"Wear this," he said, handing me the helmet.

I fitted it on my head and pulled a leg over the seat, propped my feet on the footpegs, then wrapped my arms around his middle.

"You ready?"

"Yeah, get me outta here."

www.ingramcontent.com/pod-product-compliance
Lightning Source LLC
Chambersburg PA
CBHW051205190726
48288CB00006B/1814